Praise for the Series

Foul Play at the PTA

Murder at the PTA

D0172809

WITHDRAWN

Also Available from Laura Alden

Murder at the PTA
Foul Play at the PTA

PLOTTING at the PTA

Laura Alden

AN OBSIDIAN BOOK

OBSIDIAN
Published by New American Library, a division of
Penguin Group (USA) Inc., 375 Hudson Street,
New York, New York 10014, USA
Penguin Group (Canada), 90 Eglinton Avenue East, Suite 700, Toronto,
Ontario M4P 2Y3, Canada (a division of Pearson Penguin Canada Inc.)
Penguin Books Ltd., 80 Strand, London WC2R 0RL, England
Penguin Ireland, 25 St. Stephen's Green, Dublin 2,
Ireland (a division of Penguin Books Ltd.)
Penguin Group (Australia), 250 Camberwell Road, Camberwell, Victoria 3124,
Australia (a division of Pearson Australia Group Pty. Ltd.)
Penguin Books India Pvt. Ltd., 11 Community Centre, Panchsheel Park,
New Delhi - 110 017, India
Penguin Group (NZ), 67 Apollo Drive, Rosedale, Auckland 0632,
New Zealand (a division of Pearson New Zealand Ltd.)
Penguin Books (South Africa) (Pty.) Ltd., 24 Sturdee Avenue,
Rosebank, Johannesburg 2196, South Africa

Penguin Books Ltd., Registered Offices:
80 Strand, London WC2R 0RL, England

First published by Obsidian, an imprint of New American Library,
a division of Penguin Group (USA) Inc.

First Printing, July 2012
10 9 8 7 6 5 4 3 2 1

PUBLISHER'S NOTE
This is a work of fiction. Names, characters, places, and incidents either are the
product of the author's imagination or are used fictitiously, and any resemblance
to actual persons, living or dead, business establishments, events, or locales is
entirely coincidental.
    The publisher does not have any control over and does not assume any respon-
sibility for author or third-party Web sites or their content.

ALWAYS LEARNING   PEARSON

This one is for you, Dad.
I love you.
Jack Schnell, 1931–2011

Chapter 1

"It's time," my best friend's voice said into my ear.

I glanced at the clock in my mother's kitchen. Nine thirty. The breakfast dishes were done and my two children were in the living room with Mom playing a card game. All was right with the world on this third day of spring break. I shifted my grip on the cell phone. "Why now?"

"No time like the present," Marina said airily. "Gather ye roses while ye may. A rolling stone gathers no moss, you know."

Today, clearly, was cliché day. "There won't be roses for another six weeks." I looked out the window at the snow in the front yard. "And up here at my mom's, probably not until July."

"But you don't live up there in the wilds of northern Michigan, now do you? You live in a civilized part of Wisconsin where winter is forbidden after March the second. Down here the birds are singing and the bees are buzzing and the flowers are getting all perky."

I was pretty sure she was quoting a musical, and I was also pretty sure she was quoting it incorrectly, but since I had no proof I let it go. "What, exactly, is it time for?"

"You know." She'd deepened her voice, making it

sound almost ominous. Which was a good trick for a woman who had a hard time putting two serious sentences back to back.

"I do?"

"You need to make a decision."

"And lots of them. Should Jenna get tutoring in hockey? Should Oliver take swim lessons? Should I enroll Spot in obedience training? Should I start carrying more toys at the store?"

"That's not what I'm talking about and you know it."

I did, but I'd avoided thinking about it for months, so a few more minutes wouldn't hurt. There were a tremendous number of things I didn't know; what to do about the handsome Evan Garrett was only the tip of the iceberg.

"How long have you dillydallied around this issue?" Marina demanded.

"Not very."

"Puh-leeese."

"Nine months, tops." Just short of a year, if you counted back to the first time I realized Evan was more than just a friend. But now I was getting the itchy feeling that he was going to propose and I wasn't at all sure that would be the best thing for my children.

Sure, their father and I had divorced amicably two and a half years ago. Sure, they got along with Evan, and sure, they seemed well adjusted, but what if I was wrong? What if a new marriage rocked them sideways onto a course from which they'd never recover? What if—

"You've been moaning and groaning about this for years," Marina said.

"I . . . have?" Not a good day for her math skills. Evan had moved to Rynwood less than two years ago.

"Tell me when I'm wrong," she said.

"Ready and willing." I leaned back into an inside corner of the kitchen counter, making sure to get a good view of the lake. My parents had moved here when I was seven, and twenty-odd years after leaving for college and never really coming back, I still missed seeing blue water outside the kitchen window.

"You want to make some changes in your life."

Who didn't? "Correct." I squinted out at the lake. Frozen tight from stem to stern. Happy April.

"You want to move from the Beth you are to the Beth you could be and want to be."

Had she been listening to morning talk shows again? "Correct."

"Then it's time to quit talking and start doing," she said, and I could almost see her nodding, her light red hair flopping around and her ponytail scrunchie going loose. "Tell you what," she said. "We'll make it a contest. Whoever puts up the best numbers wins."

Suddenly, all became clear. "You're talking about losing weight, aren't you?"

"What else would I be talking about?"

"Nothing," I said quickly.

There was a short silence. Marina Neff, mother of four, wasn't fooled for a heartbeat. "No weasel answers, Beth Kennedy. I want the truth."

"Oh, dear." I put on a worried voice. "Sounds like the kids are starting World War Three. Gotta go."

"You are the world's worst liar. Tell your aunt Marina all about your misinterpretations of the topic at hand."

I toyed with the idea of complete fabrication. I'd thought she was talking about my occasional desire to go back to college. I'd thought she was talking about my constant desire to stand up to the PTA vice president, Claudia Wolff. Unfortunately, the odds of getting away with a lie were slim to negative ten thousand. "You could have been talking about Evan."

"Ah-ha," she said. "Yes, I suppose I could."

"But you weren't." And since distraction was my second-best friend, I brought her into the conversation. "What's the prize for this contest? I'm not going to play for bragging rights, you know."

"Ooo, good point. It has to be good enough to be worthwhile, but not so expensive that you'll go green with jealousy when I get it."

"What makes you think you're going to win?"

"Because," she said, "I'm ready to put my nose to the grindstone. Willing to burn the midnight oil and put my shoulder to the wheel."

"You sound motivated."

"And do you know why? No, you do not. The answer to that question is, after all, the reason for this phone call. I, dear heart, am finally going to Hawaii."

My yelp of excitement caused both of my children and my mother to turn to look at me. I smiled and waved, and they returned to their vicious game of rummy. "Really truly?" I asked. "You're not making this up just to get me exercising, are you?"

"Would I be that manipulative? Okay, I could, yes, I could, but not this time," she said. "No, my little chickadee, a mere twenty-seven years, eight months, and seventeen days after our marriage, I am being taken to the land of luaus, pineapples, and sunsets. The DH is finally earning the title of Devoted Husband."

Hah. If any two people in the world were made for each other, it was Marina and her husband. Sure, he was the classic introverted engineer and she was the stereotypical fiery-tempered redhead, but their personalities mushed together like potatoes and gravy.

"What are you going to say when Evan proposes?" Marina asked.

My powers of distraction must have deserted me in my time of need. "What makes you think he's going to?"

"So young," she said, "yet such an annoyance to those of us who are interested in your life. Of course he's going to ask. Why else would he have spent the last two weekends at your house trying to figure out where that roof leak was coming from?"

"He's just trying to be helpful."

Marina snorted. "No one is that helpful unless he's after something. He's going to ask you to marry him one of these days. My money's on soon." I made a noise of demurral, but she overrode me. "Soon," she repeated. "And what are you going to tell him?"

She was my best friend, so there was only one answer I could give her. The truth. "I don't know," I said. "I really don't."

Early Saturday morning, Mom was in the kitchen packing a traveling lunch that would feed a family of ten. I schlepped suitcases and stuffed animals and blankies and tote bags from porch to car. Eleven-year-old Jenna helped by moving things from the front entry to the porch and eight-year-old Oliver helped by opening and shutting the door against the cold April wind. My sister Darlene helped by standing next to the car, huddled in a parka with the hood pulled low over her forehead.

"Now that you're leaving," Darlene said, "may I say that coming up here in April is insane?"

I shoved the duffel bag filled with dirty clothes far forward in the trunk and didn't bother turning to look at my favorite sister. "I just couldn't go another day without seeing your smiling face."

"Try selling that to someone who might believe you. And, anyway, you saw me at Christmas."

Darlene and her husband lived a few minutes away from Mom, and all three had come down to spend Christmas in Rynwood. My brother Tim and his son Max had also shown up, and it had been a lovely holiday in spite of my mother's eloquent sniffs about my house-keeping. The downside was that my mother had finally met Evan.

She loved him, of course. Who wouldn't love a man who was movie star handsome, had more money than most mortals from his former career as a corporate law-yer, and cleared the dinner dishes off the table without being asked?

A gust of wind hurried across the lake and buffeted the both of us. My lithe, athletic sister tucked her chin to her chest and rode it out, rocking back and forth. I grabbed the edge of the trunk and wished I'd put on warmer gloves.

The gust moved on and Darlene pounced with an-other question. "Are you going to marry that Evan, or what?"

If I were the conspiracy-believing type, this would be when I started thinking that my friends and family were ganging up on me. But since I believed in conspiracies about as much as I believed that long hours of playing video games would help children succeed in business, I chalked Marina's and Darlene's questions up to coinci-dence. I gave Darlene the same answer.

"What do you mean, you don't know? You've been going out with this guy for what, a year, and you don't know?"

"Nine months," I murmured. And here I'd always thought I was the math idiot in the family.

"How can you not know what you want?" she pressed. "What if he asks tomorrow? What are you going to tell him?"

"I'm not sure the kids are ready for a stepfather," I said.

"Twiddle." Darlene tried to tuck her dark hair behind her ears. Since she was wearing thick wool mittens this didn't work out very well. Her fine strands stuck to the mittens and flew out around her face. "Jenna and Oliver are so starved for a father figure that even Roger noticed how much time they spent hanging around our house this week."

I'd noticed it, too, and had put it down to the fact that Roger had been cooking maple syrup. Darlene's husband worked in construction and spent much of the winter on short hours, which meshed well with his hobbies of hunting, skiing, and maple syrup cooking. The kids had been enthralled with syrup creation and it had been hard to drag them away from the sugar shack at mealtimes. "They love their uncle Roger," I said, "but they might love maple syrup a little bit more."

Darlene put her hands deep into her coat pockets, her knuckles poking large indentations through the fabric. "What are you scared of?" she asked.

"Disease, accidents, and inappropriate friendships."

"Marina's not that bad."

I picked up a heavy cardboard box crowded with Mason jars filled with maple syrup and put it in the trunk. She knew perfectly well that I was talking about Jenna and Oliver.

"No, really." Darlene shook back her hood. Her gaze was steady and calm, which could mean only one thing. She'd turned serious. "What are you scared of?"

I couldn't tell her the truth, which was that on some

level I was scared of pretty much everything, so I just shook my head.

"Try not to be so scared, Beth," she said. "It's a dumb way to live."

"Can't help it." Once in a decade I could lie to Marina and get away undetected, but my big sister knew I'd been scared of the dark until I was twelve. She also knew that, at age six, I'd hid behind her so I didn't have to talk to strangers. She also knew that the main reason I'd become a journalism major wasn't so I could be an investigative reporter à la Woodward and Bernstein, but to become an editor so I could read all day and not talk to anyone. How I'd ended up the owner of a children's bookstore I wasn't quite sure.

"You can too help it." Darlene watched me stow a suitcase. "Just make up your mind to stop being such a 'fraidy cat."

Maybe I could make it a mantra, or something like that. Be brave. Be unafraid. Be courageous. You have no reason to fear.

But then all the reasons to be scared came rushing back. Though the sky was blue, my world darkened and tightened and clutched at me and reached out for my children and—

Darlene looked at me. "You're thinking about those murders, aren't you?"

I shook away the black thoughts. "How do you do that? You're creepy."

She laughed. "Anybody with half a brain could see what you're thinking. You're more transparent than a window that's just been washed."

"A murder is worth being scared about."

"Only if you're the victim. You were smart enough to not become one of those, remember? *And* the bad guys are in prison. Plus, what are the odds of yet another murder happening in that little town?" She spread her hands wide, palms up.

If I'd been a math whiz like our brother, Tim, I'd have been able to calculate those odds in my head. Or if I had a financial genius husband like our older sister, Kathy, I'd have been able to ask him. But since I wasn't, and didn't, I had to think Darlene's question through.

Rynwood was located directly east of Madison, Wisconsin, a city with a crime rate much below the national average. The fact that Rynwood itself, a town of five thousand, had suffered two murders in the last two years could only be a statistical anomaly.

I looked at Darlene. "You know, you're right."

"Of course I am." She nodded smugly. "I'm your big sister and I know best."

Before I could point out some of her many errors in judgment, my children pounded out of the house.

"That's all, Mom!" Jenna called.

"Nothing's left," Oliver said.

"Did you both use the bathroom?" They nodded vigorously. "Then give your aunt Darlene hugs."

While the three of them were midclutch, my mother came outside. "Don't forget this." She set a green cloth bag onto the porch. "Your lunches."

"Thanks, Mom." I picked up the bag and almost dropped it. "What'd you put in here? A twenty-pound turkey?"

"Oh, this and that."

I peered into the bag. Sandwiches. Soda, wrapped with layers of newspaper to stay cold-ish. A plastic container of pasta salad. Another one of coleslaw. Another one of broccoli salad. Another one full of what looked to be cut-up carrots, celery, cucumbers, and peppers. Clearly, my mother didn't think I fed my children enough vegetables.

"Drive carefully," she said. "Call me when you get home."

"Yes, Mom," I said automatically. "Kids, did you hug your grandmother?"

They ran over for round two, then I gave her a quick embrace. "Saddle up, buckaroos."

Oliver took the passenger's seat—it was his turn for the front—and Jenna ensconced herself in the back amid blankets, pillows, and handheld video games. I took off my coat, put it and the food in the trunk, then closed the lid. Mom had gone inside and was at the kitchen window. "Take care of yourself," I told Darlene.

She stepped close and held me tight, then stepped away and opened my car door. "Remember that night I hid under your bed and grabbed your ankles?" she asked as I settled in.

"Gave me nightmares for weeks."

"I told Jenna about it." She shut the door on my opening mouth and, grinning, trotted off to the safety of the porch.

A few hours of driving later, we were over the Mackinac Bridge, past Menominee, into Wisconsin, and past lovely little Peshtigo with its tragic Fire Cemetery and Fire Museum. Every time I thought about the horrific events of 1871, a night of bad dreams followed. Some accounts wrote about flames a thousand feet high and five miles wide rushing forward at a hundred miles an hour. Fire was something else to be afraid of, no question about it.

How could Darlene say I didn't need to be scared? She was a mother; she knew that we were scared of everything. Maybe she'd forgotten what it was like because her children were grown and gone. Or maybe she'd never been scared in the first place.

I considered the idea, then discarded it. Motherhood equals fear. No other possibility existed. A year and a half ago, when my children had brushed up against the ugly reality of bad guys and death, I'd sworn off poking my nose into things that didn't concern me. My vow had worked, more or less, and keeping my children safe and sound was the only thing that really mattered. Well, that and having the Children's Bookshelf turn a profit. And making this year's big PTA project a success.

Jenna stirred out of her nap. "How much longer?" She rubbed her eyes and flipped over to face me.

"Two hours," I said, but she was already back asleep.

Softly, gently, I rested my hand on her shoulder. Bone and muscle, skin and ligaments. If love was what it took to see this daughter of mine safely through adolescence, then I was all set. If it needed more than love, well . . .

Maybe I should summon Darlene's advice and try to apply it. "Don't be scared," I told myself. "Don't be scared."

It was good advice, really. What had the angels said to the shepherds outside of Bethlehem? "Fear not." If I'd actually paid attention in Sunday school I'd know the quote exactly, but it was something along those lines.

I caressed Jenna's hair, and wished I could do the same to Oliver's. My children, my heart, my life. The whole trip had been a pleasure from start to finish. In spite of the fact that two weeks ago I'd assumed I'd have a week without children and had planned to repaint both their rooms, clean out their closets, and have the carpets cleaned, I didn't regret one minute of this time away from home.

I'd been sitting at the kitchen table making lists of

what to pack in their suitcases when my former husband had called.

"I got a job," he'd said.

"Oh, Richard, that's wonderful!" Relief had flooded through me. No more worry about Richard's severance package running out, no more worry about the child support payments dwindling to nearly nothing, no more worry about selling the house; hardly any worries left at all. "Which job is it?"

"Not the one in Madison, unfortunately."

A chill had leached into my bones. "The one in Georgia?" The kids would hardly ever see their father. He'd become a near-stranger. They'd never learn the lessons that only fathers can teach; they'd—

"No, not the one in Atlanta. I'm going to be working in Milwaukee."

Since I'd already been sitting down, I couldn't sit down again, but the second wave of relief made me want to slide to the floor and find a wall for support. Life was so very good.

"I'll be on the west side, heading up a new branch of Smithwick Insurance."

"That's great, Richard. Just"—I had searched for the proper word and couldn't find one—"just great."

"Yes, I'm pleased."

"Are you going to move?" Richard owned a condominium just outside Rynwood. "That'll be what, an hour and a half commute?"

He'd chuckled. "The way you drive, yes. The way the rest of the population drives, it's closer to an hour. But the way the housing market is these days, I don't anticipate being able to sell for anything close to the purchase price. Besides, it'd be easier on the kids if I stayed."

"You're a pretty good dad," I'd said softly.

"They could do worse," he'd replied, reminding me of why we'd gotten divorced. "There is one small issue we'll have to deal with, however."

"How big of a small issue?" I'd asked cautiously. To Richard, a "small issue" could mean anything from being half an hour late to knee surgery. "On a scale of one to ten."

"Four."

Four wasn't bad. Four I could deal with.

"They want me to start working next week."

"That's gr—" I'd stopped. It was great. But it was also bad. "That's spring vacation."

"Yes, I know, and there's a solution. My parents want to spend time with Jenna and Oliver, correct?"

He always did this. Forcing agreement was one of his favorite management tools. Two and a half years distant from our former marriage, it still annoyed me. "We don't need to build a consensus here, Richard. What's your solution?"

He changed tactics. "My parents have been looking forward to this visit for months. The kids are looking forward to going."

My former in-laws were kind and considerate people. They were also the stiff-upper-lip type and about as likely to step out of their comfortable upper-middle-class box as Marina was likely to start wearing pearls and twinsets. But they loved their grandchildren very much and the kids loved their times in Arizona.

"I can't make the trip," Richard continued, "so I want you to consider going to Arizona in my stead."

"You . . . what?"

"It won't cost you a single dollar," Richard said. "I'll take care of the airfare and my dad will pick you up at the airport. No need to rent a car."

Trust Richard to have the details worked out in advance. And he was doing a good job of selling the idea. But then he made a major error. He said, "You'll have a wonderful time."

No, I wouldn't. I'd be bored to tears. His parents were nice people, but our overlapping interests began and ended with the kids. I grew instantly sleepy when they began describing their latest golf game, and their eyes glazed over when I started talking about the latest Caldecott winner.

"So I take it you agree?" Richard asked.

Off in the distance I could feel my future twisting around. Richard would say that Lois and Yvonne, my two full-time employees, could do without me for a week. I had orders to place, accounting to battle against, and my regular round of book deliveries to make. But I deserved a week off, he'd say. Why not take advantage of his generous offer?

"No," I'd said, and felt the clouds around my head start to clear. "No, I don't agree." It felt so good to say so that I'd said it one more time. "I don't agree at all."

"You have another plan?" He'd spoken calmly, but I could hear the irritation growing in the back of his voice. "A plan which will deprive the children of time spent with their grandparents? With their grandmother, who loves them unreservedly?"

"Not at all." If he heard my smile, all the better. "They have two grandmothers, don't they? I'll take them up north."

Now I pulled into our driveway and saw our house, all safe and sound, and let myself relax. Going away was all well and good, but coming home was even better.

I shuffled the mostly asleep kids inside to bed, tried but failed to pet the cat, who'd stayed home and been taken care of by a neighbor, then started heaving the luggage out of the trunk. Tomorrow was Sunday and laundry day, we had to pick up our dog, Spot, from the kennel, and I'd have to do some grocery shopping. I sighed. Being gone was a lot of work. Still, it had been a wonderful week and I was glad I'd stood up to Richard. I considered the thought that if I'd starting doing that twenty years ago we might still be married.

Considered it briefly, then tossed it aside. If anything, my growing a backbone would have hastened the divorce. And if I'd grown one early enough, there might not have been Jenna or Oliver.

No, things were working out, in a general sort of way. If only I knew what to do about—

My phone rang. I pulled it out of my purse, poked at the ON button, and put it against my ear while I extracted Oliver's stuffed animals from the car. "Hello?"

"Hey, sweetheart. Are you home?"

Evan. If only I knew what to do about Evan.

Chapter 2

The next morning—Easter morning—I was out of bed by eight and shepherding the kids into Sunday school almost on time. I scurried into the choir room and was donning my maroon robe when the director started warm-ups. I slid into my seat, church bulletin in one hand, folder of music in the other.

We sang up and down the scale in solfège; "Do re mi fa," and we did some ooo's and we did some aaaa's. Kay tapped her music stand with a slender baton. "The first anthem is in good shape," she said. "But the offertory is the Rutter and it needs some work. Sopranos, let's run through your descant at measure one twenty-seven."

The Rutter. I'd forgotten all about it. "Why do we have to do the Rutter?" I groused to the alto on my left. "Why does he have to write music that's so hard?"

My complaint, spurred on by driving-induced fatigue, was a bit too loud. Thanks to the proximity of the tenor section—directly behind the altos—Rynwood's police chief, my friend Gus Eiseley, overheard the comment.

"We sing John Rutter's compositions," Gus said, "because he's the best living composer of choral music."

I should have kept quiet, I should have nodded and left it alone. Instead, I turned in my seat and faced Gus.

"If he writes the best music," I said, "why isn't he more popular in his own country? Why don't the English sing his stuff? Why was the world premiere of his *Requiem* in Geneva, Illinois?"

Cold words. I loved John Rutter's music and always had. But this particular piece was difficult, I'd missed the last choir rehearsal, and I was deeply afraid of coming in early on one of the alto entrances.

"Just because you always come in early in that middle part," Gus said, "isn't any reason to criticize the composer."

Heat spread across my face. "I do not always."

He raised his eyebrows. Not an ounce of humor showed on his weathered face. Gus was one of those men whose age was indeterminate; if judging only from the vaguely gray close-cropped stubble showing on his scalp, he could have been anywhere from mid-thirties to mid-sixties. He normally wore a pleasant expression, but right now his obvious irritation was giving me a glimpse at what he would look like at eighty. Worn, lined, and downright cranky.

"Sorry," he said. "I must have been out of the room the time you got it right."

I gaped at him. Was he joking? Gus wouldn't say something like that to me. He must be joking.

"Geez, Gus." The tenor sitting next to him, a portly man with ever-present onion breath who sang like a brother of Pavarotti, bumped Gus with his elbow. "Give the girl a break. It's just a song, you know."

"It's John Rutter," Gus said carefully.

"Kay is our director," I said. "Would you care to tell her the issues you have with my performance?"

The last person who made a suggestion that contradicted her had been lambasted with more music theory than anyone saw outside a master's degree thesis. It wasn't an experience any of us wished to repeat.

"For the Rutter," Gus said, "I might risk it."

We glared at each other until Kay said, "Nicely done, sopranos. Everyone, let's start at the beginning."

I turned around to face her. There was no way, no way whatsoever, that I was going to come in early on that middle part.

That was the foremost thought in my mind, but close behind it was another thought. Gus and I, friends for almost twenty years, had just had our first fight.

"So?" Lois asked. "Did you come in early?"

It was Monday morning, and Lois, the manager of my children's bookstore, sat in my tiny office with the toes of her shoes on the edge of my desk. They were red sparkly shoes that reminded me of Dorothy's ruby slippers, but the clothes Lois wore weren't anything ever seen in 1939 Kansas.

Lois Nielson, sixty-two, mother and grandmother, had cast off her sensible shoes and cardigan sweaters when her husband died and was well on her way to becoming one of the Characters of Rynwood. Where she'd found a sari, I didn't know, but she was wrapped up in one that shimmered even in the sickly light cast by the fluorescent light fixtures. Red threads intertwined with pinks and a few blues and greens, all shiny enough that it seemed as if there were movement, even when there was none.

"In that Rutter song," Lois said impatiently. "Did you come in early?"

I looked away from the sparkly shoes. "Of course I did."

Lois laughed. "What did Gus say?"

"He didn't say anything." After the service I'd tried to talk to him, but he'd looked right through me.

The sparkly shoes whumped to the floor. "That's not like Gus. Did you talk to Winnie?"

"Didn't have a chance." Though Gus and his wife usually stayed for coffee hour, yesterday they'd melted away right after the service.

"Hmm." Lois fiddled with the pin that was keeping her sari wrapped. When she'd walked in and asked for my opinion on her attire, I'd pointed out that saris were supposed to stay in place all by themselves, and that a kilt pin dangling with tinkly charms wasn't exactly a normal part of an Indian woman's attire.

She'd replied that she wasn't an Indian woman, and did I really want to run the risk of the sudden exposure of sixty-two-year-old skin? There was, of course, no socially acceptable answer to that, so I said she looked wonderful just as she was. Which was the truth.

An even deeper truth was that I was the teensiest bit jealous of Lois's ability to wear such ensembles. Shy Beth, afraid of breaking out of her blazer and dress pants rut. Cowardly Beth, afraid of having her children giggle at her clothes. Lois, with her nest long empty, didn't have to worry about that.

"That's weird about Gus," Lois said. "You can be a little snotty sometimes, but I wouldn't have thought he'd get his undies in a bunch over some song."

"Snotty?" I asked. "What do you mean?"

"You know how you get sometimes. All prim and proper, enunciating every consonant, chin up in the air." She demonstrated.

"I do not!"

"Oh, please."

"Good morning, Mrs. Kennedy. Good morning, Mrs.

Nielson." Paoze, one of my part-time employees, smiled at us.

"Hey, kid." Lois beckoned him in. "What do you think? Does Beth here get snotty sometimes?"

"Snotty?" He touched the tip of his nose.

Though Paoze—who'd come to this country with his parents from Laos—was an English major, there were idiosyncrasies of our complicated language that continued to puzzle him. Lois, trickster that she was, occasionally made the most of this.

"Not real snot," Lois said. "Snotty like being stuck-up. Like being all high-and-mighty. Thinking you're better than the rest of us rabble."

Paoze looked from Lois to me and back again. "I am not certain what you mean."

I stood up. "Paoze, you are a gentleman and a scholar and will undoubtedly go far in life. Lois, when you're done dissecting my character, do you think perhaps we can open the store for business?"

Lois nodded. "See, like that. Snotty." But the accompanying grin took any sting out of her words. "Say, I brought in some new tea. Rooibos stuff from South Africa. Want a cup?"

"Can't. Not now, anyway." I picked up the topmost stack of papers from the corner of my desk. Invoices for accounts receivable, my favorite kind of invoice. "It's delivery day."

She made a face. "I don't know why you keep on doing that. People can pick up their own books, can't they?"

"Yes," I said, "but perhaps the goodwill generated by my personal selection and delivery service creates customers for life, customers who will recommend the store far and wide."

Lois nodded. "Snotty, but smart. You're not so bad for a girl."

"And you're not so bad for . . . for . . ."

"For a lady of a certain age." Paoze smiled, showing his bright white teeth.

Lois and I looked at him. Looked at each other. "He's catching on," I told her. "You'd better watch out."

"Age and treachery always overcome youth and skill," she said, folding her arms across her chest.

"Always?"

We looked at Paoze again. He was standing as he often did, straight as an arrow, hands clasped loosely in front of him, wearing a gentle smile that warmed the room.

"Harmless," she said. "He'll never catch me out."

I shook my head and shooed them out of my office. I had a feeling Paoze was biding his time, waiting for the perfect moment to spring a trap on Lois, a trap of gigantic proportions that would pay her back for all the tall tales she'd convinced him to swallow over the years.

With any luck, I'd be around to see it.

I'd been making deliveries for as long as I'd owned the store, but things had changed a few months ago. I'd accidentally put a copy of Brian Jacques's *Redwall* in a box for a mother who was homeschooling her three preadolescent boys and she'd fallen on it like manna from heaven.

Even marketing-challenged Beth could recognize a brilliant idea when it dropped on her head. Since that day I'd brought along a handpicked selection of books for customers to browse through. At first I'd been surprised at how many of the parents and teachers started ordering middle grade and young adult books for their own reading, but after thinking it through, I realized I shouldn't have been surprised at all. A good book was a good book, no matter who the intended audience may be. The experiment was not only building an extremely loyal customer base, it was also building my muscles. Carrying boxes of books was almost as much work as toting around a toddler.

I dropped off two boxes at Tarver Elementary's front office; one full of books ordered by various teachers, the other full of books for browsing that I'd pick up later. Then I did what I often did when dropping books at the school—I tiptoed around to peer into my children's classrooms.

Seeing the top of Oliver's head as he busily worked on a math assignment and glimpsing a bit of Jenna as she and two other children were doing something with cardboard and wood dowels gave me a warm fuzzy of the fuzziest sort. I drove out of the school parking lot, smiling.

My last stop, however, always troubled me. Every time I delivered a box to Amy Jacobson, I came away with the impression that I should be doing something more. And every time, I had no idea what that something might be.

I bumped up the long drive, parked, and went around to the trunk to get Amy's books. My feet didn't make any noise on the driveway, gravel once upon a time, but now grown over with grass and weeds. Amy cut everything back in October, but since she didn't drive, she didn't see the need for much in the way of weekly maintenance. Like, none.

Shutting the trunk with my elbow, I walked up the path that led to the house. Here, with trees growing close and birds singing overhead, it was hard to believe that Amy lived in the heart of Rynwood.

Her house sat perched on a small hill and her bushy backyard tucked up against the largest park in town. There were neighbors on both sides, but far enough away that the sound of voices rarely reached into Amy's tangle of a garden.

As I approached the house, I once again fell in love. With its diamond-paned windows, ivy growing at the corners, a pert chimney of faded red brick, and a front door arched at the top, it looked like something out of a fairy tale. Its only nod to reality was the asphalt shingle roof. I'd once jokingly told Amy that when she had to reshingle, she should turn it into a thatch roof, and hadn't known what to say when she'd unsmilingly told me it had been thatch, but her parents couldn't afford to have it fixed and had had to replace it with something cheaper.

I cast a longing look at the front porch with its friendly set of two facing benches and went around to the back. Amy wouldn't answer the front door, a fact I'd learned the hard way.

The long grass brushed against my pant legs as I walked around the house. Soon the lilacs that surrounded Amy's backyard would burst into bloom. Smiling at a scent that hadn't yet arrived, I rounded the corner of the house and stopped dead. The bird feeders. They were mostly empty and Amy was a stickler for keeping them filled.

I shifted the box in my arms. Maybe she was sick. If she'd fallen sick, she might be out of other things, too. Milk, food, medicine. I knew that Flossie, owner of the local grocery store, sent her great-nephew on weekly delivery runs, so Amy wouldn't starve to death, but if she was really sick, she might not be able to call in an order.

The back door looked as it always did—in need of paint and new weather stripping. I pulled open the wooden-framed screen door and knocked on the door's glass window. "Amy?" I called loudly. "It's Beth."

There was no answering call, but that was normal. It usually took three sets of knocking and calling to convince Amy to come to the door.

Knock, knock. "Amy?"

Knock, knock. "Hello? Amy?"

It wasn't until the fifth set that I realized what any rational person would have figured out some time ago: She wasn't home. Which didn't make any sense, because Amy was always home.

Always.

As a child, I'd pictured people who hid away from the world as men with long gray hair and beards down to their belly buttons, but Amy was female and she wasn't much older than I was.

I didn't know if she suffered from agoraphobia or if she was just the hermit type. I had the occasional tendency toward reclusiveness myself, but Amy's version was extreme. The one time I'd tried to coax her outside—"The park is just the other side of your bushes. Let's go for a walk. We'll be careful about bees and we'll stay out of sun, what do you think?"—tears had started to trickle down her cheeks and she'd covered her face with her hands.

Horrified at what I'd done, I put my arms around her. It was the first time I'd ever touched her. She flinched, then grabbed on to me as if I were the last person on Earth.

I'd murmured nonsense words and stroked her hair, wondering how long it had been since she'd felt the imprint of another person's skin. Eventually, her crying slowed to a stop. She'd pulled back, blown her nose, and the incident was closed. But ever since, I'd allowed enough time in my schedule to stay with her for at least an hour.

My knuckles were getting sore from knocking. "Amy? Amy!"

She had to be here. Any second now she'd scurry to the door and apologize for making me wait. She'd . . . been in the attic. Sure, that was it. She'd been looking for—

"Looking for Amy?"

I whirled around.

A man stood in front of a long row of lilac bushes; their waving branches on this breezeless morning solid evidence of his passage. Which was a good thing, because in this fairy-tale-ish setting, his small stature and thick white hair gave him a very elfin look.

"Yes," I said. "She's not sick, is she?"

He walked to the porch and trotted up the stairs. Somehow the fact that he carried a pair of pruning shears didn't bother me a bit. Elves just aren't threatening creatures.

"Thurman Schroeder is the name," he said. "Selling cars is the game. Or it was, until I retired. Now I clip shrubs and try to pretend I'm useful. My wife says she'll keep me around as long as I can take out the garbage, but I don't want to push my luck."

He grinned and I grinned back.

"You're not selling anything," he said. "Not dressed city enough. And you're not one of those church ladies; not old enough. You're . . . say, I know." He snapped his fingers. "The book lady. That's who you are. Amy liked you, you know."

"Today's book delivery day." I nodded at the box I'd set next to the door. "I can't believe she's not here."

The elf's cheerful smile turned upside down. "Oh, dear. You haven't heard."

"Heard what?"

His next words explained everything; why he felt free to stand on Amy's back porch, and worst of all, explained his use of past tense.

"She's dead."

Chapter 3

When I returned to the store, Lois took one look at my face and sat me in a chair. Two mugs of hot tea later, I was able to talk.

"Thurman said one of the reasons she hardly ever went outside was she was allergic to bee and wasp stings." Which I'd known, but what I hadn't realized was the severity of her allergies. To be so allergic that you could die . . . I swallowed and wanted to take back all the thoughts I'd had when Amy said she never went outside without a can of Raid in each hand. Not that I'd ever said anything, but I'd certainly thought that Amy had been overreacting.

Lois handed over the third round of tea and I set it down on my desk. "But for some reason," I said, "she went out. Thurman and his wife took their dog out for an evening walk and the dog kept whining and tugging on the leash. They found her and called 911, but it was too late." I stopped.

Lois pushed the mug toward me. I picked it up, wrapped my hands around the heat, and kept going. "She had one of those EpiPens in her hand. You know, those injection things people with bad allergies have? But she hadn't used it. No one knows why. Too scared, they're guessing."

"Poor girl," Lois said softly.

I felt Amy's panic rising in my throat. What a dreadful way to die, not being able to breathe, not being able to pull that life-giving air into your lungs, seeing dark spots in front of your eyes, seeing the dark spots grow larger and larger. . . .

"Drink," Lois commanded.

Obediently, I took a swallow. It felt so good going down that I took another. "I keep thinking that if it hadn't been for Thurman's dog, she might have laid there for hours. Days, even."

I started to lower the mug, but Lois tapped its bottom. "Drink up," she said. "It didn't happen, so quit making things worse than they are."

She was right, but that didn't make the pictures in my head go away.

"The trick," she said, "is to keep busy."

"Trick?" I repeated vaguely. Amy, terrified of bees, swatting them away, trying to run to the safety of her house, trying to—

"Here." Lois took away the mug. "You've had enough. Now it's time to get to work. Did I tell you we got that new software upgrade? I tried to install it this morning up front, but it made a bunch of weird beeping noises so I just turned the dang thing off."

"You did what?" I sprang out of my chair. If she'd halted the installation partway, it could have corrupted the store's book inventory. Worse things could happen to a bookstore, but I couldn't think of one.

"Oh, it's fine," she said airily. Then she frowned. "At least I think so. I suppose there's a chance that the blue screen it gets every once in a while means I did something wrong." Her face cleared. "But I'm sure it's nothing. Computers are pretty tough, right?"

I pushed past her. "Where are the new disks? And the documentation? Don't put any more sales into the computer until I make sure everything is working."

"Paper and pencil," she said. "Nothing wrong with paper and pencil."

In the middle of my rush to the front counter, I paused. Lois sounded a little too cheerful for what could be a medium-sized disaster. Could she be making up this whole event, just to take my mind off Amy's death?

I glanced over my shoulder. Lois was frowning at me, her arms crossed and her fingers pulling at her lips.

No, Lois might make up a story for Paoze, but she wouldn't do that to me.

I put the possibility out of my head and got to work.

Sitting in a Tarver classroom on Wednesday night, waiting for the PTA meeting to start, I was still trying to absorb the fact that Amy was gone. Bad enough when someone who had lived a long life passed away, so much worse when it was someone relatively young. So wrong for her to be dead, so wrong for all her chances at living to be gone.

Marina was sitting in the half-full room and she raised an eyebrow at my glum face. "How now the down-turned brow?"

"Still thinking about Amy," I said.

"Yeah." Marina sighed. "That stinks. I didn't know her, but what a shame. And what a nasty way to go."

She started putting her hands to her throat. I knew she was going to start fake-choking herself. "Don't you dare," I said. "It would be inappropriate, unkind, and disrespectful to Amy's memory."

There may, just may, have been a slight blush that appeared on her cheeks. She dropped her hands to her lap.

"You're such a mom," she muttered, ignoring the fact that she'd been one for twenty-odd years. Her youngest, Zach, still attended Tarver, but the rest were in or out of college.

Marina brightened. "Say, have you worked out what you're going to do about losing weight?"

Of course I hadn't. What I'd done was what I'd done for the last ten years—poke myself in the lumpy thighs, watch my index finger sink deep, and immediately put on some clothes.

"Well, what are you going to do? After all that moaning and groaning last summer when we were trying on bathing suits, don't tell me you're not going to do anything, okay? Just don't."

Our illustrious PTA president banged the gavel. I'd never been so glad in my life for a meeting to start.

"This meeting of the Tarver Elementary PTA will come to order."

Erica Hale, a silver-haired woman who could be the definition of chic, was a grandmother of two Tarver students. Her slim elegance always made me feel like an ugly duckling with zero chance of turning into a swan, and she had the enviable ability to say the right thing at the right time. After she'd retired, instead of taking life easy, she'd taken the helm of a floundering PTA and transformed it into a project-oriented powerhouse. She'd also transformed her yard into a gardening showpiece. And she'd started painting in watercolors. If I hadn't liked her so much, I would have found all sorts of reasons to dislike her intensely.

"Beth?" she asked. "Will you please take the roll?"

I called her name, then the vice president's name. "Wolff?"

"Present," Claudia said.

I didn't look at Claudia and she didn't look at me. It was best that way. Claudia was efficient and hardworking, but she also spent a lot of time telling people how efficient and hardworking she was. I could have dealt with that particular personality quirk if it hadn't been for, one, her constant campaign to ruin my reputation, and two, her vocal insistence that I wanted to be the next president of the PTA.

PTA president? I couldn't think of anything I wanted less. Secretary was more than enough for me.

I made a tick mark next to Claudia's name and moved on. "Jarvis?"

"Umm-hmm."

I wasn't exactly sure what he said, since he'd tried to talk through a mouthful of potato chips, but I marked him down as present. Randy, owner of the downtown gas station and convenience store, had been the PTA's treasurer for so long that no one remembered why he'd become treasurer in the first place. There must have been a reason, once upon a time, but I'd never heard an explanation and I didn't want to ask because Randy would be happy to tell me the reason. With footnotes. And graphic aids.

The older Randy got, the longer his stories got, and the bigger his waistline grew. He was in his mid-fifties and if he kept up the trend, by the time he turned seventy he'd have a hard time fitting behind the wheel of his car and his stories would last longer than a four-act play.

"Kennedy," I said. "Present. We have a quorum."

"Thank you, Beth." Erica put on her reading glasses and picked up the agenda. Our PTA president was a big believer in agendas and parliamentary procedure. No point in having a meeting, she said, unless there are decisions to make. No doubt she was right, but going through multiple agenda points while surrounded by construction paper tulips and posters of handwriting examples gave me the silent giggles at least once a meeting.

After we dispensed with the few invoices that needed to be paid, Erica turned to me. "Old business item number one. The senior story project. Beth?"

I bounced a little in my chair. This project was my idea. Now that it was about to start, it was hard to believe I'd been dry-mouthed nervous when I'd proposed it last fall. Silly Beth.

"Okay," I said. "We're going to be working with Sunny Rest Assisted Living. Each resident who wants to participate will be paired with a Tarver student who has signed up for the project. The students will meet their matches for the first time next week and start a series of interviews."

I bounced a little more. This was going to be so very cool. "The kids," I said, "have a list of questions to help them get started, and they'll have to take notes. By the middle of May, they've promised to turn in a first draft. What we want is the life story of each resident as seen through the eyes of the children. I'll do the editing, take the stories to Hoefler Publishing, and before the end of school we'll have softcover books to sell as a moneymaker. Sunny Rest has already asked for two hundred copies."

Marina let out a low whistle. I grinned at her. Judy, the activities director at Sunny Rest, had given me that number half an hour ago, and I was still a little light-headed.

"Good work," Erica said.

Glowing, I spun out the details of carting kids to Sunny Rest after school, arranging to have the visits supervised by PTA parents, carting kids home, all the essential things that go into a project of this size. Fifteen minutes later, I crossed the last item off my list and looked up. "That's it. The matches will be finalized early next week and the first interviews will be Thursday after school."

"One question," Erica said. "What's our profit per book?"

Rats. The one question for which I didn't have an answer. "It depends on the preorders," I said. "Until they come in, I just don't know."

"What quantity is required to get the deepest discount?" Erica asked.

"A thousand."

Marina whistled again, long and low. "That's a lot of books."

I gave her a look. "If we order a thousand, we stand to make a profit of three dollars a book. Sell them all and we make three thousand dollars."

The number echoed around the room a few times before it drifted into people's ears and sifted down into their brains.

"That's a lot of money," Summer Lang said. She was new in town and despite our ten-year age gap, we'd become friends.

"Only if we can sell that many." Claudia tapped her long fingernails on the table. "I say we order the minimum number of books so we can keep the losses small. That's if we're actually going through with this, that is. I'm not so sure it's a good idea."

I opened my mouth, then shut it. Claudia would do her best to torpedo any of my plans and arguing with her wasn't going to change a thing.

"The project was approved months ago," Erica said. "There is no question about carrying it out."

"We can vote to un-approve it, can't we?" Claudia

asked, her voice loud and piercing. "I can make a motion, right? I can make a motion that we cancel this story project, can't I?" She slapped the table with the flat of her palm. "That's what I want to do. I make a motion to cancel this."

As I did my secretarial duty and wrote her words on my yellow legal pad, I held my breath. No one spoke. Randy opened a second bag of potato chips.

"Is there a second?" Erica took off her reading glasses and looked down the length of the table. "The motion dies for lack of a second. Beth, is there anything else? Let's move on to new business."

I let out my breath in a quiet whoosh. We discussed potential projects for next year and Erica used her gavel to bang the meeting adjourned.

I noted the time, turned off the recorder, and reached under the table for the old diaper bag that held my PTA paraphernalia.

Claudia slid into the seat Randy vacated and leaned toward me. "Well, you got your way again, didn't you?" she asked.

I wanted to beat my head against the table. There was no talking to this woman. I gave her a small and very polite smile, made a sideways sort of nod, and continued to put my things away.

"You may have gotten away with it this time," she said, "but just you wait. Nominations for next year's PTA board are coming up soon, and you're not going to be the only one running for secretary."

I stopped, my legal pad halfway into the bag. "Oh?"

"That's right," Claudia said. "I have big plans for this PTA and none of them include you."

I imagined a PTA packed with Claudia and her friends. A board that would rubber-stamp every idea

Claudia came up with. A board that would happily approve pet visits to kindergarten classrooms without first checking for kids with allergies. A board that would vote to purchase wonderful new playground equipment, but would manage to forget that good equipment cost thousands upon thousands of dollars.

I closed my eyes.

Claudia laughed. "Don't like your job being taken away, do you? Well, you and Erica will just have to go try and run things somewhere else because you're on your way out of the Tarver Elementary PTA." She smiled, showing lipstick-stained teeth, and went off to join her cronies.

Marina and Summer were standing nearby, chatting about summer plans. As Claudia left, Marina turned to me. "What was that all about?"

"Um." I reran the scene and tried to include my voice in it. Would the outcome have been different? Probably not, as she would have run over anything I'd tried to say. "Nothing."

I glanced at Claudia, who was now huddled with Tina Heller and CeeCee Daniels. I expected to intercept stares of icy daggers, but they weren't paying any attention to me.

"Not normal." CeeCee's high-pitched voice rose above all others. "Poor thing, dying alone."

"She was a weird one," Tina said. "Living back there by herself."

Claudia made a clucking noise. "She didn't have to be like that. It was her own fault she didn't have a friend in the world. The woman had no life. All she had to do was get out more. How hard could that have been?"

"Not hard at all," Tina said, nodding. "You just decide who you're going to be, and live into that reality."

CeeCee frowned. "So she wanted to be lonely?"

"Must have." Claudia shrugged. "What other explanation is there?"

"Hey." Marina knocked on the table in front of me. "Earth to Beth. Did you hear anything I said?"

"What?" I blinked. "Of course I didn't. What makes you think I did?"

"Well, you agreed to bake twelve dozen cookies for Saturday's bake sale."

"I did not."

"Okay, you didn't," Marina said cheerfully. "Now finish putting away your stuff so I can get you alone. If I don't find out what Claudia did to give you that shell-shocked look, I won't get a wink of sleep."

"The last time you didn't sleep was the night you gave birth to Zach."

"Yeah, and eleven years later I still haven't recovered."

We waited until the room was empty, then walked out together into the mild spring evening. Marina made shocked and angry noises when I told her about Claudia's campaign to take over the PTA. "We must retaliate!" she shouted, thrusting a fist into air.

Even as I listened to her plans involving protest marches with linked arms, part of me was thinking about Amy. Hearing Claudia and her crew gossip had made me want to stand up and defend Amy at top volume. Only one thing had stopped me—the tight-turtleneck idea that maybe they were right. Maybe Amy *had* wanted to be lonely.

But . . . why?

Marina rambled on and I let my mind wander, coming up with ideas, discarding them, thinking about Amy's death, circling around and around like a bird in the sky. "Oh." I came to a dead stop in the middle of the sidewalk.

"What?" Marina stopped, too. "You don't like the idea of using tear gas to break up the inevitable riot?"

"No, I was just wondering . . ."

She rested both hands on her left hip and looked at me through lowered eyelids, a sign that she was going into Southern belle mode. "Mah deah, you must tell me the truth. Have you been listening to me at all?"

"About Amy," I said. "Do you know when she died?"

"Last week."

"No, the time of day."

"No ideah," she said, still in drawl. "And if Ah could make a comment, your interest in dead people is becoming dangerously close to an obsession. Have you considered getting some help?"

I looked at her.

She held up her hands. "Okay, okay," she said, back in Midwest-speak. "I might have gotten you involved that first time. And I helped out some last time. But now there's nothing to get involved *in*. It was a horrible accident, but that's all it was."

Though her consoling tone was probably meant to be comforting, I found no comfort in what she said. "The way Amy died seems a little . . . off, that's all." While I didn't know Amy all that well, I did know that she rarely went outside during the day, and was even less likely to go out in the afternoon, when the sun was strongest.

Marina threaded her arm through mine and started us walking again. I'd parked at her house and we'd walked the three blocks to the school. The proximity made her an ideal candidate for day care. Two toddlers stayed with her all day, and three grade school students—Jenna, Oliver, and another little boy—walked there after school.

"Seems a little off? Off your rocker, more like," Marina said comfortably. "It's your overdeveloped sense of justice getting too big for its britches again. I can almost smell it. You can't stand the idea of a simple accident, can you? You want there to be a reason, and you want to find out what it is."

She was right, but why did she have to make it sound as if I was too innocent to be let out alone at night? "I just have some questions. What's wrong with that?"

"Ooo, Miss Defensive." She patted my arm. "It's perfectly fine. I don't want you to be disappointed when there aren't any answers, is all. Sometimes an accident is just an accident."

I knew that. Of course I knew that. But if Claudia and her ilk were right about Amy having no social life, I may have been the closest thing she'd had to a friend.

Which meant I was the only one who knew that Amy may have been murdered.

Chapter 4

At the store the next morning I shoved aside a stack of returns, ignored e-mail, and focused my math-challenged self on balancing the March accounts. A hideously long time later, I squinted at the computer screen, rubbed my face, and looked at the computer one more time. "Huh," I said out loud. "Would you look at that?"

"At what?" Lois poked her head into my office.

Her outfit today included what looked like a vintage fifties shirtwaist dress. The small floral print and simple collar brought to mind black-and-white television shows that I'd been twenty years too young to see in prime time. I was willing to bet, however, that no TV homemaker had accessorized her dress with a red scarf wrapped twice around her neck and bright green plastic clogs.

I eyed the day's color combinations. When I first started working with Lois I suspected that she was color impaired in some way. Not true. At least not the way you might think. Lois positively enjoyed the clashing of colors. "That'll wake 'em up," she said with satisfaction the day she paired a maroon jacket and blue shirt with a leopard print skirt.

She tapped on my office's door frame. "Look at what?"

I flapped the bank statement at her. "We have money. The entire first quarter of the year—a notoriously difficult time for retail—this store actually made a profit."

"One word." Lois held up her index finger. "Yvonne."

"Yup." I tossed the statement aside. Last fall I'd fired a long-term but ineffective employee and hired Yvonne. She had a stunning knowledge of children's picture books and the magical ability to match the right book to the right customer. A native Californian, she'd survived her first Wisconsin winter with fewer complaints than most homegrown Midwesterners and said she wanted to learn how to skate. I hoped she'd never leave. "Yvonne hand sells picture books almost as fast as I can order them."

"She keeps on doing that and we won't have anything for the summer sale."

"Now, wouldn't that be a tragedy." I stood up and reached for my jacket. "A profitable first quarter calls for a celebration, don't you think?"

Lois, always perky, perked up a bit more. "I hear Alice has a new coconut chocolate chip recipe."

Alice's husband, Alan, ran the Rynwood Antique Mall while Alice baked what the *Wisconsin State Journal* called "the best cookies in the world." So far, no one had disputed the claim.

"Then coconut chocolate chip it is." I opened the bottom drawer of my desk and pulled out my purse. "There's another stop I have to make, but it shouldn't take long."

Lois clutched at her stomach. "But I'm hungry now!"

I skirted around her agony and headed to the front door. "You can distract yourself by dusting the light fixtures."

"Old women like me shouldn't be up on ladders," she called.

"If you're that old, maybe you should stop playing basketball."

"What, just when I'm getting good?"

I ignored her and headed out into the morning. The bright sun stung my eyes and the world turned white while my pupils did their best to adjust. I could almost see where I was going. Kind of. In a few more steps I'd be fine. . . .

A pair of man's hands saved me from walking straight into a light post. "Hey, sweetheart, watch yourself."

Sweetheart? But even before I finished stiffening at a stranger's touch, I recognized the voice and relaxed. "Evan. How are you this morning?"

My vision cleared and I saw tall, handsome, charming Evan Garrett smiling down at me. His dark blond hair, going gray at the temples, curled down to his collar. I reached out to give one lock a friendly tug. "Headed for the barbershop? Seems as if you said on the phone the other night that you had an appointment."

"Yes, ma'am. You?"

"Antique Mall."

"What kind of cookies are you after?"

I put up my chin—way up—to look at him. My average height didn't pair well with Evan's generous vertical distribution. "Why are you assuming I'm after cookies? I'll have you know that I'm considering the purchase of . . . of a Hoosier cabinet for a display case."

He chuckled and we fell into step. "You're still a horrible liar."

It was an accurate statement, but I felt vaguely insulted. As in, surely by your age you should be able to eke out a half-decent lie. As in, what's wrong with you that you can't manage a little equivocation?

We stopped outside the Antique Mall. Evan took my hands and they disappeared inside his. "I'm looking forward to this weekend," he said.

This weekend . . . this weekend . . .

"You can't remember, can you?"

Luckily, he sounded amused. "Not completely," I said. "We were going to . . . do something." Richard had the kids this weekend, so Evan and I had made plans. Of some sort. To go somewhere. And do something. I just had no clue what it was. After a week at my mother's with her constant dribble of suggestions of ways to improve my child-rearing skills, what I wanted was a weekend on the couch with a book, a constantly full bowl of popcorn, and a purring cat.

"Silly Beth." He leaned down and kissed my forehead. "I have tickets for the last Minnesota Wild hockey game of the season."

Then again, the couch would be there when we got back from the game. "Can I wear my jersey?"

He kissed me lightly on the lips. "You can wear whatever you'd like, my hockey-loving friend." He opened the door and I gave him a sketchy wave as I walked into the store. Two steps inside, I stopped and looked over my shoulder.

There he went, the stunningly handsome Mr. Garrett, the object of many a female swoon, a member of a group I'd always labeled the Beautiful People. With his looks and money, he could have had his choice of women. I wasn't the only one who wondered why he chose to date a slightly dumpy, mousy-haired bookstore owner and divorced mother of two. Marina said I should quit being so hard on myself and take a closer look at what Evan was seeing, but no matter how hard I looked in the mirror, all I saw was a slightly dumpy, mousy-haired bookstore owner with a warped sense of humor.

I watched Evan until he was out of sight. Then I bought a big bag of cookies and pushed open the glass door that sent me back into the fresh air. But instead of turning left and walking back to the bookstore, I turned right.

"Good morning." A young man in uniform sat behind the front counter of the Rynwood Police Department. "Can I help you?"

Budget cuts a couple of years back had necessitated the reduction of the department's staff. No longer did we have seven full-time law enforcement officers. No longer did we have a part-time receptionist. What we had were four full-time officers, all of whom took their turn at the front desk, answering phones and responding to complaints.

It had taken a period of adjustment, but the thick silver lining was how approachable all the officers were, and with that approachability, residents were growing more comfortable with confiding in the officers. The downside to the whole thing was the city council acting as if the improved rapport had been their plan all along.

Since I was a horrible judge of people's ages, my guess of the new officer's age as fourteen was probably wrong. "Is Chief Eiseley in?"

The youngster nodded. "He's in his office. If you want, just go on back." He jerked his thumb over his shoulder.

I went down the short hall. Just before I reached his office door, I came to a slow stop as I tried to think what I was going to say.

Gus and I weren't getting along. We'd had a significant

difference of opinion on Sunday. Some might even call it an argument. I'd intended, but forgotten, to call Winnie and ask for advice about approaching her husband, and the idea of talking to Gus suddenly seemed like a bad one. Maybe he hadn't heard me. Maybe I could silently reverse direction and—

"Hello? Come on in, whoever's out there." The wheels of his chair squeaked and I heard him stand up. "I won't bite."

I inched forward. The toe of my right shoe entered the doorway first, followed slowly by my right knee, then my right shoulder. Finally, I leaned around the door to look at Gus. "Good morning."

"Oh. Hello." Gus sat down. "Morning."

The greeting came half a beat late. Yes, Gus was still angry at me. Without being asked, I sat in his guest chair, my purse and the white bag of cookies on my knees. With the heels of my hands, I pushed down on my legs and stopped the nervous bouncing for almost two full seconds.

"What do you need, Beth?" Gus asked. "I have a lot of work to do."

Gus always had time to talk. He was the epitome of the friendly neighborhood policeman. He chucked the chins of babies and patted the heads of dogs, but to look at him now you'd think he didn't have a sympathetic bone in his body. You'd think stopping to have a nice little talk with him was the worst idea you'd had in a long, long time.

"Well?" He folded his hands on his desk. Suddenly he looked a lot like my junior high principal.

Unfortunately, there was no graceful way to retreat. If I were a better liar, I'd come up with a story about seeing a shadowy figure skulking in the alley behind the store. Or say I was considering a children's book festival in August and would someone from the police department be willing to spend an hour reading aloud?

"Beth—"

"It's about Amy Jacobson," I blurted out.

His gaze sharpened. I slid forward on the chair, readying myself for flight.

"What about her?" he asked.

"I was just . . . wondering."

His shoulders rose and fell. Gus had actually sighed at me. My mouth hung open. Gus occasionally sighed, but not *at* someone. In all the years I'd known him, he'd never once shown impatience. Not with the preteens who'd pulled out all the daffodils on Main Street just for the fun of it, and not with elderly Mrs. Furbisher, who'd driven the front end of her Cadillac through the wall of the grocery store. Flossie, the equally elderly store owner, had volubly demonstrated extreme impatience, but Gus had radiated such a sense of calm and understanding that peace had quickly descended.

"Please don't tell me," Gus said, "that you think she was murdered."

His voice had an edge that cut at me as surely as if he'd been wielding a knife. I was not a hysterical female shrieking at the sight of blood. I did not see danger at every turn, and I did not routinely call the police when a car drove slowly down my street. I didn't do any of that, and never had. So why was he acting as if my presence were an irritation and an annoyance?

"Since I am a taxpaying member of the City of Rynwood," I said, "it doesn't seem like it should be too much of a burden for you to answer a few questions." My words should have come out as a joke, but instead they came out sarcastic and ugly and I wanted to redo them as soon as they left my mouth.

"Yes, you pay my salary," Gus said. "So do four thousand, nine hundred and ninety-nine other people."

All the life went out of the room. Of all the things that I wanted—my children to be happy, my mom to stay in permanent good health, my Christmas cactus to bloom at Christmas—none of that came close to how much I wanted to leave Gus's office.

"Are you saying you won't answer my questions?"

Gus sighed again. "Amy Jacobson died of anaphylactic shock. A severe allergic reaction. She had multiple stings on her face, neck, and arms. Yes, she carried an EpiPen, but she must have panicked. The EpiPen was in her hand, but it hadn't been used. It was an accident."

He spaced out his last words evenly, giving them the import of a commencement speech.

"When did she die?" I asked.

"Last Wednesday."

"No, what time of day."

His mouth tightened. I almost felt like crying. How could that offhand remark about a composer have done this to our friendship? What else had I done? Whatever it was, I hadn't meant it. Whatever it was, I wanted to take it back. "Gus . . ."

But he whipped his chair around, putting his back to me. "Amy Marie Jacobson was pronounced dead at"— he opened a filing cabinet drawer and ticked through some folders—"at seven thirty-five p.m. on Wednesday, April fourth. The EMTs were summoned to the scene by a neighbor who spotted Amy lying on the ground. They called 911 immediately." He paused to turn a page.

"Upon the EMTs' arrival, the EMTs commenced revival procedures, to no effect."

Poor Amy, dying scared, frightened, and lonely.

"The medical examiner's office," Gus droned on, "gave an estimated time of death between two and four p.m."

I closed my eyes. She'd been lying there for hours before Thurman had found her. All by herself, lying on the ground, useless EpiPen in hand, the day sliding past—

My eyes snapped open. "Two and four p.m.?"

"That is correct."

"What was the weather like that day?"

"The . . . weather." Gus didn't make his sentence into a question, he made it a flat, uncaring statement.

"Yes, the weather." I inched forward in the chair. "Amy never went out in the sunshine. Said it made her break out into a rash. Maybe she was allergic to that, too, I don't know, but she never would have gone out into bright sunlight voluntarily. Don't you see? That means—"

"It means nothing." Gus slid the folder back into place and shoved at the drawer with the heel of his hand, slamming it shut. He swung back around and met my gaze. "All it means is she went outside during the afternoon. What an unusual occurrence," he said sarcastically. "Someone going outside."

"But it was," I said earnestly. "For Amy. She never went out."

Gus looked at me. "Never?"

"Well." I fiddled with the strap of my purse. Amy had talked about doctors' appointments. And once she'd mentioned going out to buy birdseed. "Not very often, but I know Amy never went out in bright sunlight. If it was sunny and she went outside voluntarily, she'd have been wearing a hat and long-sleeved shirt and probably gloves. We need to know what she was wearing."

"We don't need to do anything." Gus stood. "What I need to do is get back to work. Don't you have a store to run?"

All sorts of sharp answers rushed into my head, ranging from "that's none of your business" to "what on earth is wrong with you?" I waited for those knee-jerk responses to fade. "Then I can assume you're not going to look into Amy's death?"

"Look into what?" His voice rose, swollen with impatience. "A woman walking outside on a spring day? A woman with a severe allergy dying from what she's allergic to? Be realistic, Beth. I'm sorry Amy's dead, but there's no mystery here."

Former friend or no, I was not going to let Gus bully me into leaving before I was ready. "What if there is? What if Amy was . . . ?" I didn't want to use the *M* word, didn't want to bring the possibility that close to the surface.

"If you find evidence of murder, by all means bring it to me." He pushed at the outside corners of his eyes with his fingers, stretching his eyelids to thin taut lines. "But until then, I don't see that we have much to discuss." He sat back down and started shuffling papers.

I stood, walked a few steps toward the door, hesitated, then turned back. "Gus, is there — "

"Beth, I'm very busy." He moved a folder from one side of his desk to the other. Picked up a pen, clicked it on, and started writing on a yellow sticky note. "If you come across any information call the department. Someone will follow up."

I almost heard it — the shutting of an imaginary door and the construction of an invisible yet impenetrable wall.

So this was how men ended friendships. I'd never known.

For a long time, I stood there, staring at the top of Gus's close-cropped gray hair. I thought about not leaving until he acknowledged my presence again, until he let me talk to him, until he let me apologize. But he was stubborn, so we'd probably end up in our respective positions until I passed out from dehydration and hunger. Which would probably irritate him even more.

"Good-bye, Gus," I said softly, and walked out.

Chapter 5

That afternoon, I fluttered the stack of papers in my hand, trying to catch the attention of twenty-five grade school children. "Okay, kids, listen up!"

Two youngsters focused their attention on me. The other twenty-three, including my son, continued to talk and giggle or look around wide-eyed at their surroundings. It was a large room, paneled in dark-stained wood. Hung on one wall were portraits of long-ago Sunny Rest board members. All men, complete with the requisite dark suits, crew cuts, and glasses so out of fashion they were almost in again.

"Kids!" I got the attention of one more set of eyes, but that was it. I wet my lips, found the proper position of tongue against teeth, and gave an earsplitting whistle.

The kids talking to friends whipped around to face me. The kids already facing me put their feet flat on the floor and their hands in their laps. Even the loyal carpooling moms chatting in the back of the room sat up straight.

All fell silent.

I smiled at everyone. "Thank you. That's much better." Whistling girls and crowing hens may always come to some bad ends, but I'd found the judicious use of a loud whistle a valuable tool. "In a few minutes, Mrs. Judy

will be here to take everyone to meet their story partners. Are you ready?"

Some kids shrugged, some nodded, some stared at me.

So, not ready. Using my finely tuned Mom Senses, I
deduced that they were scared. Reasonable—this was a
big new thing. Clearly, I had to take away some of that
fear if this project was going to get a good start.

How, was the question. A nice rousing fight song would
be excellent, but Tarver Elementary didn't have a fight
song. If I'd had a decent memory, I might have sung "Climb
Ev'ry Mountain," but the only song I could reliably recall
from beginning to end was the theme to *Gilligan's Island*,
and that wasn't exactly a song of inspiration.

"Mrs. Kennedy?" Sydney, a girl with long dark blond
hair, stuck up her hand. "What if, well, like, our story
partner, um, falls asleep while we're in there?"

I smiled at her, trying to ooze a contagious confidence.
"You'll have either a mother or a nurse's aide with you.
If your partner falls asleep, just ask in a quiet whisper
what you should do."

Sydney squirmed in her seat. "Okay," she said. "But
what . . . ?" She hunched down in her chair. "What if . . .
well, you know."

I had no idea what was bothering the girl. I glanced
around at the other kids, and nearly all of them were
wriggling as if every inch of their skin suddenly needed
scratching. I looked at Oliver, but he was busy knocking
his shoes together. What on earth . . .

Then, suddenly, I understood.

"None of your partners," I said firmly, "is going to die
any time soon."

Sydney, whose long hair had come out from behind
her ears to cover her face, looked at me between the
loose strands. "They won't?"

Suddenly all the children were giving me their full attention. Bingo! Three cheers for Beth, who was at last understanding the common fear uniting these kids.

"No," I said to the children in front of me. "Each of your partners is perfectly healthy."

Sydney's intelligent face started taking on a questioning cast. She started raising her hand.

"They need help, sometimes," I added hurriedly. "After all, they're at Sunny Rest for a reason." As in, duh. "But none are in danger of dying any time soon." Or so I fervently hoped.

"That's right." The activities director, Judy Schultz, stood in the doorway, her stocky softball-player frame filling it nicely. She grinned at the kids. "No dying allowed for the next six months. It's not on the schedule."

Sydney nodded seriously. "Thank you."

Problem number one solved. Onward and upward. I flapped the sheaf of papers. "Does everyone have their notebooks? Hold them up, please." Twenty-four kids held up PTA-purchased spiral notebooks.

Oliver sat on his hands and looked glum. Poor Oliver. The school had decided that story project students shouldn't be any younger than nine. At eight, Oliver hadn't made the cut, but he'd wanted to come along, "Just to watch," he'd pleaded. I'd let him, but twenty minutes in, I was questioning my decision.

I handed one paper, a list of questions to ask the residents, to each child. "Does everyone remember the name of their resident? Sienna?"

"Um, Mrs. Parker, I think."

"That's right. Sydney?"

"Mrs. Burgoff."

I checked the names against my own list, ticking off

each one. When I'd crossed off the last, I turned. "Mrs. Judy, are we ready?"

"They're rarin' to go," she said. "You wouldn't believe how much the residents are looking forward to this."

Behind Mrs. Judy was a smiling column of nurse's aides. Young and old, mostly female with a smattering of males, all were dressed in cheerfully colored scrubs. In less time than it takes to tell, each aide collared two children and trotted off with them to environs unseen, the PTA moms trailing behind.

"Well, that's that." Mrs. Judy dusted off her clean hands. "Got anything else you want me to do?"

"Yes."

Mrs. Judy and I turned, for I wasn't the one who'd answered. It was the diminutive Auntie May, aka May Werner, aka the terror of Rynwood, Wisconsin. At ninety-one years old her memory of every embarrassing incident in anyone else's life was sharp and clear. Maybe she couldn't always come up with the name of her latest whippersnapper of a doctor, but she could recall in great detail the lukewarm chicken dinner she'd been served at the Ladies Auxiliary luncheon in 1952.

One of her favorite things in life was to catch people lying. The possibility of hearing Auntie May's cackle of delight and ensuing "Liar, liar, pants on fire!" had kept falsehoods in the entire town to a minimum for decades.

I didn't want to think about what would happen to Rynwood when there wasn't an Auntie May around, so instead I thought about her bright purple wheelchair. Every warm day, she convinced an aide to push her the two blocks downtown. After cookies at the Antique Mall, her favorite stop was, for better or for worse, the bookstore.

"I need a kid to do a story," Auntie May pronounced, thumping the arm of her wheelchair.

Judy and I exchanged glances. Both of us had been pleased last month when Auntie May had opted out of the story program. "Don't need no one to tell my story," she'd snapped. "I can tell my own. Say, did I ever tell you about the time I caught little Mackie Vogel skinny-dipping?"

I'd backed away, stammering excuses. The image of our staid and portly school superintendent swimming in the buff wasn't one I wanted burned into my brain.

"Kid." Auntie May was pounding. "Story. What part don't you two understand?"

"May," Mrs. Judy said, "the residents are already matched with students. We don't have any children left."

"What about him?" Auntie May stabbed a gnarled finger in Oliver's direction.

"He's here to keep me company," I said. Oliver was doing his best to be invisible, but Auntie May was nothing if not persistent.

"I need a kid," she said, "and he's a kid. Yours, isn't he?" She skewered me with a look. "Thought so. What's his name? Bring him over here."

Mrs. Judy angled herself between the wheelchair and Oliver. "Now, May—"

"Kid," Auntie May commanded. "Come here."

My son slid off his chair and slouched across the room. I tried to catch his eye—I wanted him to know that I wouldn't let the old bat eat him—but he was too busy studying the floor to see my encouraging look.

He reached the side of the purple wheelchair. Since I'd never seen Auntie May standing up, I had no idea how tall she was, but if her birdlike frame was any indication, she'd never reached five feet tall. My son was on the small side himself, and the top of his head was just above the top of hers. He looked slightly down into her eyes.

"Hi," he said. His voice shook only the slightest bit and I wanted to cheer his courage. "My name's Oliver," he said. "What's yours?"

And then he smiled.

When Oliver gives out his real smile, it's a thing of beauty. First, the ends of his mouth curl up, giving a hint of what's in store. Then those ends move higher and higher, the curve of his mouth deepens, his lips part slightly, and, finally, his whole face shines with goodness and purity and light.

Auntie May sucked in a breath over her loose dentures. "Well, well, well," she said. "Bet you're the apple of your momma's eye."

Oliver watched her, his head tipped slightly to one side. "What's your name?"

"May Werner." She held out her hand. "But you can call me Auntie May. Now, I need you to write out a story. Can you do that?"

"I think so."

"You think so? How old are you?"

"Eight years and eleven months."

Auntie May chortled. "Still young enough for months to matter. Ha! Can you write a half decent sentence?" He nodded. "Then you're my boy." She slapped him on the shoulder and he rocked back on his heels.

"But I don't have a notebook," he said, recovering his balance. "Or a pen. Or the questions."

"Patooties, that's not a problem." She glanced around. "Judy, Beth. Get this young man what he needs. There's a story to be told."

"Last week you said you didn't need your story written out," Judy said. "What changed your mind?"

"Who said we're talking about my story?" Auntie May cackled and thumped Oliver on the shoulder again. "This gentleman's going to be writing the biography of my friend Maude." She twisted her head around and looked behind her.

For the first time, I noticed that someone had come into the room behind Auntie May. Someone with apple cheeks and snow white hair. Someone with a lace-trimmed hand-kerchief tucked into the sleeve of her pink cardigan.

"Now, May," she said. "There's no need to browbeat people. You can catch more flies with honey than with vinegar, you know."

Auntie May made a snorting noise of disgust, but didn't say anything; Maude smiled like a cherub might if it were a female octogenarian in a wheelchair, and Judy and I looked at each other and nodded. Maybe, just maybe, this would work out.

That night at dinner, there were two parallel conversations. In my left ear, I was hearing a minute-by-minute recap of Jenna's first hockey lesson. In my right ear, I heard Oliver's interpretation of his first visit with Maude Hoffman.

"Mom, you wouldn't believe how fast Coach Sweeney is. He has skates made just for him. Do you think if I got my own skates made I'd be able to go faster?"

"Mom, Mrs. Hoffman was born in 1825. That's really, really old, isn't it?"

I swallowed a bite of pork chop. "Jenna, you play goalie. You don't need to skate like Coach Sweeney. And Oliver, Mrs. Hoffman was born in 1925, not 1825."

They blew past my motherly comments.

"Yeah," Jenna said, "but maybe really good skates would make me a better goalie."

"Being born in 1925 is still really old," Oliver said. "I bet Mrs. Hoffman is one of the oldest people in the world!"

I speared a piece of broccoli. Eddie Sweeney played in the National Hockey League for the Minnesota Wild, but he'd had a knee injury and hadn't played since January. His NHL contract allowed him to give clinics, and the first Sweeney Youth Hockey Workshop was here in Rynwood.

Jenna had been overjoyed that one of her heroes was coming to her town. "That means we're special, right?" she'd asked. I didn't tell my daughter that the determining factor for Sweeney's decision was probably the cheap ice time at Rynwood's Agnes Mephisto Memorial Ice Arena.

Oliver was waiting for a response to his statement. "Not many people get to be as old as Mrs. Hoffman," I said. "But there are people who are older. Auntie May, for one."

"She's mean," Jenna said.

"Take one, please." I held out the tray of fresh vegetables. "Why do you think she's mean?"

Jenna scrunched her face, took the smallest piece of carrot on the plate, and waved it around. "She's got this big high voice that goes right through you, you know? And this one time Bailey and I were on the sidewalk and she just starts yelling at us for no reason."

When Bailey was involved, "no reason" could involve anything from banging fences with sticks to having a screaming contest at nine in the morning.

"I like her." Oliver took a sliver of celery. If the boy didn't start eating more, I was going to have to start stuffing him with protein drinks. "Auntie May, I mean."

Jenna and I shared a long glance. I was pretty sure

that in the history of Rynwood, no one, but no one, had ever admitted to liking May Werner. I respected her age and valued her life experiences, but the concept of liking her wasn't something that had ever occurred to me.

"I'm glad," I said. And I was. If Auntie May was going to have a new friend, who better than Oliver? Empathic and intelligent, he was also loyal and thoughtful. How he'd gotten that way, I had absolutely no idea.

"Can I go back tomorrow?" Oliver looked at me over the top of his plate. When I didn't answer right away, he took a bigger piece of celery and bit hard. "Mrs. Hoffman wants to tell me about being really depressed."

"The Great Depression?" I asked.

He nodded, chewing. "She must have been really sad, to call it great."

Gently, I started to correct him, but the phone rang.

Jenna jumped up and tossed her napkin on the table. "I'll get it."

"We're eating," I said automatically. "Take a message."

"I *know*, Mom," she said as she picked up the receiver. "Hello? Kennedy residence." She turned and pointed at me. "I'm sorry, but we're eating dinner right now. Can I take a message? Oh, hi, Mrs. Hale. Sure, I'll tell her. Good-bye." The phone went back into its cradle with a solid thump. "Mrs. Hale wants to have a PTA call at seven."

"Those were excellent phone manners," I said. "You earn a gold star for the day."

She slid back into her chair and retrieved her abandoned napkin. "Does that mean I get out of doing dishes?"

"What do you think?"

"I think . . ." She slid a glance my way, read my expression, and slumped a little. "No."

I patted her on the shoulder. "You're learning, kiddo."

"Beth, are you taking notes?" Erica asked.

It was seven o'clock. Dinner was over, the dishes washed, the dog walked, and the kids were ostensibly in their rooms working on homework. From the giggles and dull thumps that straggled down the stairs, I had my doubts about their efficiency, but as long as I didn't have to drive anyone to the emergency room, I was willing to let them toil at their own pace.

"Pen at the ready," I said. Through the magic of technology, the four PTA board members were on the phone for what Erica called a work session. I found these calls more of an Erica Keeping An Eye On What's Going On session. But it wasn't a bad idea, really, though it had been much more pleasant before Claudia became vice president.

"Then let's get started."

We slid through a few issues concerning other projects and discussed options for the end of the year PTA gift to students. Then: "If I recall correctly," Erica said, "today Beth took the students to Sunny Rest for the first time. Beth?"

As the chances of Erica recalling incorrectly were roughly seven million to one, I interpreted her use of my name as a call for a report and not a memory confirmation.

"We arrived at Sunny Rest ten minutes before scheduled." Which I'd planned. Inevitably, half the kids on any group trip would plead for a bathroom upon arrival, even if we'd made sure the restroom had been visited before departure.

"Why so early?" Claudia asked.

I started doodling in the margins of my legal pad. Hatchets dripping a dark liquid. Bull's-eye targets and arrows. "Just the way it worked out."

"Well, I hope you didn't mess up anyone with getting there so early."

"It worked out," I said mildly. "The kids all had their notebooks, I handed out the questions, and the Sunny Rest CNAs took the kids to the residents' rooms. We regrouped in the meeting room after an hour, and the carpool moms did their thing."

There was a grunt, which I assumed was Randy Jarvis giving a vague sort of approval, then Erica asked, "Any glitches?"

"Not that I can—" Then I remembered. "There was one little thing."

I could almost feel Claudia perking up. "What?" she demanded. "Bet it wasn't as little as you think. Sometimes you really don't pay enough attention to other people, Beth. Like last fall. You hurt my feelings when—"

"Back to Sunny Rest, please," Erica said. "Beth, go on."

I doodled a face with X's for eyes and a tongue sticking out, and described the scene with Auntie May and Oliver.

"You let Oliver be part of the project?" Claudia asked. "He's not approved. You shouldn't have let that happen."

Randy guffawed. "Like to see anyone tell May Werner she can't have what she wants."

"It couldn't be that hard," Claudia said stiffly. "You should have simply told her Oliver wasn't approved to do a story."

My face doodle expanded to include an anvil dropping out of the sky. I tried to imagine telling Auntie May that her friend Maude would have to go without a story-teller. Imagined Mrs. Judy, Oliver, and me deaf from her screeches. Imagined her apoplectic fury. Envisioned the Four Horsemen of the Apocalypse riding me down.

"I disagree," Erica said. "Dealing with May can be . . . difficult."

At that, my own ears perked up. Could Auntie May be the one person Erica couldn't handle?

Claudia sniffed. "Whatever. If I'd been there, this never would have happened."

"You're probably right," I said. Because if Claudia had been there, Oliver wouldn't have come within a mile of the place. "She yells at kids," he'd told me when we'd opened the birthday party invitation for one of her sons.

Oliver had looked up at me beseechingly, and I'd mussed his hair and telephoned Claudia that, sorry, Oliver would be with his dad that Saturday, and they had something special planned. Which wasn't a lie, because eating take-out pizza and watching Disney DVDs could be very special.

"So what are you going to do about this?" Claudia demanded.

I drew a noose around the face doodle. Started drawing another face, one that was watching the death, and smiling. "I'll talk to the school," I said. "If they give permission for Oliver to be a part of the project, will this board object?"

There was a loud swallowing noise. "Not me," Randy said.

"Given what I know of the boy," Erica said, "he'll do fine."

Claudia cleared her throat. Cleared it again.

The margin on the left side of my paper was full, so while I waited for Claudia to bow to the inevitable, I moved to the right margin. Time to draw something nicer than nooses. Say . . . flowers. Flowers were always nice. I drew a bloom that somewhat resembled a rose and added a sun shining down from on high. Tried to draw a drop of dew. Added a bee in search of pollen. Added a—

My pen stopped. I stared at the bee.

Amy. And bees.

Amy, who, the single time I'd seen go outside, had been armed with a fresh can of bee killer spray in each hand, both uncapped and ready for killing. It was the only way she'd go out in the day, she'd said, she was that allergic.

So . . . had Amy had cans with her when she died? And if not, why not?

Chapter 6

"Are you going to ask Gus?" Marina asked. "You know, about Amy and the cans of bee killer?"

"Umm . . ." It was Monday and I was leaning against Marina's kitchen counter, watching as she plopped spoonfuls of dough onto a cookie sheet. All three kids—Jenna, Oliver, and Marina's youngest-by-far, Zach—were outside. After Marina's last day care kid had been picked up by a harried father, the trio had run out into the cool early evening air to play a complicated version of tag.

Marina had opened the kitchen window a few inches, letting the shouts and laughter slip inside. It was getting close on to dinnertime, and by rights I should be grabbing the kids and heading home to start cooking, but a few more minutes wouldn't hurt.

"Are you in there?" Marina rapped her knuckles against the air a few inches from my head. "Are you going to ask Gus, or what?"

Go back into that unwelcoming office and be greeted with an antismile? Mention the possibility of an absence of spray cans, get a reply of raised eyebrows and a comment of "Anything else?"

"No reason to rush over there," I said. "I'm thinking

of waiting until I have a better idea of Amy's everyday habits."

As a diversion, it was good one. Marina, however, had known me for a long time. "Is Gus still mad at you?" she asked.

"When I stopped by the other day to ask him about Amy, he said . . ." I felt the muscles at the back of my neck tighten with unhappiness and closed my eyes against the memory. "He said he was sorry she was dead, but that there's no mystery. He said if I find evidence of murder, to bring it to him, but until then we didn't have anything to discuss."

I opened my eyes to see Marina staring at me, her mouth hanging open. "But . . . but that's . . ." Her mouth flopped a few times. "That's not like Gus."

"No." The bowl was now empty of dough. I took it to the sink and turned on the faucet. "It's not. I tried to apologize about the thing at choir, but he wouldn't let me. Just said he was busy and to shut the door behind me."

"There's only one answer," Marina said.

"What's that?" I looked over my shoulder and saw her strike her Roman senator pose. This was the one where one hand held her invisible toga closed while the other stroked her chin. I turned back to the sink.

"Gus's body," she stated in round tones with an English-y accent, "has been taken over by aliens."

"No doubt."

"It is the only possibility."

"Or it could be that he's mad at me."

"Oh, please." Marina cast off her imaginary toga and grabbed a dish towel. "So you made fun of some composer. So what? When have you ever known Gus to get bent out of shape about anything?"

"Well, never, but —"

"No buts." She flicked the towel at me. "You're nuts to beat yourself up with a big heavy hammer because of something you said. There's something else wrong with the man."

I wanted to believe her. I tried to believe her. I stared at the soapy dishwater running out of the sink and concentrated on believing her completely and thoroughly. I was almost there, I could feel the beginning of comfort, but then my brain reversed itself. I hated my brain sometimes. "If that's true, why is he so angry at me?"

Marina started to say something. Stopped. Started again. Stopped again.

"I don't know," she finally said. "And you know how much I hate saying that."

A half-formed idea sent out a tendril. "Maybe it's something about Amy that's bothering him."

"Maybe." Marina peered through the oven's window at the flattening cookies. "But he was mad at you before you started asking about her, remember?"

So much for that tendril. I couldn't even garden in my head. "Maybe it's all related."

"Call Winnie." Marina grabbed a pot holder, opened the oven door, and rotated the cookie sheet one hundred and eighty degrees. "If anyone knows, it's Gus's wife."

"Marina Neff," I said solemnly, "you are the smartest person on the planet."

She tossed her loose ponytail over her shoulder. "About time you recognized that."

I walked around the end of the counter and rooted around in my purse for my cell phone. Marina rattled off Eiseley's phone number and I punched in the numbers. When Winnie answered, I said. "Hey, it's Beth. How are you this lovely day?"

"How am . . ." Winnie's normally cheerful voice faded into flat silence. "Why are you asking?"

Frowning, I walked into the study that Marina's Devoted Husband had created out of the bedroom their oldest child had vacated almost a decade ago. "It's what I ask everyone. It's what everyone asks everybody."

"Oh." A couple of short breaths forced themselves into the phone. "Then, yes, I'm fine. Of course I'm fine. Why wouldn't I be?"

It didn't even require shutting my eyes to picture my friend Winnie. Comfortably round and permanently red-faced, she'd be sitting at her kitchen table, TV turned to the Weather Channel, her hands busy with crocheting or knitting or quilting. Either that, or she'd be studying the classifieds for garage sales, but it was a little early in the week for that. "No reason," I said slowly. "Actually, I was calling about Gus."

"He's nasty busy these days, what with all those budget cuts. Seems I hardly ever see the man."

Now that sounded like Winnie. "Yes, but is there anything else wrong?"

"What makes you think there's something wrong?"

And that didn't sound like her. "Well, he's not speaking to me, for one thing."

She chuckled. At least I assumed it was a chuckle. It didn't sound very humorous, but I couldn't think what other noise it might be. "Now, Beth, you know Gus doesn't get mad at anyone. You must have gotten the wrong end of the stick, that's all. I'll tell him you called. I'm sure everything's fine."

And she hung up before I could get in another word.

I went back to the kitchen and returned the phone to my purse.

"What's the matter?" Marina asked. "You look befuddled. Or bewildered. What's the difference, anyway?"

I didn't answer, but Marina didn't care, because she started singing "Bewitched, Bothered and Bewildered," using the words from the stage musical, not the movie that had come years later.

The woman was a marvel, but the puzzle of the source of her knowledge was nothing compared to the puzzle of that phone call. Gus wasn't talking to me, and now Winnie was being evasive. Gus always talked to everyone and Winnie's transparency was legendary. Something was up, and—

"Mom!" Oliver banged in the kitchen door. "I'm hungry! When are we going to eat?"

"Yeah!" Jenna barged in after him. "I'm starved."

Zach came in last. He made a beeline for the cookies, but Marina snapped him lightly with a dish towel. "Back, young sir. Yourst dinner preparations have begunest. And shall commence soonest if the table is set."

We headed home, the kids chirping happily about school and sports and friends, and my prickles of unease about Gus and Winnie and Amy's death almost dropped out of my thoughts.

Almost.

Thursday afternoon, I stopped by Tarver Elementary with a load of books. "Hey, Lindsay." I plopped the heavy box on the office counter with an "oof" and a smile for the secretary. "Orders for Mrs. Pattengill, Ms. Burke, Mr. Adler, and Mrs. Lehrer."

Lindsay got up from her desk and peered into the box. Last year Tarver's secretary had retired and the unanimous choice for a new lifer was the six foot tall, thirty-ish, model-skinny, fashion-blind, über-competent

Lindsay. I hoped she'd stay at Tarver forever. "Lots of goodies." She squinted at me. "Are you singing?"

"Oh. Sorry." I felt a tinge of red tiptoe up my neck. Once again, evidence of my father's addiction to Tom Lehrer's music had snuck out. "Just an old song." Echoes of "New Math" banged around inside my skull and I shook them away. "Is Gary in?"

Lindsay picked up a copy of a Newbery winner, *Moon Over Manifest*. "Is this any good? No, our esteemed principal is out meeting with the superintendent and if I tell you what the topics of discussion are, I'll have to lock you in the attic until fall."

Since Tarver didn't have an attic, I wasn't overly worried. "Do you know what it's about?"

She opened the book. "Budget cuts. Again."

"And I heard Gary say something about expanding middle school orientation." A round-faced woman stood in the doorway that led to the back offices. "He's had parents complaining their children are scared about moving to the big school."

Lindsay turned a page. "We already have one meeting in May, one in June, and another right before school opens. Beth, you got the announcement, didn't you?"

She looked at me, at the newcomer, then back at me. "Have you two officially met? Beth Kennedy, this is Millie Jefferson. Millie, Beth owns the Children's Bookshelf and is secretary of the PTA. Beth, Millie is the new school psychologist. New-ish, anyway."

We shook hands and said the polite things people say to each other. Millie wore a denim jumper over a bright yellow knit shirt, and had a comfortable smile that gave me the impression that if we knew each other a little better I'd be getting a great big hug.

"Sorry I haven't introduced myself before this," Millie said, "but soon after I was hired, I had a family issue that required a lengthy stay back in Charleston." Her voice had the attractive soft vowels that come from the Carolinas. I wanted to ask her questions just to keep hearing her talk.

"What do you need Gary for?" Lindsay asked me.

"There's a little glitch with the senior story project."

"I hear this was your idea," Millie said. "And I must say it's a wonderful one."

"Unfortunately not everyone thinks that way."

"Who could think it's a bad idea?" Lindsay leaned against the front of her desk and crossed her ankles. "No, let me guess. Someone on the PTA board?" She grinned at Millie. "Bet it's Claudia Wolff."

Millie's face flickered, then went back to its former pleasant expression.

"Hah!" Lindsay laughed. "I saw that. Beth saw it, too, didn't you, Beth?"

"The reason I need to see Gary," I said, "is a Sunny Rest resident wanted in on the project at the last minute and Oliver was handy. Claudia says eight is too young for a project like this, so I said I'd get the school's permission before a second session."

Lindsay laughed. "And you think Gary's going to have an opinion on this? He sits on the fence so long that he's going to get a permanent crease in his behind."

"He's still adjusting to being principal," I said. "After being vice principal for so long, it's bound to take a while."

"Been almost a year." Lindsay rolled her eyes. "Say, Millie, you've talked to the kids about this project. Do you think Oliver's too young?"

"Oliver Kennedy," Millie mused. "About this high" — she held her hand up where the top of my son's head would be — "light brown hair, normal kid skinny."

Lindsay laughed. "That's him." She cocked her head, and her eyes went distant. "Uh-oh. That sounds like the UPS guy. I'd better get the door." Her eyes refocused and she headed for the attractions of a young man in brown shorts.

I looked at Millie. "What else can you tell me about Oliver?"

And Jenna, too, come to think of it. But only tell me good things, please. I don't want to hear anything bad. I'm sure there aren't any bad things, naturally, but I don't even want to hear semibad.

"What else?" Millie looked at the ceiling. "Hmm. Serious eyes. More a watcher than an instigator. Smart. A little inward. I wouldn't be surprised if he'd had an imaginary friend around age three or four."

I stared at her. How had she known?

Millie hummed a little tune. "Math isn't his strong suit, as I recall, but he does just fine with everything else." She smiled at me. "He's a wonderful kid. He and Jenna both. And regarding his participation in the story project, well, he may be only eight, but I imagine he'll do just fine."

"Tristan," I blurted out. "His imaginary friend was Tristan. And I have no idea where he got the name."

"It's Claudia who's objecting to Oliver?" Millie asked.

I nodded. "Erica and Randy are both fine with it. Especially since the senior citizen in question is a good friend of Auntie May's."

"Is this your aunt?"

"Oh, no." I recoiled at the thought of having May Werner as a blood relative. I flapped around for an explanation. "Not mine. Not anyone's. It's more of an honorific title." It was a good question, though. Did Auntie May have real nieces and nephews? At her age she'd probably have great-nieces and nephews. Great-greats even. And if she didn't have any of those relatives littering the landscape, why had the title of "Auntie" been bestowed upon her in the first place?

Millie smiled. "We have a lot of those down in Carolina."

"I certainly hope not," I said fervently.

She threw back her head and laughed, a big, rolling, contagious bubble of joy. "So you're the source of Jenna's sense of humor. I wondered where it had come from."

If not me, it must have fallen from the sky. Poor Richard's laughter had devolved to the strained type that always sounded as if he was trying too hard.

Millie glanced at her watch. "Time for me to get to the next school."

Tarver shared a psychologist with three other elementaries. It worked out well, budgetwise, but the turnover rate for psychologists was higher than the average bear's. It flabbergasted me that Millie already knew my two children so well. How many kids was she semiresponsible for? Hundreds, at the least. The woman was a keeper.

"Thank you," I said impulsively.

"You're very welcome." She looked at me with a quizzical smile.

Thanks for what, exactly, was her question, but she was too polite to ask it out loud. "It's nice," I said, "to have you here, that's all."

"And nice of you to say so. Unless I'm in private session, I have an open-door policy." She gestured with her thumb back to her office. "Tell your children to stop by any time they'd like. The same goes for you, too. I'm always happy to talk with parents."

A small, wicked part of me wanted to ask, *Even if the parent is Claudia Wolff?* Instead, I nodded. "Thanks. I'll remember that."

I sat on the edge of Maude's loveseat, listening raptly.

"We couldn't just walk into a store and buy bags of groceries and walk out," she said. "Not during the war."

Oliver, freshly approved for the story project by his principal, was sitting on a stool by Maude's feet and frowning. "How come?"

"Rationing." She tapped the arms of her wheelchair. "But you don't know about rationing, do you? Oh, dear." She sighed. "You don't know much of anything, do you?" Her words could have sounded harsh, but since they were delivered with a soft voice that breathed kindness, it was impossible to take offense.

"Not really." Oliver sighed back. "I'm only eight."

"When I was eight, it was . . ." She sucked in her lips. "Let me see, it was 1933. Things were bad because of the Depression, but I didn't know that. My dad owned the only service station in town. Even with the gas rationing, we never went hungry. Sold gas for ten cents a gallon, back then."

"What's a service station?" Oliver asked.

Maude smiled, showing bright white dentures. "Something I bet your mother doesn't remember, either."

I leaned back and clasped my hands around one raised knee. Leaned back carefully, because the loveseat was upholstered in a smooth brocade fabric that would be happy to see me slide off onto the floor. "There was one service station in town when I was a kid," I said. "But by the time I started driving they were all gone."

"Where are you from, dear?" Maude asked.

Oliver spoke up. "She grew up near Petoskey, Michigan. Here, see?" He held up one hand in a mitten shape and pointed to the tip of his ring finger. "Grandpa Emmerling ran a newspaper."

I smiled at my son. People rolled their eyes every time Michiganders pulled out their hands. Michiganders— and their offspring, apparently—saw it as the easiest way to communicate geographical information.

"You know a lot about your mother," Maude said.

Oliver nodded. "And my dad. We had to learn it last year in school. My dad was born in Milwaukee in 1968, but my mom was born in 1970, and . . ." He stopped. Opened his eyes wide. Turned to look at me, panic setting in around his mouth.

Because Maude's eyes were filling with tears. One drop had started to trickle down her wrinkled cheek and a host of others were making ready to follow.

"Oliver," I said quickly, "why don't you go down the hall to the dining room and see if you can find a paper cup and a straw for Mrs. Hoffman." Another teardrop cascaded down. I stood. "And do you remember Tracy? Mrs. Hoffman's aide? Find her and ask if there's a special snack Mrs. Hoffman might like."

He looked at Mrs. Hoffman, his lower lip trembling. I put my hand on his head. "Go, sweetie," I said. "It'll be all right." I leaned down and whispered in his ear. "It's not your fault."

His face cleared slightly. "Okay." He stood, headed for the door, then ran back and patted Maude's hand as gently as if he'd been patting a kitten's head. "I'll bring you something to make you feel better."

I sat on Oliver's stool and took Maude's thin palm between my own.

We sat. I patted her hand. She cried.

And cried.

After a few minutes, I pulled a facial tissue out of the box next to her bed and offered it to her. "Thank you," she whispered and blew her nose delicately. I took the tissue from her, dropped it into a nearby wastebasket, and handed her a new one.

When she'd used up a third tissue and was wiping her eyes with a fourth, I settled myself in Oliver's listening position; elbows on knees, chin in hands. "Is there anything I can get you?"

"No, dear." She wiped at her eyes. "So embarrassing to sit here, bawling like a baby. You must think I'm a silly old woman."

"I think you're wonderful. But if there's something you don't want to talk to Oliver about, let me know. The last thing we want to do is cause you any upset."

"You are a lovely girl, aren't you? So kind and considerate. Your mother did a good job." She reached forward and patted my knee. "And you're doing a lovely job raising Oliver. Such a nice young boy."

"Thank you," I murmured. Wasn't me, it was sheer luck, but I was finally learning to accept compliments. I didn't have to agree with them, after all.

"Now." She settled back in her wheelchair. "I owe you an explanation for my little scene. No, please don't argue. What I hadn't told Oliver yet is that my husband and I never had any children. Back in those days you never knew why and my husband didn't care for the idea of adoption." She paused to wipe her eyes, and went on.

"One of my sisters lived down the street from us. Her children, my nieces, were in and out of our house so much they were almost like our own children." She looked at her lap. "Almost, but not quite."

Her pain was so obvious it was almost visible. It would be a deep and burrowing kind of pain, pulsating with different colors: white with heat, red with fire, then black with the kind of sorrow that comes at three in the morning when there's nothing, and no one, who can comfort you.

"I'm so sorry," I said softly.

"Thank you. We do the best we can with what we have, don't we, and at least I had children in my life, and they were my own flesh and blood, even if they never called me Momma."

"I'm sure you were the perfect aunt," I said, handing her another tissue, for at the word "Momma," more tears had started to brim over.

"It was all so long ago, you'd think I'd hardly remember."

On the other hand, even at less than half her age, some of my sharpest memories were hurtful ones. The time the neighborhood boys put pine cones in my hair. My sister Kathy walking down the street with her friends and ignoring my eager wave.

"When you get to be my age," Maude said, "most things were a long time ago. But in here?" She tapped her chest, a small thumping noise that could have been the echo of her heartbeat. "Some things happened yesterday."

I nodded. I could feel how that was going to happen. It was already happening.

"You were born in 1970." Maude twisted her tissue so hard that small white pieces shredded onto her lap. "And so was my niece." Her voice was trembling, a bird beating its wings against cold air. "Kelly," she breathed. "My little Kelly. She was so beautiful."

"Was"? I didn't want to hear this. I wanted to shut my ears to this poor woman's story, which clearly wasn't go-

ing to have a happy ending. "What happened to her?" I
asked.

"Oh, my dear." Maude gave a sad, sad smile. "You
already know, don't you? She's dead."

I nodded. "How old was she?"

Maude's clear eyes lost their focus. "My sister and her
husband moved to a condominium after the girls were
grown, and my niece and her husband stayed on. Their
girls grew up just like my own nieces, in and out of our
house every day. Kelly was the youngest. Long blond
hair in braids, then ponytails, then loose down her back."
She trailed her hand down the back of her arm. "Her
hair, it was the color of morning sunlight."

I didn't want to hear what happened. I wanted Kelly
alive and well and living in her mother's house with her
own sunlit-haired children. "What happened?"

"She didn't do it," Maude said. "They say she did, but
I knew Kelly. She wouldn't do a thing like that." She
looked at me earnestly.

I nodded. Not that I had any idea what she was talking about, but she was waiting for some sort of reaction,
so I had to do something. Nodding was easy. And subject
to interpretation.

"It was all whispers, afterward." She dropped her
voice to a rasp. "Did you hear about Kelly? It's so sad
what Kelly did." Her head came up, her chin firm. "Kelly
didn't do it, I tell you. She didn't!"

I was getting a bad feeling about this.

"She was only eighteen." The tissue lay in pieces on
her lap. "Just turned eighteen. Why would a girl with
everything ahead of her take her own life?"

And there it was. It lay there in front of us, sallow and
limp and big enough to pull all the air out of the room.
Suicide, that sad, ugly word, no one ever wanted to hear.

"Why would she?" Maude insisted. "Why?"

But she didn't meet my eyes. She knew as well as I that there were almost as many reasons for a teenager to commit suicide as there were teenagers.

I edged forward and laid a hand on her knee. "What happened?" I asked.

She took hold of my hand with a grip that ground my bones together. "How could she drown herself?" she asked fiercely. "She couldn't. That girl was part fish. Swimming before she was three. Winning ribbons at summer swim meets when she was six. Drown?" Maude made a noise in the back of her throat. "Might as well say Johnny Weissmuller could have drowned."

"Did it . . . ?" I looked over my shoulder, through the walls and in the direction of Blue Lake, the lake where all young Rynwoodites learned to swim.

Maude followed my gaze. "It was in late May, not long before her high school graduation. They say she was depressed from her boyfriend breaking it off with her on the night of her prom."

The poor girl.

Maude pulled at my hand and I turned back to look at her.

"She was going to college. Kelly was going to get her biology degree and work at a doctor's office in the summers." Maude's pride in her great-niece shone in her ringing tones. "She had straight A's always. She was going to be a doctor. Does that sound like a girl who would drown herself over some boy?"

"No," I said. "It doesn't." But did we ever know who was likely to take her own life? Sometimes. Not always. Not nearly always.

"Find out," she said.

I blinked at her. "Excuse me?"

"You've done this before." Maude leaned close. "May Werner told me about it. You've hunted down killers and put them in jail where they belong. Do it for Kelly."

"I . . . what?"

"Now, no need to be shy. It was in the papers, both times. You do realize, don't you, that you have a gift for talking to people?" She patted my hand in much the same way I'd patted hers. "And a tremendous gift for listening. That's the most precious gift of all."

What I had was a gift for incredibly bad timing. Including this particular moment. If I hadn't sent Oliver off, would I have heard all this? And the incidents that Maude had mentioned, I'd stumbled half blind into things that if I'd been using my brain properly, I wouldn't have come within miles of.

"No one remembers Kelly." Maude's shoulders curled forward. "Just her parents. And old Aunt Maude." She sighed. "I'm not sure even her sisters really remember her."

"That's . . ." I searched for the right words. Couldn't find any.

"Yes," Maude said, her head hanging down. "But life goes on. For some of us, at least." Her lower lip trembled. "Please tell me you'll find out what really happened to Kelly. You're the only one who'll care enough. Please help me."

She pulled my hand tight to her chest. I felt her heart beating fast through her thin sweater. *Thud-thud. Thud-thud.* "Maude, I—"

"Please?"

So close, I could see the veins in her neck pounding in time almost with her heartbeat. So close, I could see the texture of her skin. So close, I could see how small red veins were branching out through the whites of her eyes. So close, I could see how badly she wanted me to do this.

But how could I? I was just a middle-aged mom. A bookstore owner. Secretary of the local PTA. How could I tell this good woman that I'd help her when in all likelihood I wouldn't be able to find out a thing? Her greatniece had died more than twenty years ago. How on earth could I uncover anything new?

"Please?" she whispered.

Then again, how could I not?

I squeezed her hand. "Maude, I'll—"

"Got her talked into it yet?"

I whirled around to see Auntie May wheeling herself into the room.

"You told her you'd do it, right?" She pointed at me.

"Well, I—"

"Better have." The left front wheel of her chair rolled on top of my foot. "Maudie needs you. If you don't help her and she dies without finding out what happened to Kelly, you'll never forgive yourself. Bet on it."

"Auntie May, I—"

"Don't 'Auntie May' me, young lady. And don't give me any song and dancing about being too busy. I see you traipsing down the street to talk to that pretty Evan Garrett all hours of the day. Spend a little of that time working on something constructive and the world would be a better place."

I felt heat inch up my neck. "That's not fair, I—"

"Pisher-doodle," she said. "Maudie comes to you for help and all you think about is your boyfriend. There's trouble in that, real trouble. What kind of example are you setting for that girl of yours? What kind of mother are you . . . eh? What's that?"

"I said I'll do it," I said loudly.

"You bet you—" Auntie May stopped and cupped her hand around her ear. "Did you say you'll do it?"

"Yes. I can't promise anything, but—"

"Oh, goody!" Maude clapped her hands. "She's going to do it, May!"

"I heard." Auntie May stared at me so hard I flexed my hands to make sure I wasn't turning to stone. "No shirking, young lady. Do a good job, you hear? Otherwise you'll be hearing from me." She thumped her chest with her fist.

Maude smiled. "She'll do fine. I have complete confidence in Beth."

"Hmmph." Auntie May speared me with a glare.

She would make my life miserable if I couldn't help Maude. She'd haunt the store like an avenging angel. She'd stalk me on the sidewalks. She'd cackle and point and become the screaming harridan who hovered on the edges of all Rynwoodian nightmares.

But, if I failed, even harder to bear would be Maude's disappointment.

Maude nodded at me, her kind smile flaming the embers of my deeply embedded and ever present guilt. If love made the world go around, then I was pretty sure guilt was what started the spinning.

"You'll do fine, honey," Maude said, still smiling. "I know you will."

I smiled back.

And didn't say anything.

Chapter 7

"How was your week?" Evan reached across the table for my hand.

It was a wide table and had a large expanse of white tablecloth between the two of us. Evan's generous arm length allowed his hand to reach past the halfway point with ease, but clasping his hand required that I lean forward until my chest rested on the tabletop. It wasn't exactly uncomfortable, but it wasn't a position in which I wanted to spend a lot of time, either.

"My week? Um, fine, I guess. How about yours?"

Jenna and Oliver were with their father, watching the latest Pixar movie for the fifth time, and I was having dinner with Evan. His hardware store was in the black, and as a reward to himself he'd joined the local country club. Not that the hardware store was paying for the membership. As a retail storeowner, I knew the chances of that were zero to negative quad-zillion. It was Evan's former life that had purchased the hardware store, paid for his condominium, leveraged his vacations, and bought him a new car every year.

I looked around. Everything in the room was done in a big way. Big chandeliers. Big flower arrangements on the accent tables. Big windows with a big view of the golf course. Everything larger than life, everyone good-looking. Or if not good-looking, then dressed as if they were, which was almost the same thing.

A waiter soundlessly laid menus on the table, took our drink orders, and wafted off. I detached myself from Evan's hand and opened the leather folder.

"My week," Evan said, paging though the wine list, "was spent listening to reps from three different paint companies, each of whom was trying to convince me to carry their new, improved products. Paint has changed—" He stopped. "What's the matter?"

"This menu." I flipped the thick pages. I'd heard about menus like this, but I'd never seen one. "It's missing some key information."

"Oh?" The outside corners of Evan's mouth turned down. "Let me get you a new one." He looked for our waiter and started to raise his hand.

"Don't bother. I bet he brings me one that's just the same." I laid the menu flat on the table and pointed at the right side of the pages. "See? No prices."

Evan chuckled. "Priced menus are only given to the club members."

"I know. It's just"—I turned the pages, each one looking like a printing mistake—"just weird."

"That's how it's done," he said, reaching for my hand again. "You know you can order anything you like, don't you?"

My politeness reflex kicked in. "Yes. Thank you."

He stroked the back of my hand with his thumb. "I hear a 'but' in that sentence."

"No, no buts." I put on a smile. "See? All happy."

Laughing, he squeezed and released my hand. "You always make me laugh. No matter what my day's been like, you make it better."

My face went warm and I buried myself in the menu. Most of the words I'd seen before, but pronunciation was going to be a problem. Salmon was easy enough to say, but *Le Filet de Saumon au Beurre Rouge* presented a bit of a challenge. Maybe I could just point.

Evan was still looking at me. "This is okay, isn't it?" He gestured at our surroundings. "It's really the golf course I care about. We don't have to come here again if you don't like it."

"I'm fine." It wasn't a complete lie. I didn't feel sick, and I wasn't angry, or upset, or worried that I'd use the wrong fork. No, I just felt a little . . . itchy.

"You're sure?"

I looked up and fell deep into his blue eyes. Evan was a kind, thoughtful, incredibly handsome man and I was doing my best to enjoy the places he took me. Okay, it was easy to have a good time at the hockey games, but that was my thing, not his. On a regular basis the two of us ate at restaurants where children weren't part of the normal clientele. We went to art gallery openings. We'd been to cocktail parties and dinner parties. Though I rarely made a complete idiot of myself, time after time I never felt as if I truly fit in. But how could I explain that feeling to someone who'd always fit in? I wasn't sure there was any way to make him understand.

"I'm fine," I said. And, for a moment, smiling into his eyes, I almost believed it.

The waiter advised us on dinner choices, the wine steward helped Evan choose the bottle that would best enhance our meals, and we were left to our own devices.

"Alone at last." Evan fingered the lapel of his jacket and I had the sudden, horrifying thought that he was going to pull out a ring and propose, right there and right then.

Not in public. Please, not in public. Please don't turn me into a spectacle. I don't even like anyone to watch me open birthday presents. I really, really don't want you to go down on your knee with a restaurant full of people watching. Please . . .

"What do you think of this?" He slid a piece of paper out of his inside pocket and pushed it across the table.

No, not paper. A small-ish, white, rectangular piece of cardboard. White cardboard on white cloth, it was almost invisible. "Um."

Evan turned it over. "This is from the new paint line that sales rep number two is touting. What do you think?"

I eyed the colors. "They're, um, nice."

"Do you really think so, or are you just being polite? If this is boring, just say the word and we'll talk about something else."

"No, I like paint." What a stupid thing to say. "I mean, these colors don't offend me." Though I couldn't think of a color that would. Some might make me squinch my eyes shut and others might make me feel vaguely ill, but finding a color offensive didn't seem possible.

"Is that the one you like best?" Evan asked.

I looked down to see my index finger pointing to a shade somewhere between light off-white and medium off-white. "It's a color worth considering."

Evan nodded. "Not too dark, not too light. It's good for public areas." He talked on about the value of a neutral background for artwork, and I faded away.

Also worth considering was Auntie May's vague threat. Or was it a curse? Either way, thanks in large part to my fear of a ninety-one-year-old woman, I was about to embark on a journey twenty years into the past.

But how on earth was I going to find out anything

about a death that had happened so long ago? Sure, most of the major players were still alive, but how accurate was anyone's memory at such a distance? I couldn't remember what I'd eaten for breakfast on Sunday, let alone something that happened when I was still in high school.

Yes, tragic events loom large in a memory, and their edges can stay razor sharp, but isn't it the pain that lingers longest? Does the clarity include events leading up to the cancer diagnosis? Do the precise recollections include reliable accounts of what your grandfather said the week before he died?

I didn't know. Sadly, there were an awful lot of things I didn't know, including the difference between Italian and vinaigrette dressings. Figuring out a way to find out what happened to Kelly Engel was just one more on a long, long list.

"You don't like it, do you?" Evan asked. "That look on your face is a dead giveaway. Here, how about this one?" He reached into his jacket for another sample.

Then again, making lists was one of the things I did best. Marina, my children, my former husband, my siblings, my fellow PTA board members, and my employees might all make fun of my lists, but how many of them had asked me to put something on a list? Every one of them. Over and over again.

Making a list would help me help Maude. Even if I didn't unearth anything new, lists would at least be something I could wave at Auntie May. Here, I'd say. I tried, I really tried. I did my best. See all that I did?

"Not that I'm telling you what to do," Evan was saying, "but if you were going to repaint your bookstore, what color would you want?" He fanned the samples out on the table.

I'd missed the switch from darker shades of pale to bright pastels. "Um . . ."

"Yellow could be a good option." Evan poked at the color. "Though we'd have to see how it looks under those halogen lights."

I nodded. "Those lights do funny things. It's hard to know ahead of time what a color's going to look like."

Of course, it was hard to know ahead of time about anything. Impossible, really, without the ability to see into the future. What was Jenna going to be when she grew up? A wife, a mother? Dedicated to her career? What about Oliver? A husband, a father? Good at golf for the sake of his profession?

For that matter, what was I going to be? At forty-one, I still hadn't figured it out, not really. Growing up, I thought I'd wanted to run a newspaper, like my father. Growing up, all I'd wanted to be—

Be? Or bee?

I rubbed my upper arm, touching the place where I'd been stung by a bee last summer. The bee had been lurking in my dying rosebushes and when I'd pushed leaves around, looking for clues to their illness, it had buzzed out and defended itself. I'd melted an ice cube on the bite and forgotten about it in two days. No need for me to carry an EpiPen, no need for me to tiptoe outside warily all summer. For me, a warm spring day was cause for rejoicing, not for fear.

Poor Amy. What had she wanted to be? Had she seen any of her dreams come true?

Was I nuts to think she might have been killed? Cans of bee killer or no cans, were my suspicions just the daydream of a woman who didn't have enough going on in her life, a woman who was so bored that she'd manufacture murder out of an accidental death?

Gus thought so. And, if I mentioned any of this to Evan, he'd likely agree with Gus. He'd give me that concerned look, warn me about interfering, and push more paint samples at me. Here, Beth. Let me distract you.

Neither one would want me poking my nose into Amy's death. And it didn't do to think about what would happen if either one found out what I'd promised Maude Hoffman.

"You did what?" Evan's eyebrows would zing halfway up his forehead. "Beth, helping people is a commendable trait, but how can you make accurate conclusions about an event more than twenty years old?"

And the new Gus would say something along the lines of, "Don't be an idiot. Kelly committed suicide. Maude just doesn't want to admit it. Go back to your kids' books."

I didn't like keeping things from Evan. He deserved better than that. But Amy deserved better than to have her death written off as an accident without more questions being asked. To me, Amy's needs topped Evan's.

Plus, I'd made a promise to Maude. And with Auntie May as a glowering witness there was no wiggle room. I was lucky she hadn't made me swear to deliver daily progress reports.

"I know that smile," Evan said. "You must like this green the best."

The thought of my store painted that pale green made me slightly queasy, but I kept smiling anyway.

Because I had half a plan.

Sunday morning came with a rush of rain. I stood at the kitchen window, listening to the thunder, watching the lightning, wondering what Richard was going to do with Jenna and Oliver. So much for his plans for playing miniature golf. They'd probably end up in front of the television, playing video games and shortening their attention spans by another few seconds.

I, on the other hand, was going to spend the afternoon looking over copies of the papers the story project kids had handed me on Thursday. With only a few short Thursday sessions to go before the stories needed to get to the publisher, I needed to keep on top of the kids' progress. The height of the stack of paper, however, indicated that I'd be spending more time editing than trying to elicit words to be edited. The children were writing more than anyone had guessed, and I was looking forward to telling Claudia so.

I glanced at the clock. Time to get going.

"Don't want to," I muttered, then got into my raincoat, into the car, and backed out of the driveway.

I slid into my chair just as Kay started warm-ups. Between aaaaa's and eeeee's, my left-hand neighbor leaned over. "Where's Gus?" she whispered, tipping her head toward his empty seat.

"Don't know." The words came out a little short. Just before we launched into iiii's, I added, "Tried calling Winnie yesterday, but no one answered." The answering machine had clicked on and Gus's voice had started the spiel. I'd listened to the sound of the old and friendly Gus, and had swallowed down the urge to cry. After he'd said "Please leave a message. We'll get back to you soon," the machine had beeped. I'd stood there, phone tight in my hand, listening to myself not talk.

What should I say?

What was there to say?

I'd hung up, not saying a word, feeling like an idiot, feeling miserable. Feeling sad.

And now Gus wasn't at choir. Gus was always at choir. He could get a gold star for attendance and was punctual to the point of irritation.

I knew the earth didn't revolve around me. I'd known that from a very young age. Both of my sisters had made that very clear. But it was hard to look at the seat behind me and not think that I was the cause of its emptiness.

Kay ran her fingers through her hair. "That was awful. Let's run through the gradual anthem and see if we can sound anything like a choir. Tenors, you need to be—" She looked at the tenor section, then looked at me. "Where's Gus?"

I shook my head and shrugged, shame creeping through my skin. For in addition to being clueless about his whereabouts, I was also glad he wasn't there.

The sun came out as the minister made the benediction, a good omen if there ever was one. By the time I got home, replaced the dress, nylons, and pumps with jeans, a sweatshirt, and running shoes, I'd finished thinking through my half a plan.

"And half a plan," I told George the cat as I polished off the leftovers from last night's dinner, "is better than no plan at all."

George, who was sleeping on Jenna's chair, opened his eyes to small slits, gave me a measured look that clearly said, "If you say so. Just leave me alone," and closed his eyes.

Spot, on the other hand, was very interested.

"You're a pretty good dog," I told him, "but are you good enough to behave properly with strangers?"

Spot barked and jumped up, raking the air with his front paws.

"I'll take that as a 'no.'" The fur on the top of his head was soft under my hand. "Maybe next time."

I picked up my purse and took a stagger step at the weight. I put said purse on the kitchen table and turned it upside down. Away across the table rolled loose change and pens and pencils. The checkbook bounced one way, my wallet went another. The cell phone bounced left, the car keys bounced right. Then came the rest; rubber bands, bookmarks, scraps of paper, a deck of cards, paint samples, a small calculator, yellow sticky notes, adhesive bandages: the dozens of oddments that end up in a mom's purse.

The program from last winter's school play went in the trash, as did Evan's paint samples and six pens that didn't work. But the rest?

I studied the pile. The fairly large pile. Everything in it was useful.

"That didn't help much, did it?" I asked Spot.

He cocked his head and looked at me with big brown eyes.

"What am I going to do?" I asked him. "That is the question of the day. As someone once said, problems can't be solved by the same level of thinking that created them. What's needed here is a new approach."

Spot gave a small whine and ran to the back door.

While I was taking him on a short walk in the backyard to do a little bit of dog business, the new approach I needed popped into my tiny little brain. "Got it," I said out loud. Spot looked back at me over his shoulder. I gave him a pat, which seemed to reassure him, and he went on with his work.

After I escorted him back to the house, I headed to the garage and rummaged through the bin of sports paraphernalia. Not the soccer ball or the inline skates or Wiffle bat or croquet mallet or . . . there!

I reached down to the bottom of the bin and extracted a very flat and slightly tattered backpack. Richard had used it in Jenna's stroller days since no power on this earth could have made him carry a diaper bag. For a moment, I stood here, looking at it. Saw Richard kissing Jenna on the top of her head, saw him picking her up and lifting her high. Heard her giggles. Felt the love the three of us had shared.

"Don't." My voice echoed off the cement floor, off the hard walls and hard ceiling. "Just don't." I replaced the bin's lid with a loud thump and stabbed the garage door opener with my thumb. The door rattled up and light flooded in.

I stepped outside. The temperature had risen ten degrees in the short hour since the rain clouds had blown off, and the streets were almost dry.

It was the end of April, a beautiful spring afternoon, and the sun was out.

Time for another new approach. Two in one day, which must be a world's record for me. Marina would never believe it.

I bicycled the two miles to Amy's house, the backpack's straps resting comfortably against my shoulders. Fresh air sang through my lungs and I felt a rush of freedom that was like a memory.

An approaching car honked and a man's hand stuck out the window. "Hey, Beth!"

Since I was hopeless at vehicle recognition, I gave a half-hearted wave. Then, as the car passed, I saw who it was. "Hi, Pete!" I called just after he'd gone by.

But he wouldn't take my sluggish response personally. Of all the people in Rynwood, Pete Peterson would be at the top of the Least Likely to Take Offense list. He owned and operated Cleaner Than Pete, a company that cleaned up all those truly icky things no one wanted to touch. He'd started with sewers that had backed up into people's houses, expanded to skunk cleanup, and finally branched out into the lucrative crime scene cleanup.

We'd met almost two years ago while he was cleaning a murder scene, and, last year after his sister had moved to Rynwood with her seven-year-old daughter, Alison, we'd started running into each other more often. Even more so this spring when Oliver and Alison had played on the same soccer team.

Pete was one of those friendly guys who didn't seem to have a worry in world. Standing on the soccer sidelines one day, I'd tried to get him to admit to at least one worry, but the only thing he came up with was a mild concern about the way his milk had smelled that morning.

His typical stance was a round-shouldered comfortable slouch, hands in pockets, smile on his face. Just looking at him made my neck lose a few degrees of tension. Medium height, balding, and cheerful as a chickadee, Pete was one of those people who made you feel good just by walking into the room. No, Pete wouldn't take offense at my nonwave. He'd probably already forgotten about the whole thing.

I turned left onto the road that went around the park. My hair blew back from my face as I rode, feet spinning, legs pumping, knees going up and coming down, up and down. The rhythm was soothing, in a hard work sort of way, and it was easy to think of absolutely nothing at all. Easy to be nothing, easy to do nothing except be.

With my mind clear of pretty much everything except the pleasures of the season, it was inevitable that I zipped right past Amy's driveway.

Halfway up the block, I woke up to where I was, braked hard, turned in a wide arc, and went back to where'd I just been, scolding myself mildly for being such a moron. Though, as I approached the driveway, I realized I was being too hard on myself.

Not even a month since Amy had died, and already her mark on the earth was disappearing. The rains of spring had sent the uncut grass knee high. The shrubs had taken on an untended look. Even the trees looked shaggy.

Technically, this wasn't much different from the way Amy's driveway normally looked, but it didn't . . . well, it didn't *smell* right. Not that anything smelled bad. Not that there was any smell at all other than the overwhelming scent of spring. No, what I sensed was that something was wrong.

Halfway up the steep drive, my thighs decided they'd had enough. I swung off the bike, put one hand on the handlebars, the other on the seat, and pushed it up the hill, thinking.

It wasn't the raggedy grass that was different. Couldn't be. Raggedy and unkempt was Amy's favorite landscaping style. I'd often wondered, but never asked, how she avoided citations for violating the town's lawn ordinance. And now I'd never know.

I kept on up the hill, still trying to pinpoint what was different. It wasn't the closed curtains behind the diamond-paned windows. Amy always had them closed during the day, opening them only at night, the reverse of the rest of the world. And it wasn't the absence of a car, since Amy didn't have one. What, then? What was shrieking at me, telling me that something was wrong, that something was ...

I stopped. The bicycle stopped. My breathing stopped. Tears touched the corners of my eyes and I stood there, staring.

The bird feeders. They were empty.

A light breeze caught at the back of my neck and sent the feeders to swaying. Back and forth, back and forth.

I watched them for a while, thinking sad thoughts about life and death and lost opportunities and things not done and all the roads not taken.

The breeze fell away, touching my cheek with its last breath. I leaned the bike against the peeling white paint of the ancient detached one car garage and shrugged off the backpack. Inside were the bare minimum: keys, wallet, checkbook, comb, cell phone, pens, and a brand-new spiral bound notebook. I zipped it open, reached down into the depths for my favorite pen and—

"Hello, there."

I shrieked and dropped everything.

"Sorry about that," said a male voice.

Rustling leaves gave me a clue to his whereabouts. I turned and saw a small face peering out of a lilac bush.

"You're that book lady. No, don't tell me, I never forget a name. Meg. Yep, that's it. Meg ... Murphy? Kavanagh? O'Neill!" he said triumphantly.

"Beth Kennedy," I said apologetically. "You were close."

The elf spread the branches and walked through. "Bet you don't remember my name, do you? Hah, you don't!"

Thurman Schroeder. Smiling, I shook my head.

"That's what made me such a success in car sales, you know. People remember the people who remember their names."

"I'm sure you're right."

"Of course I am!" He walked close and looked up at me. "You know Amy's dead, don't you? Died last spring."

"She . . . did?"

"Or was it last winter?" He frowned, and his eyes went vague. "Meg, did you say your name was?" His right hand reached out, halfway to a handshake, halfway to a plea for help.

"Thurman?" A woman crashed through the bushes. "Thurman? Oh, there you are!" She stood, panting, with her hand flat against the base of her throat. "Goodness, you scared me!" Her hair, curled tight to her head, was whiter than a fresh snowfall.

"Sweets," he said, "this is Meg Murphy. Meg, this is my wife . . ." The eyes went blank and his hands started to tremble. "My wife . . ."

"Nice to meet you," I said quickly. "My name is—" Stepping closer to the woman, I lowered my voice. "I'm Beth Kennedy."

The woman took Thurman's hand in hers. "Nice to meet you. I'm Lillian Schroeder."

"Lillian," he murmured. "My wife."

"That's right, honey. I'm your wife. Lillian."

He nodded. "Lillian. Wife." He started whistling a tune that sounded almost familiar. I tried to follow the melody, but he lost the thread and it turned into an aimless humming.

Lillian watched him. "This morning was so good," she said quietly. "I tried to get him to take a nap after lunch, but he said he wanted to sit on the patio." The strain of caretaking showed in the lines around her mouth. "He seemed happy enough with the newspaper. I turned my back for just a minute—a minute!—and he was gone."

"Who's gone?" Thurman snapped to attention.

"No one," Lillian soothed. "Everyone is where they should be."

"Shipshape?" he asked.

"And seaworthy." She smiled, but it was a smile that could break your heart.

He cupped his hands around his mouth. "Anchors aweigh!"

"Anchors aweigh," she said softly. To me, she said, "We used to have a sailboat. For years we spent all our weekends on Lake Michigan. But I had to sell it last summer. He . . . we just couldn't do it any longer."

I nodded. And wanted to cry.

"Well." Lillian stood tall, making the top of her head come almost level with my shoulder. "Beth Kennedy. You own the Children's Bookshelf. I've been in there a few times, buying books for our grandchildren." She glanced at Thurman. "That new girl, Yvonne. She's very . . . understanding."

"I'm glad she could help."

"You used to deliver books to Amy," Lillian said. Thurman started to walk away, but she tugged him back to her side. "Just a minute more, honey."

I saw her question coming and hunted around for an explanation of my presence. Couldn't come up with a very good one. Decided that telling the truth was the only real possibility.

I stooped to pick up my dropped pen and notebook. "Amy's death has been bothering me. So—"

"You're going to journal about it?" Lillian nodded in an approving way. "That's an excellent idea. My pastor recommended journaling as a way to deal with . . . with my situation. All I have to do is remember to burn it before I die." She laughed. "If any of the children get hold of it my image would be shattered."

Without thinking, I said, "Not possible. You're the closest thing I've ever met to a saint."

She smiled. "Aren't you a sweetheart? But you don't know what I'm like inside." She closed her eyes briefly. "Some days are harder than others."

"Have you . . ." Then I stopped. How could I offer up advice to this woman? She didn't need someone half her age giving her options about dealing with her beloved husband. She was clearly smart and savvy; she'd have long ago investigated the facilities at Sunny Rest.

"Don't worry about me," she said. "We'll be fine. As long as Thurman's happy, I'm happy, and for now he's happy here at home."

Thurman started humming "Wouldn't It Be Loverly." Lillian stroked his hand and hummed along with him. I swallowed, not quite sure why I was so sad. They weren't, so why did I have the urge to throw my arms around the both of them and bawl my eyes red?

"Um," I said. "Is it okay to sit here a while?" I gestured at Amy's backyard, hefting my notebook. "It's a little weird, I know, but . . ."

Lillian took up the slack I'd offered. "But you feel close to Amy," she said. "Makes perfect sense. And I suppose it's all right if you spend some time here." She looked at the house, frowning. "I have no idea what's going to happen. Her parents are long gone, of course. This was the house she grew up in, you know, and she was an only child. I suppose she must have some other relatives, but I'm afraid I really don't know."

Thurman's face lost its formless look. "Miss Amy had a first cousin on her mom's side. He lives in Montana. No idea what he does for living. Sells ice to Eskimos for all I know." He grinned.

The elf was back, and the smile on Lillian's face was wide and deep. "Takes coals to Newcastle."

"Furnaces to Hawaii." He took her hand and twirled her in a circle.

"Potatoes to Idaho," she called, midspin.

"Baked beans to Boston." He pulled her close and took the lead in their waltz. Around the yard they went, laughing like young lovers, calling out phrases that got more and more ridiculous.

"Cable cars to San Francisco."

"Arches to Saint Louis."

"Wind to Chicago."

They ducked back through the lilacs, and were gone.

I waited until I heard nothing save the wind in the trees. Then I opened the notebook and started writing.

Chapter 8

By the middle of the following week, I'd filled a dozen pages with bits and pieces of Amy's life. I started with the scraps that I knew and the few things the Schroeders had told me and moved on to my normal sources. Each person told me something new, and each thing went down in the notebook.

"Amy? That poor girl." Flossie Untermayer, running the local grocery store at age eighty-one and looking perfectly capable of running it for another eighty years, slid her pencil into the clipboard she carried everywhere. "Amy left town the day after high school graduation and didn't come back for years. Not until her dad got too sick to take care of her mom."

"I heard she was an only child."

"Did caretaking for both parents until her mom died, then watched over her dad. Every time I delivered groceries I told her to get some help." Flossie lifted her shoulder expressively, conveying in that one gesture sympathy, regret, empathy, and a small bit of irritation.

Clearly, her years as a professional ballet dancer had given her more than just a career. All my single year of ballet lessons had given me was an inferiority complex because I couldn't figure out the difference between fourth and fifth positions. When I kept asking about a sixth position, the instructor had a long talk with my mother and the next fall I started swim lessons. Flossie had told me that in some schools of ballet thought, there is a sixth position. One of these days I'd have to tell my mother.

"But Amy said she didn't want help." Flossie's mouth made a tight, frowning movement. "And what can you do then?"

My hair stylist, Denise, said she'd cut Amy's hair before Amy left town. "After she came back I don't think she cut her hair." Denise chopped at her waist with her flat palm. "Last time I saw her it was down to here. Not a good look for most women, you know?"

What no one seemed to know was how Amy made ends meet. And no one knew what she'd done in those years she'd lived away. No one even knew for certain where she'd lived. Some said the East Coast, some said the West, some said down south. Over the phone, Marina had guessed Venice, but when I pinned her down, she confessed she'd made the guess in hopes that we'd travel there to investigate.

"So you don't have any reason to think Amy lived in Venice?" I'd asked.

"Everyone wants to live there," Marina said. "It's one of the most beautiful cities in the world. She must have visited, at least. We can go and check hotel registers. We can take her picture to all the cafés. We can stop at the Doge's Palace and interview the docents."

She rattled on for a while without any response from me. Finally, she stopped. "We're not going to Venice, are we?" she'd asked sadly.

"Not this year," I'd said, and hung up before she started fantasizing about next summer.

"May I ask?" Paoze indicated my notebook.

For the moment, we were the only two people in the store. It was the post-lunch lull, and Lois and Yvonne were out getting something to eat. When they'd first started lunching together I'd spent a fair amount of time staring out the front windows, my index finger over my lips, wondering what tall tales Lois was telling Yvonne. Stories about Wisconsin winters. Stories about Paul Bunyan. Stories about cheese. About the Green Bay Packers.

Any of those stories could turn Yvonne against the fair state of Wisconsin. There wasn't anything or anyone to keep her here, after all. Scare her too much and she'd be gone.

But every time they came back from lunch, Yvonne would give me an oversized wink, so I'd eventually stopped worrying.

I smiled at Paoze. "Of course you may ask. I'm starting a sort of a journal."

"This is a good thing." He nodded. "In my literature classes, the professors say many authors begin by a journal. I have a journal for three years."

"It's more like, um, therapy for me." Not exactly a lie. "Have you started writing that book of your family's history? If you haven't—"

The phone rang. Paoze's reactions were younger and faster, so he was first to reach the receiver. "Good afternoon, Children's Bookshelf. How may I help you?" His eyes slewed over to me. "Hello, Mrs. Wolff. Let me see if Mrs. Kennedy is available."

I crossed my eyes and stuck my tongue sideways out of my mouth. Not very adult, but Paoze had witnessed too many Claudia scenes to believe that I'd be happy to talk to her. I held out my hand for the phone and, grinning almost Lois-like, Paoze passed it over.

I forced my face into a semblance of a smile. "Hi, Claudia, what's up?"

"PTA phone conference. Tonight. Seven o'clock."

"Tonight? Okay, but what's the—"

Click.

"Hello?" But I heard nothing save the faint humming of a half-open phone line. She'd hung up on me. Really, truly, hung up on me. Even in the dark days when Richard and I were on the verge of separation, we'd been scrupulously polite to each other.

"Can't say I care for it." I handed the receiver back to Paoze.

"There is something you don't like?"

"Pea soup," I said, and was rewarded by his wide smile. White teeth against brown skin. Big brown eyes and black wavy hair. The kid was a heartbreak waiting to happen. He seemed to have no clue how attractive he was, though, which only added to his appeal.

"Cottage cheese," Paoze said. "I do not find it like-able."

"Just like Claudia Wolff," I muttered.

Paoze's grin flashed bright. "She is difficult," he said, then his grin faded out of view. "But there are friends for her."

Tina the Terrible, as Marina would say. And CeeCee Daniels, and Cindy Irving, and a host of others. "What are they seeing in her that I don't?" I asked.

"Maybe she is similar to pea soup," he said.

"Um . . ."

"Yes, very like pea soup, I think. To you, pea soup is not something you like, but other people do like. Are there things in pea soup that you care for?"

"I like ham," I said cautiously. "And carrots."

"So the main ingredient is what you do not like. Peas.

But other people like peas very much." He pointed at himself. "The main ingredient in Mrs. Wolff, herself, is what you do not like. But other people like her."

The clock above our heads ticked time away as I thought about what he'd said. Finally, I asked, "But how does that help?" Because in forty-one years of living, I still hadn't learned to like pea soup. It was one of the few foods that made my gag reflex take over. I couldn't even stand the smell of it. Once, when eating at the Green Tractor, four people in the booth behind me all ordered the mushy green stuff. I'd had to box up my lunch to go.

Paoze shrugged. "I do not think it does help," he said. "But the analogy is interesting, yes?"

I looked at him a little sourly. "You are an English major. You probably dream in similes and metaphors."

"Themes and plots," he said, nodding. "And symbolism. We are reading now about green lights at the end of a pier."

He went off into a description of *The Great Gatsby*, complete with sweeping arm gestures and widened eyes. I half listened, the rest of me split between wondering about the upcoming PTA call and wondering what F. Scott Fitzgerald would have written about Amy.

"Where's your list?" Marina was examining Oliver's unlikely sketch of George the cat and Spot the dog sitting next to each other with smiles on their furry faces. "You must have one, don't tell me you don't."

It had been such a warm afternoon that Marina had taken her day care kids to a local petting zoo after school. Afterward, she'd dropped them off at their respective homes, and my house was last on her route.

"The grocery list is right here." I tapped a half sheet of paper. A couple of years ago, I'd read a tip about preprinting your own grocery list. People usually buy the same items over and over, the article had said. Why not save yourself time and customize your own list? That made a lot of sense to me, so I did. I still thought it made a lot of sense, but I'd received nothing but grief from anyone who ever saw it. Overly organized was the nicest thing I'd heard.

"Not that list." Marina made a show of pawing through the papers on the kitchen table. "Wait, wait . . ." She peered at a small square of paper. "But, no. This is a list of NHL hockey teams that Jenna would be willing to play for. Where, oh where, is the real list?"

I opened the oven door. "They're all real lists. Please be more specific." I slid the pan of chicken inside.

"Your weight loss list."

"What makes you think I have a list for that?"

Marina gave me a "don't make me get out my flying monkeys" look. "Unless I'm gravely mistaken, the world has not yet ended. Therefore, you have a list. You make lists for everything from Saturday morning chores to stopping at the grocery store for three measly little items."

She pulled out a stool, sat at the kitchen island, and started using a bowl of fruit as a visual aid.

"You make a list for going on a weekend trip." A banana plopped on the counter in front of her. "You made a list for your Thanksgiving menu." An apple settled next to the banana. "You write up lists for PTA projects and school craft projects and projects you have going on at the store." Three oranges were added to the pile. "I bet you have a list of things for the kids to do this summer. A list of books for them to read. You've shown me that list of places you want to go someday. And I'd lay money you've already started a Christmas list."

She laid a large cluster of grapes across the top of the fruit pile and the whole pile shifted. "Know what this is? It's the listing pile of lists." She chortled. "Get it? Hah! Funny again today, aren't I?"

I leaned against the kitchen counter, arms folded, ankles crossed. "Are you going to eat all that? Because if not, I'd like to put the grapes back in the refrigerator."

Marina popped one into her mouth. "All in good time, my dear. All in good time." She picked up her imaginary foot-long cigarette holder and blew an invisible smoke ring. "Since you are not flapping this weight loss list about, I can come to only one conclusion."

"That you've made a tragic error and the world has, in fact, ended?"

"Which would explain the high grades of my youngest son for last marking period. But, no. My conclusion is that you haven't yet made a list."

I pushed myself off the counter. That chicken didn't seem to be cooking very fast. Maybe the oven wasn't working right. Maybe—

"Once again," Marina said, "I am correct. Conclusion number two is that in spite of your promise roughly a month ago, you haven't done a single thing to lose weight. How, pray tell, are you going to lose those twenty pounds you so cavalierly said you'd lose?"

"I never said I'd lose that much weight." I wanted to, of course I did, but reality was different from simply wanting. Too bad, really.

Marina waved off my protest. "Did I ever tell you about the prize?"

"Prize?"

She sighed. "Once again, your overloaded brain has failed you. Remember I called you during spring break? Remember that I said we were having a weight loss contest? Remember that I said I'd come up with a worthwhile prize?"

"No."

"So much potential, and she's wasted it all."

"Have you been talking to my mother?"

"It's time to announce the prize." She thumped the oranges back into the bowl. "And it's such a good one that I'm going to win it."

"How nice for you."

"Yes, indeedy." She beamed. "Hawaii is coming, you know. Say, did I tell you this is an open weight loss contest for anyone in Rynwood?"

I stared. No, she hadn't told me it was any more than the typical Beth vs. Marina contest, which was no contest at all because neither one of us ever lost weight for more than two months in a row.

"Oh, dear." She put her finger to her lips. "I see I haven't. Which means I also haven't mentioned who else is in the contest."

Lots of people lived in Rynwood. There was no reason to suspect that any one person in particular would be joining the weight loss game.

"I've started a Yahoo group," Marina said. "Didn't you get the e-mail?"

I had, but since I didn't realize what it was, I'd deleted the message without reading it. Bad Beth, for not paying complete attention to what she was doing.

"And it's the second of the month already." Marina held up one, then two fingers. "What have you done so far to change your lifestyle?"

"Yesterday morning I got up at five and did an hour of aerobics. Ate a single egg for breakfast, walked to the store instead of driving, ate a salad with no dressing for lunch, walked home, and ate a small and very plain chicken breast for dinner."

Marina's eyes went wide. "Really?"

"Please. Can you honestly picture me getting up at five in the morning to exercise?"

"Not to work out. But to finish reading a book? Sure."

"Well, I haven't found time to exercise. And I don't know when I will. When would I?" I started to do a run-down of my daily schedule, but if the way she put her hands over her ears was any indication, she didn't want to hear about my busy life.

"Not listening," she said. "La, la, la, I can't hear you, but I can talk to you, so listen up." She dropped her arms and folded them across her chest. "Like I said when you were up in the wilderness during spring break, it's time to quit talking and start doing. If you don't start making a serious effort to lose that poundage, I don't want to hear you complain about being fat ever again."

I piled up the papers from the kitchen table. "Oliver?" I called. "It's your turn to set the table."

"And it's time to start taking care of yourself," Marina said softly. "Lose the weight, sweets, it's not good for you."

I stopped. "But I thought this was all about you. About you not wanting to hear me whine. About you getting ready for Hawaii."

"Of course it is. But since you care more about my opinion than anything else in the world, I thought I'd try concern as a motivator."

"Marina the Manipulator." I opened the refrigerator door and peered inside. Leftover mashed potatoes would work for a starch. But what to do for a vegetable? I shut the door. "There's that old saying about people in glass houses and stones. I'm not the only one in this room who could stand to lose a few pounds."

She picked up her purse. "But I, dear heart, am content, satisfied, and in a general way am happy as a clam with my fitness and appearance. I'll send you another invitation to join the Yahoo group." And before I could ask her why, if she was so at peace with her weight, had she joined a weight loss contest, she was gone.

"Mom?" Jenna and Oliver pounded down the hall and into the kitchen. "When's dinner?"

"Check the timer," I said absently, and opened the refrigerator door again. There was nothing wrong with a plate of raw carrots, broccoli, and green peppers for a vegetable. Nothing at all. And if I put a bowl of sour cream and onion dip on the table, well, there was nothing wrong with that, either.

"Why are we going for a bike ride?" Oliver asked over his shoulder.

Because your mother is fat. "Because it's fun," I said.

The three of us pedaled along in silence. We were riding single file, Oliver in front, Jenna next, Mom bringing up the rear with her backpack of emergency essentials. I wasn't sure if it had been Marina's dig at my health, her convincing tone that she didn't want to hear any more complaints, or the fifth piece of broccoli that I'd pushed deep into the dip, but something had tweaked my brain.

One minute I'd been resigned to carrying an extra twenty pounds the rest of my life. The next minute I realized I was being a horrible role model for my children, especially Jenna. I should be showing her that adult women could be active and strong. I should be leading by example, demonstrating daily that exercise was a lifetime activity, that it didn't end when you left school.

"Hey!" I called. "You're getting too far ahead." Or at least that's what I wanted to say. It came out as a series of single-word sentences with two huffs of breath between each one. My bike ride to Amy's house had left me thinking that I wasn't in such bad shape, but I'd been deluding myself once again. My pace on that trip had been snail-like compared to the speed my children were pedaling.

Maybe this was why some mothers didn't go out on activities like this with their fast-growing kids. It was downright embarrassing to have my eight-year-old outperform me. Me, a former athlete. Sure, I'd been a swimmer, and it had been back in high school, but still.

Jenna and Oliver coasted until they were just ahead of me. "Mom, you're such a slowpoke," Jenna said. "Can't you go any faster?"

"Sorry. When we get to the park, we'll—"

I cocked my head. Either my cell phone was ringing or I was having an audio hallucination that involved Vivaldi's *Gloria*. "Hang on a second, you two." I stopped, straddled the bike, and slipped one arm out of the backpack's straps. The phone was still ringing when I found it in the bottom and turned it on. "Hello?"

"It's seven o'clock," Claudia said.

Rats. I'd forgotten all about the work session. "Um, I'm out riding bikes with my kids, can we do this later? In an hour?" Or never, whatever.

"Seven o'clock is the time you agreed to," she said in a precise voice.

She was right. Bad PTA secretary, for neglecting her duties.

There were a few clicks, and Erica and Randy were both on the line. "This is going to be short and sweet," Erica said. "Claudia, you called for this session. What do we need to discuss?"

"It's Beth's story project. I'm concerned about its progress. It's already the second of May, and what have we seen? Nothing! How is all the writing and the editing and the printing going to get done by the end of school? I don't see it happening, I just don't. I'm sorry to say this, but this was a bad project from the beginning. We should never have agreed to do it."

"The vote to do the project was unanimous," I pointed out.

"Whatever," Claudia said. "What I want to know is, how do we know it's going to get done?"

"Beth?" Erica asked. "Do you feel that the project will be completed on time?"

"Um . . ." Why hadn't I brought my schedule? Or, better, why didn't I have it memorized from stem to stern so I'd be able to summon details at the faintest of Claudia's sniffs? "I think so."

"You think so?" Erica's repetition of my reply made it sound very lame. "That's not a reassuring answer."

I watched my children play some sort of complex game. They'd propped their bikes up against a large maple tree. Oliver had found a small stone, and he and Jenna were kicking it back and forth to each other. Their point totals seemed to jump faster depending on how much body English the kicker used. Jenna had an edge because of her alternate life as a goalie, but Oliver had the creativity of someone who'd never found much attraction in rigid rules, so it was a fairly even game.

"It'll be done on time," I said. "If I had the schedule in front of me I'd be able to give an accurate summary."

"She's not prepared," Claudia said. "If she's not ready for this meeting, how can she possibly do this project?"

Randy grunted. "Maybe it's too big."

I waited for Erica to reassure the others that I had

excellent command of the situation, that Claudia was overreacting, that there was no need to worry, no need at all.

"Well, Beth?" Erica asked.

"I ..." The pavement under my feet suddenly felt unstable and, with my free hand, I gripped my bike's handlebars tight enough to make my hand hurt.

"Give us some assurance, Beth. Update us on the progress. Tell us about the targets you've achieved. Are you meeting your stated goals?"

"Um ..." Each of Erica's short, focused sentences sent my thoughts in a different directions. I felt like a puppy trying to catch the first snowflakes of winter. "I've done a lot of work on this."

"No one is questioning your commitment," she said. "Our concern is if your expectations have been realistic. If the book cannot be completed on time, the Tarver PTA will be publicly embarrassed. We've sent out press releases to news media all over the state. I've even been talking to PTA National about this project. If it isn't done on time, our reputation will be damaged."

My heart thumped hard against my ribs. I was disappointing Erica. Thanks to my own grandiose ideas, I was going to ruin Tarver's PTA.

"I think she bit off more than she can chew," Claudia said.

Erica made a noncommittal noise. "Do you have a suggestion on how to proceed, Claudia?"

"Oh, well, I guess ..." Her words trailed off into silence.

"Randy, how about you?" Erica asked.

He grunted a response that sounded negative.

"I see," Erica said. "Well, we have a situation, don't we?"

A situation. I'd always hated that phrase. Why not just

say "we have a problem"? "No, we don't," I blurted out. "The project is going just fine."

"Then you need to show us," Erica said. "E-mail a progress report as soon as possible. On a project with this much scope, we cannot simply take your word."

"I want to see some of the stories," Claudia said. "Anybody can write numbers in a spreadsheet. I need to see what the kids are writing. And not Oliver," she added. "Her son's stuff doesn't count."

My breaths turned hot and sharp. Claudia Wolff was saying I would turn in a falsified progress report. She was calling me a liar. "Are you calling me—"

Erica cut in. "Not an unreasonable request," she said. "Beth, we'll give you a week to come up with what three children have written to date. Three stories, with the recognition that they need not be complete, and a solid progress report. You do realize how crucial the timing is for this project, don't you?"

Of course I did. I was the one who'd kept harping on that very point all winter and half the spring. I was the one who'd drawn up the calendar and the schedules and the drop-dead deadlines. All of which were far out of reach, at home on the computer. "Yes, I—"

"Then you have a week to bring this together. Show us solid evidence of progress and we won't shut this down."

"Sounds good," Randy said. "See you in a week."

"But I can gather up all that by tomorrow. I'm not at home, that's all, and—"

"They're gone," Claudia said.

"Oh." Yet another reason to hate conference calls.

"I hear you're supposed to be part of Marina's weight loss contest."

"Um, I guess so." Whether I wanted to be or not. Marina didn't always present me with a choice.

"You guess?" Claudia laughed. "You don't know? It's already the second of May. I've lost over five pounds already. Better make up your mind or you'll never catch up."

"You're in the contest?"

"Well, duh. Who wouldn't want that prize, a day at that fancy spa in Madison? Talk about a motivator. Massage, facial, manicure, pedicure, the works. Want to make a side bet? Twenty bucks says I win."

My response was unthinking. "I don't bet."

"Hah. I knew you wouldn't. Not a chance you're going to win, anyway. But hey, that extra thirty pounds doesn't look too bad on you, considering."

"Considering what?"

"Well, how old you are. At your age you can't expect to look that great. Fact of life, you know?"

"I don't bet," I said. "But there are always exceptions. Twenty dollars says I win."

"You're on," she said triumphantly. "And you're going to lose."

A thought popped into my tiny little head. "How many people are in this contest?"

"Last time I checked the Yahoo group it was up to fifteen."

"If we both lose," I said, "the overall winner gets our money."

"Doesn't matter, because I'm winning. A certificate to the spa and twenty bucks of Beth's money to spend. Sounds like the perfect day." She laughed. "Did I tell you I've lost over five pounds already?" She laughed again and hung up.

I ended the call. There was motivation and there was motivation. A day at the spa would be nice, but even nicer would be seeing Claudia's face when I won the contest.

"Let's go," I called to the kids.

They abandoned their game and hopped back on their bikes. "Where are we going?" Jenna asked. "Are we still going to the park?"

I glanced at my watch. Looked at the sun and gauged how much daylight was left to us. "To the moon, Alice!"

Jenna looked puzzled. "Who's Alice?"

"That's a really long ways," Oliver said.

"Maybe it is a little too far." I grinned at my children. "How about to the lake and back?"

It'd be a three-mile round trip, but whatever Claudia's secret weapon might be, there was no way it would be exercise. My secret weapon would be sensible meals combined with a reasonable amount of exercise. No wacky diet could beat that, not in the long run.

Yep, good sense and exercise. How could I lose?

The next morning it took a lot of groaning and a long, hot shower to get me moving. Three miles. How could three lousy miles of bike riding make me hurt so much? As a kid I'd ridden that far, one way, to buy a bottle of soda. As a teenager I'd ridden twice that far to get to the good beach. When and how had this ill fitness happened to me?

"Are you all right, Bethie?" Maude Hoffman looked at me.

Thanks to Auntie May, I was now known throughout Sunny Rest Assisted Living as Bethie. No one, not even my younger brother in his very youngest days, had ever called me Bethie. "Fine, thanks."

"Oh, dear, I'm not sure you're telling the truth." She turned to my son. "Oliver, does she look fine?"

"Um." His face squinched up as he looked at me. "She has been moving kind of funny. Did you see how slow she sat down?"

"Yes, indeedy. I also noticed how tight she held on to those chair arms." Maude reached forward and patted my knee. The slight thudding made me wince. "It was a beautiful night last night," she said. "Did we go for a long walk?"

"Bike ride." Oliver bounced a little on Maude's bed. "A long, long one. Jenna and Mom and me all went."

I wanted to correct his grammar, but I lacked the energy. Just getting through the day had taken a lot out of me. Three miles, for crying out loud. Three!

"What a nice thing for a family to do." Maude smiled. "My sisters and I all had bicycles. In the summers we rode all over town. To the soda fountain, to the movies, to the train station to see who was coming in."

I tapped Oliver and made scribbly writing motions with my hand. He stared at me blankly, then his eyes opened wide. He bent over his notebook and started taking notes.

Maude went on talking. "The girls were just starting to wear pants back then. Not to school, of course. Never to school. And if we'd worn pants to church surely God would have stricken us dead. But most parents let their girls play outside in jeans. So much easier for riding a bicycle than a dress." She paused and looked at Oliver. "Where did you go on your long bike ride?"

"We went to the lake and back."

"Blue Lake?" Maude asked.

Too late, I remembered where her great-niece had drowned. I steeled myself for another bout of tears and damp handkerchiefs.

Maude leaned forward in her wheelchair. "Did you find anything? See anything?"

"Did I . . . ?"

"You're starting the investigation, aren't you?" She sat back. "That's why you biked all the way out there instead of driving, isn't it? Keeping a low profile." She clasped her hands and her lower lip trembled. "And now you hurt yourself trying to help me. When this is all over, I'll find a way to repay you."

Oliver stopped writing. He looked at me with a puzzled expression. "But, Mom, we didn't—"

"Honey," I said, "could you do me a favor? Do you think you can find Mrs. Judy? The activities director? Can you ask her if we can use the Sunny Rest copy machine at the end of today's session? Thanks, sweetie."

He scampered off. I turned back to Maude. Studied her, saw hope and expectation shining on her face. She'd believed me when I'd told her I'd try to help. I'd pushed her request to the back of my mind, vaguely hoping for a small bout of amnesia, and now I was being hoist on my own petard.

I reached for Oliver's notebook and turned to a fresh page. Fetched a pen from my purse and uncapped it. Smiled. "What else can you tell me about Kelly?"

A light voice coughed. In the doorway stood Tracy, the nurse's aide for Maude's wing of Sunny Rest. "Maude, do you mind if I borrow Beth for a couple minutes?"

Maude held up two fingers. "That's all you get."

"You're a peach." Tracy blew her a kiss. "I'll bring her back safe and sound, I promise."

Maude tapped her watch. "One minute and fifty seconds," she said with mock severity. "I'm not so old I can't tell time."

Out in the hallway, Tracy beckoned me over to a small alcove just big enough to hold a table and two chairs. A fresh jigsaw puzzle was spread out over the tabletop. My fingers itched to start putting edge pieces together, but I put my hands in my lap.

"The residents are just loving this story project," Tracy said. "The ones who didn't sign up are jealous of the ones who did. Lots of the residents have asked if we're going to do this project again next year."

This was something I hadn't once considered. But since I rarely managed to think ahead more than twelve hours at a time, the fact that the idea hadn't crossed my mind shouldn't be a surprise. "I don't know. We'll have to see. I'll talk to Judy and the PTA board and we'll see." Or not. Whatever.

"Sounds good."

The words could have been delivered in an emphatic and decisive way. Instead, she let them out vaguely as she put two fingers on two puzzle pieces and slid them up and down. It didn't take a rocket scientist to figure out what was going on.

"Tracy, is there something you want to talk to me about?"

"Well . . ." She glanced over my shoulder, back toward Maude's room. "It's about Maude. There's something you should know."

I went very, very still. She'd been diagnosed with a degenerative muscle disease. She'd just this minute been diagnosed with a contagious disease and Oliver was at risk. She had cancer, had only three months left to live, and her nieces were moving her to Florida this weekend.

All this ran through my worried brain cells in a fraction of a second. If leaping to conclusions were a form of exercise, I'd be the fittest woman in Wisconsin. "She looks good for being eighty-something." She'd told me that she'd broken her hip and it wasn't healing quite right, hence the wheelchair and the assisted living.

"She is, mostly." Tracy fiddled with the puzzle pieces. "Maybe I shouldn't really say, but—" She slapped her

hand to her waist. "Oh, drat. It's my beeper." She unclipped the black plastic rectangle, pushed some buttons,
and stood. "Sorry, there's a call I have to answer." Her
white plastic clogs padded down the carpeted hallway.

I watched her go. Don't worry about Maude, I told
myself. If there was a real problem, you'd know. Judy
wouldn't have Tracy give me the bad news, she'd tell me
herself. Don't worry.

It was good advice. Unfortunately, there was no way I
was going to take it.

Chapter 9

Flossie tossed a black plastic garbage bag over the edge of the Dumpster. "Kelly Engel? Good heavens, that was a long time ago. Why on earth are you asking? You were still a child back then."

I let the Dumpster's lid slam shut. "We're the same age." Or would have been, if Kelly hadn't died.

"Really?" Flossie studied the sky. Partly cloudy, the forecast had said. Which, to me, implies that it should also be partly sunny, but obviously partly cloudy meant something different to weather forecasters since the sky was coated with low, thick clouds. We watched the clouds slowly form, break up, and reform, until Flossie finally said, "Time is an odd thing."

She paused, but since I couldn't think of anything sensible to contribute, I stayed quiet.

Flossie dusted her hands against each other. "Kelly died just before I moved home from Chicago." She shook her silvery curls. "Everyone wanted to forget what happened, you know. The lake was a safe place up until then. Rynwood was a safe place. Kelly drowned not long before the summer started. Hardly a kid swam in that lake until the heat came, in August."

It was hard to imagine. The swimming beach at Blue

Lake was a friendly space with an eagle-eyed lifeguard perched high on a chair that was painted white every spring. There was a swimming raft with a floppy diving board, buoys bobbing where the water started turning deep, and a pavilion for shelter when it rained. Picturing it empty throughout June and July was like picturing a deserted downtown two days before Christmas.

"Why the questions about Kelly?" Flossie asked. "I'm surprised you've even heard of her."

I gave her a snapshot summary of the PTA senior story project. "And Oliver's match is Maude Hoffman."

Flossie nodded. Though she'd spent thirty-odd years in Chicago, she'd grown up in Rynwood. Local knowledge flowed through her blood and was impregnated into the marrow of her bones. "Maude had a hard time with it, from what I heard. She was almost as much a mother to those girls as Barb was."

"I'd say she's still not over it. She's convinced something happened that night that the police never discovered."

"And she wants you to find out what? Hmm." Flossie pursed her lips, creating an array of small vertical lines around her mouth. "Maude. Lovely lady, but there's something you should—"

"Hey, boss?" A young man's face peeked out of the grocery store's rear entrance. "We got a problem up front. The scale won't work and we got customers getting cranky about me not knowing diddly."

"Be right there." Flossie looked at me. "Give me a call, Beth. We need to talk."

I watched her jog up the short run of steps, wishing that I could move with her grace, but even more, wondering what everybody thought I needed to know about Maude.

*   *   *

Ruthie, intrepid owner of the Green Tractor diner, shut the cash register with a light bang. "Kelly Engel? Now that's a name I haven't heard in years."

She got a faraway look on her face, then shook it off. "Here, come sit with me. We'll have a nice cozy chat about Kelly and I'll get Ian to bring you a cup of that tea you like so much. Ian? Can you get Beth here a carafe of hot water and a chai tea bag? Thanks, hon."

I slid into the vacant booth she was patting. "Ruthie, you don't need to fuss over me."

"Yes, I do. I love to fuss, why do you think I opened this restaurant?"

Ian deposited tea and fixings in front of me, a mug of steaming coffee in front of Ruthie. We thanked him, and while I bobbed my tea bag, I watched Ruthie.

Ruthie's age was in the vicinity of seventy. Not quite in Flossie's range, but close enough to make me wonder where the stamina these women had came from. If it was genetic, I was out of luck. But maybe the city's water supply was a secret source of energy for people over the age of sixty.

"So. Why Kelly Engel?" Ruthie asked. "And why now?"

Before I was halfway done with my explanation of the PTA's story project, she was nodding, having made the mental leaps far faster than I could talk.

"Maude Hoffman. Is she partnered with . . . oh, Oliver?" A smile sent wrinkles shooting in new directions across her cheeks. "How nice for them both. I'm guessing Maudie wants you to find out what really happened that night. She's a newspaper reader, front to back, and knows how you and Marina Neff have helped clean up this town. Quit denying it. You know it's true. So. About

Kelly." She sipped her coffee, looking at me over the mug's bright green ceramic rim. "What do you know already?"

"Just what Maude said. Blond, pretty, headed for college with plans to go to medical school. That she drowned in Blue Lake, right before her high school graduation. That people say she committed suicide."

Ruthie sighed. "She didn't tell you about Keith, did she?"

"Um . . ."

"Sounds like Maude." She set her coffee mug down with a thump. "Keith Mathieson and Kelly had one of those storybook romances. When she was five and he was seven, he rescued her from being attacked by a dog. Happened at a neighborhood party."

I listened, rapt.

"Kelly was off in a corner of the backyard, playing with someone's German shepherd. Dog turned nasty for some reason. Knocked her to the ground and stood over her, growling, lip curled up, looking like he was about to take a big bite out of her. She started screaming like only little girls can. Keith was the closest. Ran over there fast as he could, grabbed one of those green plastic chairs, and pushed it at the dog until Kelly could get away."

"He was only seven?" I breathed. "Amazing."

"Yup." Ruthie nodded. "Keith was the man of the hour. Got his picture in the paper and everything. After that, hardly a day went by without seeing those two together. Hero worship, at first, on Kelly's part, but she grew out of that fast enough."

"Not a good basis for a lasting relationship," I murmured.

Ruthie waved at Ian with one hand while pointing at her coffee mug with the other. "Unless it's the boy wor-

shipping the girl. In my experience that works just fine."
She winked, laughing. "Anyway, those two grew up hand
in hand. Went from the playground to junior high to high
school without looking at anyone else. Everyone figured
they'd get married someday. Kelly picked out her brides-
maids by the time she was thirteen."

"But . . . ?"

Ian appeared with coffeepot in hand. "More hot water, Beth?" I shook my head and he went away.

Ruthie sniffed her mug. "The boy served me the bottom of the pot." She took a sip and made a face. "Keith
and Kelly. Remember Keith was two years older? They
had it all planned out. Keith was enrolled in Wisconsin
on the Milwaukee campus. Kelly could do her undergrad
there, then she'd go to the Medical College of Wisconsin.
All the plans they had." She shook her head. "Makes you
wonder, sometimes."

Lots of things made me wonder. For instance, why
was the number one button on a telephone on the upper
left, but the number one button on a calculator on the
lower left? And why did we always get one last snowfall
the week after I put the snow shovels away?

"What was Keith studying?" I asked.

"Business." She gave a short, barking laugh. "A busi-
ness major. Hah! Give me those kids for six months and
I'll teach them more than they'll learn in four years.
Business. Please."

"So what happened to their plans?" I asked.

"Her parents said Kelly came home from a date with
Keith, crying, and wouldn't talk about it. The next weekend she was dead."

No wonder there was so much talk of suicide. "What
a dreadful thing."

"In a nutshell. Everybody in town blamed Keith for

Kelly's death. Her family had a heckuva time dealing with it. None of them would believe suicide. Kelly was a good Catholic, they said."

"They must have suffered terribly."

"Still are. At least her mother is. Her dad? Well, men can be hard to figure when grief comes around. Kelly's sisters all moved away soon afterward, poor things. Home just wasn't the same anymore, they said."

No, how could it be? There'd always be a raw hole where there once was a living, breathing, laughing girl. And no matter how thick the scar, the pain would always, always be there.

"So I'm guessing Maude's come over to Barb's point of view?" Ruthie asked.

"She wanted me to find out what really went on that night," I said slowly. "Barb is Kelly's mother? What does she think?"

"That Kelly was murdered."

I stood inside the door of the Rynwood Antique Mall, looking across the street at the police department. Rain dripped down onto the brick sidewalks, onto the heads of the people walking past, onto the green shrubberies lining the street, and onto the windshields of the passing cars.

Cindy Irving, who did most of the landscaping work for the downtown businesses, was the only person not hurrying to get inside. In a bright yellow rain slicker and rubber boots, she was also the only person dressed properly for the weather.

"Beth, do you want to borrow an umbrella?" Alan, co-owner of the mall, stood at the counter holding a black collapsible version. "I don't think that rain's going to quit for a while."

"No, thanks." I reached back, pulled up the hood of my light jacket, and renewed my hold on the bag of chocolate chip cookies that had been my excuse for leaving the store. "It would take me ages to remember to return it, and the guilt would ruin my sleep for weeks."

Alan laughed, but it was an indulgent laugh at what he assumed was a joke. Clearly, he had no idea that I was serious.

With a deep breath for courage, I pushed open the door and splashed out into the rain. Wet, wet, wet. I tiptoed across the street, head down, trying to keep muddy splashes off my light beige pants. The rain poured down and by the time I made it to the police station, all I wanted was to be inside out of the weather.

"Hi, can I help you?"

I shook off the rain onto the floor mat, tried to remember the new officer's name, and couldn't come up with even a bad guess. "Hi, I'm Beth Kennedy. I don't think we've officially met."

"Sean Zimmerman." Standing, he held out his hand. "You own that bookstore."

He was a few inches taller than my own five foot five, and had hair so short it was hard to determine its color. The square-ish shape to his face suited his solid body, and suited the uniform. He looked like a policeman should look.

"Did you grow up wanting to be in law enforcement?" I asked, shaking his firm—but not anywhere close to painful—grip.

"Every single Halloween I went as a cop," he said, smiling.

How strange to always have known what you wanted to do. Maybe it was a guy thing; my physicist brother had been the same way. But, no. Marina always said she'd known she was destined to be a stay-at-home mom from the age of thirteen when she'd taken an occupational questionnaire and had no idea how to answer most of the questions.

"I mean, honestly," she'd told me. "How was I supposed to answer a question like 'What would you do if two superiors gave you different instructions?'" Rolling her eyes, she'd flicked her cheek with her index finger. "Do the work requested by the highest authority, do the work requested by the one I feel closest to, or ask for more time?" She'd made a buzzing noise. "I wrote in my own answer of 'do nothing until those two get their act together' and the next week the counselor called me into her office for a little chat."

I smiled at Officer Zimmerman. "A framed set of your Halloween pictures would fit in nicely over there." I indicated the wall of current officer photos.

"Yeah, as if I don't look young enough already. Are you here to see Chief Eiseley?" the young man asked. "Because he's not in right now."

A fact of which I was well aware since I'd watched him walk down the street and into the Green Tractor. Whoever he was meeting there, he wouldn't be back for at least half an hour, not if the last twenty years of Friday morning cinnamon rolls meant anything.

"Then maybe you could help me," I said. "What can you tell me about a teenager who drowned in Blue Lake twenty years ago?"

"That's a ways back. Wow, twenty years. Well, I can look and see if we have anything on the computer. Otherwise, you'll have to talk to the chief."

I gave him the date and name, and Sean sat back down at his desk. "Engel, you said? Hang on." He started humming a tuneless tune. "Kelly Engel? She died in

May, looks like they were calling it an accident . . . huh. That's weird." He frowned at the computer screen. Using his index finger and thumb, he tugged on his lower lip hard enough to show his closely spaced bottom teeth.

"What's the matter?"

"There's some stuff in the memo field . . ." A troubled looked settled on his face. "Probably I shouldn't tell you this."

I wanted to know what he was reading so badly that I was tempted to fake a fainting spell, send him for a glass of water, sprint over to the computer, and speed read until I heard his approaching footsteps, then quick as a wink sprint back and resume my swooning position.

Marina would do it. She would have already started to sway and moan. But I lacked the chutzpah to carry out subterfuge on that scale. My dissembling techniques began and ended with Santa Claus, the Easter bunny, and the Tooth Fairy. And since, in January, Oliver had broken the news to me that he hadn't believed in Santa for two Christmases, I didn't even have do that any longer.

"Don't do anything you're not comfortable doing," I said.

"It's not that so much." He twisted his lip. "It's . . . well . . ." He tapped a few keys. On the other side of the room, a printer whirred to life. "Did you know Ms. Engel?"

"No. It's her great-aunt who would like to know what happened that night. She's at Sunny Rest. That assisted living place down the road."

Sean nodded. "Okay, I get it. She's getting up there in years and wants to know what really happened. Makes sense to me. It's just, well . . ."

He dropped back into pensive mode, and I got a gray, dull feeling. Poor Maude. She wouldn't want to hear this.

She wanted a different ending, one that didn't change her great-niece from a strong, vibrant, young woman to pallid maiden unwilling to live without her knight in shining armor.

"The notes say she took her own life, don't they?" I asked quietly.

His gaze slid away from mine. "Um, sorry, but yeah."

"Don't be," I said. "Start apologizing for things that aren't your fault and you'll spend the rest of your life saying you're sorry." I spoke with the confidence of long experience.

"Okay," he said, nodding. "I see what you're saying. But I am. Sorry, I mean." He glanced at the computer screen. "She was really pretty. It's too bad. Kind of a waste, you know?"

I thanked him, and stood to go. "One more thing. Does the computer tell you who made those notes about Kelly?" Chances were, it was an officer long gone from Rynwood, but still.

"Initials are, hang on a sec, G.E. Looks like Chief Eiseley wrote it up." He looked up and behind me. "Do you remember this one, Chief?"

"Very well."

I jumped. "Gus. I didn't hear you come in."

His glance skidded over me and away. "Beth. Officer Zimmerman here has work to do. If I hear you've been wasting his time with your crackpot theory that Amy Jacobson was murdered, I'll have him cleaning toilets for six months."

The trepidation I'd felt five seconds earlier vanished. "Seems to me he's doing a fine job," I snapped. "Seems to me that answering somebody's questions has more to do with police work than eating cinnamon rolls. Does Winnie know how many of those things you eat?"

"Leave Winnie out of this." His voice was hard. "I don't want you bothering her."

Winnie was my friend. There was no way Gus was going to keep me from talking to her. He had no right. None whatsoever. "We don't always get what we want, do we?"

Emotion flashed across his face, but it was gone so quickly I was left with only a memory.

Gus strode past me, down the short hallway to his office, and shut his door with a bang.

I made half a move to go to him, to beg him to tell me what I'd done wrong, to ask forgiveness for whatever it was, to plead to have things back the way they'd been. Instead, I sighed, thanked Officer Sean for his time, and left the suddenly stuffy air of the police station.

Outside, I splashed down the sidewalk, not thinking of anything at all. Then, since not thinking wasn't a state of mind that ever lasted very long, I started thinking about what to do next. Behind me was a short walk to Sunny Rest and Maude. Could I look into her gentle eyes and give her the news she so desperately didn't want to hear? Could I tell her that no matter what she wanted to believe, Kelly had taken her own life?

Someday, maybe. Just not today.

I kept walking back to work. Back to where Lois and Yvonne and a whole host of beloved books were waiting for me. Back to where happy endings outnumbered unhappy ones by ten thousand to one.

Chapter 10

The weekend and the following week blurred past in a rush of work, kid activities, and PTA duties. I'd e-mailed away the Erica-required stories to keep Claudia's breath off the back of my neck, but I was getting the panicky feeling that life was whizzing by too fast. I said as much to Lois and Yvonne one day.

"Send your kids out for adoption," Lois suggested. "They're cute enough that someone will take them."

"Lois!" Yvonne stared at her, openmouthed. "How can you say such a thing?"

I patted her shoulder. "She's just joking."

Lois gave an evil chuckle. "Are you sure?"

"Yes," I said firmly. "And quit with that creepy laugh. You're scaring Yvonne. She's not used to you yet."

Lois slung her arm around the younger woman's neck, grinning. "Sure she is. We're the best of buddies. She knows I'd never steer her wrong."

"Then why did you send her down to the hardware to get a shelf stretcher?"

Lois sniffed. "A life lesson. Humility is good for the soul. Speaking of what's good for you, you should learn to relax more. You're looking uptight these days. When's the last time you and that Evan of yours had a nice relaxing dinner out?" She waggled her eyebrows and Yvonne put a hand in front of her mouth to cover her laugh.

"Tomorrow night," I said. "The kids are with their dad this weekend."

"So convenient." Lois nodded wisely. "If you need a chaperone, I'm sure I can rearrange my bingo night."

For a moment I was tempted. Having Lois along could make for a very interesting evening. I pictured her entertaining Evan and me with her talent for storytelling. Last winter I'd challenged her to make up a story about a box of tissues and she'd risen to the challenge grandly with a sad tale of a child who'd lost her favorite, but very small, doll. The poor little girl had broken down in tears, reached for a tissue, and joyfully found little dolly inside the box. Happy ending. Which was a welcome change. Most Lois stories ended in death, destruction, and mayhem.

"Hello, Beth?" Lois waved her hands in front of my face. "Ah, there you are. Nice to see you back in the here and now." She tossed one end of her chenille scarf (in bright stripes of orange and yellow) over her shoulder. "I have a recommendation to make. Yvonne, you be witness."

"Why," I asked, "am I getting a bad feeling about this?"

"No idea. All I'm going to suggest is—"

"I'm not flying to Las Vegas for the weekend." It was one of her more popular recommendations. "Or taking a road trip to the Baja peninsula. Or gorging myself on cheese. I'm trying to lose weight, you know, not gain it."

"—is that you take the day off tomorrow."

"Don't be silly." The last few months I'd slid into working on the Saturdays that I didn't have the kids. It gave me time to work on the things that never seemed to get done during the week. "There's too much that needs doing."

"Matter of fact, take this afternoon off, too. It's a gorgeous day, you're caught up with work, and Sara will be here any minute to give us a hand."

I looked at her. At my office, where piles of work waited. At the young adult books, where I'd planned to analyze the benefits of face out versus spine out. At the dangling and dusty cobweb in the high back corner of the store, something that had been annoying me for weeks, a chore that I'd finally written down on my Saturday To Do list. "There's too much to do." I looked out at the blue sky and sunshine. "I should pay some bills, and the new catalogs are here."

Outside, a youngster in baggy shorts and a T-shirt ten sizes too big for him whirred past on a skateboard.

I turned away and tried to focus. "No. Thanks for the suggestion, but I just can't."

"Oh, yeah?" Lois yanked off her scarf. "First step is hold out your hands so I can tie them together with this. Yvonne, get the rope. We'll need it for her feet."

"Very funny." I put my hands behind my back.

Lois swung the scarf back and forth like a long, snaky pendulum. "You need to take some time off. Time off. Time off."

I batted it away. "I'm not going to be hypnotized by a striped scarf."

"How about a polka dot one? I have it in my car."

I blew out an exasperated sigh. "Look, I know you mean well, both of you, but there's too much to do."

"And what will happen if it doesn't get done until Monday?" Lois asked.

"Well . . ."

"Please, Beth." Yvonne touched my arm. "You've

been looking awfully tired lately. Please go home and get some rest. I don't want you getting sick. We need you."

It was her last words that tipped me over the edge. I looked at Lois. "The world won't end if I don't come back until Monday?"

"If it does, I'll let you know."

"Well, okay." But I still hesitated. "You're sure? I mean, sure sure?"

Lois drew herself tall, stretched out her arm, and pointed with a long and bony index finger to the door. "Go!"

I went.

"You did what?" Marina stared at me, her jaw dropped so far that, if I'd wanted to, which I didn't, I could have examined her tonsils.

I leaned against her kitchen counter and tried to look casual. "Took the afternoon off."

After my staff had sent me home, I'd spread a blanket out in the backyard, packed myself a snack of celery sticks and unsweetened iced tea, lugged out a pile of books I'd been meaning to read, lay flat on the blanket, and fallen asleep. Which was why I'd shown up at Marina's house for our Dinner and a Movie half an hour late. I hadn't woken up until the sun had sunk low enough to cast shadows across the yard, chilling my body enough to bring me back to life.

"Almost any other story I'd have believed, but this?" The cooking magazine in Marina's hand waggled at me. "Not with your work ethic. Not with your obsessive intent to always do the right thing. Not with the way you commit to work before pleasure, every freaking second of every freaking day."

I pushed up the sleeve of my polo shirt and pointed at the faint color change. "See that?"

Marina gasped. "Is it, could it be, could it truly be, a *tan* line?" She put her nose an inch away from my bicep. "Why, it is! Beth Kennedy, you sly dog, you. You really did take the afternoon off! Wonders never do cease, do they? Don't tell me you went to the lake."

"Okay, I won't."

Her eyes went round. "You went to the lake? On a weekday?"

"No, I fell asleep in the backyard."

"You said . . ." She stopped and replayed the conversation. "Oh, aren't you the funny one. I knew you couldn't have done anything all that exciting, not without me to lend a hand."

"I can't do anything fun on my own?"

"Sure, you can. You just don't."

I opened my mouth to start listing all the fun things I'd done by myself. Closed it when I couldn't come up with anything better than "in January I spent a Saturday night reading the latest Laurie R. King mystery." Fun for me, but it wouldn't even rank a one on Marina's one to ten scale.

Her ones were structured activities like riding roller coasters. A five might be crashing a country club wedding reception and leading the conga dance out to the club's swimming pool and off the end of the diving board. Nines looked a lot like the movie *Ferris Bueller's Day Off*. Ten, she was saving, but it would probably have something to do with either the president of the United States or Hugh Jackman. Maybe both.

"Have you talked to Winnie yet?" Marina pushed my sleeve back down and patted it in place. "You know, about what's eating Gus?"

"Sent her an e-mail asking her to call me, but she hasn't yet." Both Winnie and Gus had been acting so out of character that I wasn't sure there would even be a phone call. I said as much to Marina.

She scoffed. "Please. It's Winnie. She's worse than you are about doing the right thing, if that's possible.

"Why do you make it sound as if doing the right thing is something to be ashamed of?"

"For most people, it's not. Normal people don't hold themselves to some freakishly high standard of conduct. Most of us play by the eighty-twenty rule. You know, do the right thing eighty percent of the time and choose custard-filled long johns over broccoli the other twenty percent. Your percentage is ninety-nine to one. It's not right and I'm pretty sure it's against the law."

"I bought out Alice's M&M cookies this morning."

Marina lifted her hand for a high five, but just before our palms slapped, she pulled hers back. "How many did you eat?"

"Three."

"That's my girl!" Her hand went up again. Pulled back again. "What did you have for lunch?"

"Well . . . I kind of didn't."

"Too busy, or intentionally, to make up for the cookies?"

I wanted to lie, but knew I'd never be able to pull it off. What it said about me that one of my deepest wishes was to improve my lying skills I didn't know, but it probably wasn't good.

"Intentionally, then." Marina lowered her hand and shook her head sadly. "A flicker of hope, blown out forever."

"You're the one who started this weight loss contest," I said. "You're the one who expanded it to the entire town, and you're the one who got that spa trip as a prize, so you shouldn't be surprised if I want to put a little effort into winning, especially with Claudia in the running."

"All in your best interest, mah dear," she said, slipping into Southern belle-speak. "Ah'm just trying to help." She opened the refrigerator door and extracted a stick of butter. "Ah'm doin' this for you."

"Then you should put that butter away and use canola oil instead."

She looked at the half cup of fat, cholesterol, and calories. "No butter?"

"If it's not good for me, it's not good for you."

"Sure, but you're the only one who cares."

"Back." I pointed at the fridge.

"Don't make me." She turned her hands palm up, presenting the butter to me like a small trophy. "You do it."

"Think of how much better for you a little oil would be." I took the butter and swatted her hands away when she tried to get it back.

"Think how much better butter tastes."

"Nothing tastes as good as thin feels," I said, quoting a long-ago coworker.

"And I would know that how?" She thumped her well-rounded hips. Stabbed her midriff with her thumbs. Held up her hand and flopped the flesh on the underside of her arm.

"Stop that. Some things you just have to take on faith."

Muttering, she opened the cupboard door and rattled around until she found an unopened bottle of olive oil. "I have a lot more faith in the healing power of butter." She plopped the bottle on the counter. "Fat equals flavor, you know, and flavor is what it's all about."

"Have you lost any weight?"

"With the weight of the world on my shoulders?" She struck an Atlas pose.

I took that as a no. "How much has anyone else lost?"

"If you'd joined the Yahoo group, you'd know that already."

"Maybe tomorrow. How much has Claudia lost?" Horrible person that I was, I was hoping for her to have gained weight. Childish Beth.

"Was it six?" Marina poured a dollop of oil into the frying pan. "No, not six."

I let out a breath of relief. Maybe my four pounds was still in the running. If I started exercising twice each day—back to the two-a-days of high school swim team—I'd be able to beat Claudia. Win the prize, even.

A day at a spa had never been one of my fantasies, but I could probably deal with a few hours of doing nothing. Especially if they let me bring in the eReader Evan had given me for Christmas. A day of self-indulgence wouldn't be complete without at least a couple of hours of uninterrupted reading. He'd also given me a gift card that had let me download a number of e-books, and I still hadn't read Lorraine Bartlett's latest, or the Margaret Maron. And wasn't Lee Child releasing a book soon? Maybe I could time my spa trip to coincide with—

"I remember now," Marina said. "Claudia's lost ten."

"Ten pounds?" My voice rose to a near-shriek. "It's only been a few weeks. How could she have lost ten pounds?"

Marina shrugged. "Probably just water weight. You know how some people lose lots of weight when they stop eating all that salt and gunk in so much prepared foods. She'll probably gain most of it back when she starts eating normally again, but if she keeps it off until the end of the month, well, weight is weight."

"Ten pounds," I said dully. No way would I be able to compete with that.

"Or was it eight?" Marina hummed as she studied her spice rack. "Basil, oregano, and garlic? Or garlic, oregano, and basil?"

"I thought we were making tacos."

"Change in plans, mah dear. If you're going to catch up to that wretched woman, we need to feed you properly, and tonight properly means small amounts of pasta and large amounts of vegetables. Say . . ." She turned to face me. "Maybe Claudia killed Amy. If we can prove it, oh, like this weekend, she'll get slapped in jail." Marina's face lit up. "Wouldn't that be perfect? The food is bound to be fattening in there, so there's no way she'll win. And I bet that Tina helped out with Amy. Those two never do anything on their own. Tina's only lost five pounds, but put her in a cell next to Claudia and I bet they do nothing but eat and eat and eat."

Clearly, Marina had a different idea of what jail was like than I did. "And why would Claudia have any reason to kill Amy?"

Marina pointed a jar of rosemary at me. "Tina went along with Claudia, like she always does. And Claudia goes off half-cocked all the time. It could have been because Amy took Claudia's parking space."

"Amy didn't have a car."

With another wave of spices, Marina disregarded my objection. "Then she was still mad about something from twenty years ago. People like Claudia don't need a good reason to kill, you know. Any old justification will do."

I looked at her. "You've been trying to pin a murder on Claudia for years."

She nodded furiously. "Wouldn't we all be happier if that woman was tucked away where she couldn't do any more harm? Last year she started that boycott of your store and almost put you out of business. The year before that she incited mob justice over the school addition. And remember the Claudia-inspired Troubles of the Tarver Tater Tots? How, I ask"—Marina tucked her thumb into the armpit of her invisible vest of an imaginary three-piece suit—"how can this woman still be roaming around free to do more damage to this fine country of ours?"

"Since you're such an expert," I said dryly, "how do you suggest we go about proving any of this?"

She lifted one eyebrow. "That, mah dear, is where you come in."

Saturday morning I woke up with the sun streaming onto my face. The cat and the dog lay snuggled together at the foot of the bed. George opened his eyes to the thinnest of slits, saw that I was watching him, and bolted off the bed as if seven demons were chewing on his tail. He didn't mind cozying up to the dog, but he didn't care to be caught doing it.

I reached down to scratch behind Spot's ears. "What should I do today, buddy?"

His deep brown eyes told me that he'd like me to spend the rest of the day scratching his ears, with perhaps an occasional rub on his tummy.

"The possibilities are wide open," I told him. "If I were the paragon of virtue Marina says I am, I'd spend the day working on the papers the kids handed in for the story project."

"Mrr." George's face appeared over the edge of the bed.

"Exactly," I said. "Plenty of time for that tomorrow afternoon, when it's supposed to rain. Today is sunny and supposed to get to seventy. Not a day to spend inside."

I pulled George up onto the bed. He made a show of struggling, but then allowed that a human's lap wasn't such a bad place to be. Kneading my legs with claws I should have clipped a week ago, he settled down with a loud purr.

"And again, if I were the person Marina claims I am, I'd spend the day outside doing yard work." I glanced down at my arm, eyeing the tan line halfway up my bicep, which was about the only tan line I ever got.

"But you know what?" I scratched George's chin with my left hand and rubbed Spot's belly with my right. "I'm not going to do any of that. I'm also not going to clean the house, do laundry, pay bills, or figure out the June work schedule. Lois and Yvonne are right. I could use a day off."

George stopped purring and looked up at me.

"Shocking, isn't it?" I rubbed my knuckles under his chin. He closed his eyes and the intensity of his purr went up by a factor of two. "And we can blame Marina, which is always nice."

Her arch comment of "that's where you come in" had been followed by a long litany of possibilities for me to explore. When I'd pointed out that she, too, could examine some avenues, she'd claimed to have done half the work just by coming up with the ideas. Plus, it was her in-laws' anniversary. "Of course," she said thoughtfully, "you could come to the party with me, feign an upset stomach, and then I'd have to take you to the emergency room."

I'd passed on the idea. I'd also passed on the whole concept of Claudia and/or Tina as killers. While I was willing to believe that, given certain circumstances, anyone could kill, I just didn't see how it fit in here. That wasn't any sort of proof, of course, but I wasn't about to twist and warp the facts to fit Marina's wacked-out theory. If there was any warping and twisting to be done, it would be to fit my own ideas.

"So if Marina's theory is out, what's left?" I asked George. The question was pointless. Cats don't have opinions on anything that doesn't have a direct bearing on their comfort. I looked at Spot. He heaved a doggy sigh and put his chin on his paws. In five seconds, he was snoring.

"You two are no help." I slid out of bed and headed for the shower.

An hour later I was clean and breakfasted. In spite of my ambitions to do a total of zero chores, I backslid enough to bring the dirty clothes downstairs to the laundry room and to check e-mail. I started to log on to Yahoo to join the weight loss group, but the connection was slow and I gave up. Easy enough to do that later. All I had to do was remember.

After I took Spot for a short walk, I packed the backpack with a lunch, a beach towel, and my notebook, and wheeled my bike out of the garage. "Off like a dirty shirt," I said, quoting a great-aunt. I swung my leg up and over and headed to Amy's house. While I was sorting whites from darks from good-heavens-how-did-that-get-so-filthys, I'd realized something so very basic that I suddenly felt sorry for Jenna and Oliver, to have such a moron for a mother.

Basic fact #1: Amy's neighbors were Lillian and Thurman Schroeder.

Basic fact #2: I'd already talked to the Schroeders,

told them what I was doing (more or less), and enlisted their support. They knew how to reach me if something about Amy's death turned up.

Basic fact #3: The Schroeders were Amy's neighbors to the north.

Basic fact #4: There was a whole other set of neighbors to the south.

I dismounted from the bike, slid out of the backpack, and threaded it over the handlebars. The house south of Amy's was what, once upon a time, had been called a starter home. What they called them now in this age of a bedroom and a bathroom for every person in the house, I didn't know. Nearly unsellable, probably.

But though tiny, this particular house exuded an air of contentment. Maybe it was the lemon yellow shutters that were slightly oversized, giving an impression of generosity. Or maybe it was the perky annuals spilling from the terra-cotta pots. Or maybe the house really was content with its place in the world.

I wheeled my bike up the driveway, thinking that Richard would have had me committed if I'd ever said such a thing out loud. Which was one of the reasons he was now my former husband. Evan, on the other hand, would smile and say . . .

"Hello?"

I was so startled that my legs forgot they were next to a bike. My right shin ran hard into a pedal and I bit back a word that would have gotten my children into trouble. "Um, hi."

A young woman had stepped out of the shadows between the detached garage and house. Her bright green tank top was filled out nicely by what she'd been destined for at birth, and the low-rise shorts showed off a waist that had never seen pregnancy. Youth bloomed in her cheeks and shining blond hair. She smiled. "Don't tell me you're selling something. I'm a real sucker for door-to-door salespeople."

"Selling . . . ?" I blinked at her, then saw that she was looking at my backpack. "Oh, no, I'm not selling anything. I'm horrible at that sort of thing. That's my lunch, is all."

"And here I was in the mood to buy something."

I pushed at the backpack, setting it to swinging. "Five bucks will get you a half a peanut butter sandwich, some celery sticks, an apple, and a bottle of water."

"That's your lunch?" She made a face. "Sounds more like a snack to me."

"Honey, who are you talking to?" A young man came around the corner of the garage, a rake in one hand, a pair of limb loppers in the other. "Oh, hi." He stopped at his wife's side, half a step in front of her.

I beamed at the pair. Though I was clearly no threat, he was instinctively taking the protective position. And, though I was at least fifteen years older than he was, she was threading her hand through the inside of his elbow, taking possession. First house, first yard, first garden. First love, maybe. I sent up a quick thought to whoever might be listening that their happiness last forever.

"Beth Kennedy," I said.

"Travis Heer," the young man said. "This is my wife, Whitney."

There was a pause. The Heers looked at me. I looked at them. Since I was the one on their property, I needed to open the conversation. Unfortunately, since I'd somehow expected to meet another elderly couple, my brain was stuck.

"Um, I was a friend of Amy's." I tipped my head in

the direction of her house, which was a fair distance away. At least one vacant lot sat between the homes, maybe two. Modern life being what it was, and Amy being what she'd been, it was possible they'd never even talked.

"That poor woman." Whitney put her head against her husband's shoulder. "I felt so bad for her."

"Yeah." Travis transferred the rake to his other hand and put his arm around his wife. "We were just starting to talk to her, and then . . . well, you know."

"How long have you lived here?" I glanced at the sparkling clean windows. Once upon a time, I'd had windows like that, too. "I own the bookstore downtown and delivered books to Amy."

"Oh, you're the book lady!" Whitney said. "Amy talked about you."

"She did?"

"Sure," Travis said. "I remember. You brought her new friends, is what she said."

It was simultaneously rewarding and incredibly sad. "She was a nice lady."

"We moved in just after Thanksgiving," Whitney said. "We took over a loaf of banana bread and asked her to dinner, but she said she was too busy."

"Busy?"

"Yeah." Travis let the loppers drop and rested the business end of the rake on the ground. "Said she had deadlines to meet, so she couldn't do anything until spring. Then it was spring, and we went over and she said maybe in June, once it was really warm out. I kept thinking she was blowing us off. Whitney said she was just shy." He looked at me, clearly wanting me to weigh in on the topic.

"Deadlines?" I asked.

"That's what she said." Whitney adjusted a strap of her tank top. "I figured maybe she was taking classes at Wisconsin. Lots of older people are doing that these days."

The possibility of Amy venturing out of Rynwood, into Madison, and onto a large university campus was about as likely as me losing that twenty pounds. "She never said anything about taking classes." But how much did I really know about Amy? "She didn't talk about herself much, did she?"

They shook their heads in agreement. "We hardly spoke to her," Travis said. "Just a few times. The only time she said much at all was a few months ago, just before the time change. It was really warm out that day, remember? Everyone in town was out doing yard work until it was pitch dark. Just when we were about to go in, Amy came out."

Whitney nodded. "She looked like a ghost, all dressed in white like that."

She'd almost always worn white. That, or very light pastels. More than once I'd been tempted to call her Emily, but if she knew about the habits of the reclusive Emily Dickinson, she didn't need me to remind her.

"Yeah." Travis grinned. "Scared the you-know-what out of me the first time I saw her wandering around at night like that."

"She did that a lot?"

The pair glanced at each other. "I don't know about a lot," Whitney said slowly. "Amy wasn't out there more than once or twice a week." She paused. "Three times, tops."

They were protecting Amy's memory. I felt a warm rush of emotion toward these two youngsters. "I'm glad she had you as neighbors."

"I guess." Travis shifted his weight. Looked at the ground. "But it's not like we did much."

Yes, they had. They were too young to know it, but they had. "There's nothing like a good neighbor," I said. "Just knowing someone is there, keeping an eye out, is a very comforting feeling."

Travis didn't look convinced. "Not that Amy needed help. I mean, it's not like she went away anywhere, or had lots of people coming over."

"Just that one time," Whitney said.

Travis and I both stared at her. "What time?" he asked.

"I told you about it, remember? That guy who walked all the way up the driveway? He looked like an insurance salesman, but she let him in the back door." Whitney shrugged. "I only saw because I was coming home from work late that night."

"When?" I asked.

"Oh, geez." Whitney squinted. "Maybe the week before she died."

"What did he look like?"

"Like an insurance salesman."

I would have laughed, but her face was straight. "Um, what does an insurance salesman look like to you?"

"You know, insurancey." She hunched her shoulders and dropped her chin to her chest. "A little squirrelly, a little weaselly."

Must be she'd never met Glenn Kettunen, owner of the company that took care of most of Rynwood's insurance needs. A former college football player, and bald as the proverbial billiard ball, Glenn was also the extrovert's extrovert.

"That's not an insurance guy," Travis said. "That's an accountant. Insurance guys are sales guys, really. Not squirrelly at all."

"Whatever." Whitney didn't seem to care that Travis had corrected her in front of a near stranger. "He wouldn't have turned my head in a crowd, is what I'm saying." She grinned up at her husband.

"Did it seem as if she knew him?" I asked.

"All I know is she let him inside her house at seven o'clock at night."

"Do you remember what he was driving?" I asked. "Size, age, make? Anything?"

She shook her head. "A sedan, I think. I don't remember cars much. Sorry."

There was no use being annoyed at her. It wouldn't help, and besides, I had the same tendency regarding cars. "Color?" I asked hopefully. Sometimes I remembered a car's color. Well, if it was yellow or red. Almost all the other car colors looked pretty much the same to me. I couldn't even consistently name the color of my own car. In the sun it look greenish-gray, when cloudy it looked grayish-green. Did that make it green, or gray?

"Maybe white." She looked over at Amy's driveway. "Or silver. Could have been that funky beige color."

Which was basically no help at all.

"Do you think I should tell the police?" Whitney asked.

"And tell them what?" Travis blew out a short puffy sigh. "That you saw some skinny guy go into Amy's house? That he might have been driving a white car? No, wait. It was silver. No, beige. Give me a break." He rolled his eyes. "Go to the cops and they'll start laughing before you walk out the door."

Whitney looked at him. "Don't be a jerk, Travis. I'm just trying to help."

"I know, honey, but—"

They had a short stare down. Whitney won, of course.

"Yeah, okay," Travis muttered. "I didn't mean to make fun of you."

"Yes, you did," she said comfortably, sliding her hand into his. "And at some point tonight you'll have to fall asleep."

"Aw, Whitney, don't be like that."

She patted his arm, smiling. "Then quit making fun."

I smiled back at her, wishing I'd had her husband-management skills at her age. If I had, maybe I wouldn't be divorced now. Of course, if I hadn't been divorced, I wouldn't be enjoying Evan's company every—

"Uh-oh," I breathed.

"What?" Whitney's sharp-eyed gaze went a shade sharper. "Did you think of something?"

Oh, boy, had I.

"Just something I forgot to do." Like calling Evan first thing this morning to discuss dinner plans. I fished a business card out of the backpack. "Here. If you remember anything about Amy's visitor, or anything about Amy that you think might matter, give me a call. I know, um, people at the police department and I can talk to them."

"Good." Whitney slid the card into her minuscule front pocket. "I've never actually talked to a cop, you know? Not like a real conversation. They seem scary, somehow, in those uniforms, and all that stuff on their belts. Like they're not real people. I'm sure they are," she said quickly. "If they're friends of yours, they must be, right?"

I gave my head a single, sharp shake. "More like acquaintances."

"Oh, I get it," Whitney said, not getting it at all. "Hey, do you really think that guy had something to do with Amy dying?"

"It was accidental," Travis said. "She was allergic. How could anyone have anything to do with it?"

I didn't know. But there was something wrong about how she died. Amy would never have gone outside at that time of day unless something was terribly, terribly wrong.

Unfortunately, I was the only one convinced of that.

Chapter 11

Though Sabatini's was crowded every evening of the week, on Saturday night the line snaked through the lobby and out onto the sidewalk. The scent of oregano, hot tomato sauce, and cooking pizza dough permeated the air so thickly that I was pretty sure I was consuming calories just by breathing.

Evan and I chatted with the other Rynwoodites standing in line for the forty-five minutes it took us to get seated, learning that Stephanie Waldress's son was doing well in the 800 meter this track season, and that Carol and Nick Casassa were planning on a trip up the Alaska Highway. Small talk in small towns. It was the glue that held us together. I'd once thought of it as gossip—and some topics I still considered so—but I'd come around to the belief that it mattered why Mr. Brinkley stopped a fifteen-year tradition of having breakfast at the Green Tractor.

After all, if I hadn't heard that he'd been diagnosed with an advanced case of stomach cancer, I wouldn't have stopped by his house for a visit. We wouldn't have started talking about his Depression-era childhood. I wouldn't have made a vague comment about how children never really understood how different life had been for their grandparents. Mr. Brinkley wouldn't have laughed and told me to send them over, that he'd tell them all about hand pumps in the kitchen sink and helping his mother can tomatoes in August heat. And I wouldn't have come up with the idea for the senior story project.

"So what do you think?" Evan asked.

I blinked, and had no idea what he'd been talking about, none at all. "A glass of diet soda?"

He laughed. "No, what do you think about this?" He tapped a collection of brochures that had magically appeared on the table. Judging from the creases, they had been in his pocket. "What do you think?"

I fanned through the glossy trifolds and tried to figure out what was going on. "They're all . . . nice." As in Hawaii nice. Mexico nice. Alaskan and Caribbean cruise nice.

"That they are." Evan smiled at me, that crooked grin that melted my heart into a puddle. "Anything else?"

Was he saying . . . ? No, he couldn't be. We'd never truly broached the topic of . . . of . . . "Um, I've never been to any of these places. Have you?"

"Did you see this?" Evan turned to the back of the Hawaii brochure. "On Kauai there's a train ride that takes you through a working plantation and—"

My cell phone trilled out a digital rendition of the theme song for *The Twilight Zone*. Over Christmas, Jenna had declared that the standard ringtone I'd been using was embarrassing her to death. I'd said she could change it to anything she wanted, not anticipating that she'd actually spend the time to figure it out, and then keep changing it on a random basis. But as I told Marina, it could be worse. She could download the "Chicken Dance."

I dug deep into my purse. "Sorry," I muttered. "Forgot to turn it off. Do you mind?"

Evan made a go-ahead gesture, and I looked at the number. "This won't take long," I said, and put the phone to my ear. "What's up?"

"The temperature, the grass in my yard, and Zach's height," Marina said. "Do you realize that boy has grown three inches since last fall?"

"You called to tell me that?"

"Of course not. That's the kind of really important stuff I save for telegrams." There was a pause. "Do you think there still are telegrams?"

"Marina, I'm in a restaurant. With Evan."

"And answering your cell phone?" She tsked. "Goodness, how rude of you."

"You're right. I'd better go."

"No, wait! I found out something."

"On a scale of one to ten, how big a something?"

"Um . . . ten. Or maybe a zero. Depending."

"On what?"

"On whether or not this is actual proof that Amy was murdered."

In an instant, the sights and sounds around me receded to the back of my consciousness, and I was once again in Amy's backyard, seeing her porch and lilacs and bird feeders. "Tell me."

"The cans of bee killer you were so curious about? Well, thanks to your friendly neighborhood busybody— that's me, by the way—we now know that Amy had one can with her."

One? One didn't make sense. If she had one, she'd have had two.

"You can thank me later for my hard work," Marina said. "The sweat of my brow is as nothing."

I made appropriate noises of admiration, then, "How did you find out, anyway?"

"Thought you'd never ask."

She was well launched into a long tale of finding out that her neighbor was the sister of the cousin (or was it the brother-in-law? She couldn't remember for sure) of one of the EMTs that was called to Amy's house when Evan tapped the back of my hand. Our waitress was fast approaching and I hadn't even looked at the menu. Not that I needed to. Tonight was a salad night, dressing on the side, please. I made my good-byes and set the phone on my lap.

"What can I get for you?" The waitress stood with pen poised over an order pad.

I placed my low-calorie order and listened to Evan ask for a medium pizza with pepperoni and Italian sausage. Men.

When the waitress left, he reached across the table and took my hands in his. "There are so many places I'd like to take you. This could be just the start."

I looked into his light blue eyes. Dove down in. My grandmother Chittenden had always said handsome is as handsome does. As a child I hadn't known what that meant, and I still didn't, not for sure. But I did know that the handsome man across the table made me feel different than I'd ever felt in my life. The problem was, I hadn't quite figured out what that difference was. As soon as I did, I'd know what to do, but until then, I had to slow things down. For me, yes, but for my children's sake even more.

"As in, this could be the start of a beautiful friendship?" Smiling, I pulled my hands away. "Traveling is something I've always wanted to do, but it's hard with the kids so young." I opened the brochures and looked at the pictures of sandy beaches. If I managed to lose those twenty pounds I might wear a bikini like that, but I doubted it.

My thoughts wandered away. I wondered what kind of swimsuit Kelly had been wearing that night. Wondered if Amy had owned a swimsuit. If she'd even known how to swim . . .

Evan watched me. "Beth, is something bothering you?"

I blinked. "Like what?"

"That's what I'm trying to find out. You seem preoccupied. I know you're always busy, but lately you're farther away than ever. Is there something on your mind?"

There were all sorts of somethings on my mind. If he was asking me to discuss all of them, we'd be here until midnight. On Tuesday.

"You've been looking preoccupied in a very focused way," he said. "Like you looked last Thanksgiving after Sam Helmstetter was murdered and you took it upon yourself to do something about it."

He was making it sound as if I'd become a vigilante. I hadn't really wanted to do anything, but circumstances had pushed me too hard.

"No one in Rynwood has been murdered," Evan said. "So there's no investigating going on, correct?"

This whole conversation was making me feel very prickly. "And what if I was?"

"Then I'd ask you to stop. It's not your place. We have laws and law enforcement officers to enforce those laws."

"What if they're not doing their job?"

"There are more appropriate ways to—"

My phone rattled against the plastic laminate tabletop as we were once again treated to the *The Twilight Zone* theme song.

"Sorry," I muttered. "Thought I'd turned it off." But, weak person that I was, I looked to see who was calling. I jumped to my feet. "Evan, I need to take this call. I'll be right back, okay?"

I hurried through the restaurant, trying to get outside, trying to get somewhere that wasn't so packed with background noise. "This is Beth."

"And this isn't," said an old, crackly voice. "You got any answers yet? Or is Maudie going to have to die knowing you didn't lift a finger to help her?"

When I'd seen the number for Sunny Rest on my phone's screen, I'd expected bad news, for how could any call from there on a Saturday evening be anything else? But I hadn't prepared myself for something worse than bad news: A phone call from Auntie May.

"I've been working on it," I said. "I'll stop by tomorrow to talk to Maude." But tomorrow I had church and I needed to finish up the story project stories that had been handed in. Plus it was Mother's Day and Richard was dropping the kids off early. "Or Monday. Tuesday at the latest. And what do you mean, about her dying. Is she sick? She looked fine the other day."

"At her age, you can't expect much," Auntie May said. "Now tell me. Have you been doing your best? Maudie deserves it, and if you aren't doing your darnedest I want to know about it."

Her snide words cut at me. "Well, I—"

She rode right over the start of my explanation. "Ah, I knew you were shirking. Don't waste your breath denying the truth. Makes you look stupid."

"But I have done something. I've talked to the police.

The official report said it was an accident." I paused. "Auntie May? Hello?" No answer; nothing but an empty phone line that was giving a very good impression of censure.

I stared at the phone that I was beginning to hate. Auntie May's taunt stung because she was, as per usual, correct in her accusation—I hadn't been doing my best. And I'd promised Maude I would.

Vandalism, cheating, stealing, wanton waste, cruelty, greed—I hated all of these, but I hated hypocrisy even more. It was too late to take back the promise I never should have made, but at least I could do something about my hypocrisy.

John Engel, Kelly's father, stirred his decaf coffee and smiled at me. "We've heard a lot about you."

I hated when people said that. It made me feel slightly naked, for one thing. For another, whatever they'd heard was probably wrong. And wrong for different reasons, depending on where the information had come from.

"Yes," Barb Engel said. "Aunt Maude hasn't talked about anything except you and your son since this story thing got going."

Taken straight, her comment was a simple statement of fact. The vocal inflections she'd colored it with, however, gave her words a harsh edge that made me want to squirm.

I didn't reply for a moment. The woman had lost a child, after all. There couldn't be anything in the world harder to bear, and I couldn't imagine what it would do to someone's heart and mind.

I busied myself with pouring a substantial amount of milk from the tiny pitcher into my exceedingly dark coffee.

When I'd called right after church, John had answered the phone. I'd introduced myself as a friend of Maude's and he'd immediately issued an invitation to afternoon coffee. I'd expected us to sit around a kitchen table with clunky, mismatched mugs. Instead, the three of us were settled into a living room that looked like something straight out of the furniture store. Sofa, chairs, loveseat, coffee table, and end tables all showed an equal amount of wear, which was to say none. Barb had carried in the tray of coffee accoutrements and the three of us had sat equidistant from each other, the husband and wife in facing chairs, me in the middle of the sofa.

One of my intentions in stopping was to find out what everyone else seemed to know about Maude, but the brittle atmosphere in the room wasn't going to make that easy.

"So." John sipped his coffee. "Maude says you're going to figure out what happened the night Kelly died."

"Be nice if someone did."

John ignored his wife's sour comment. "The police said it was an accident, as I'm sure you know," he said. "I'm not sure what you expect to find out after all this time. It's very nice of you to help Maude, she's something isn't she, but I'm afraid you'll be wasting your time."

"It's her time to waste," Barb said. "What are you afraid of?"

"Now, Barb—"

"Don't 'now, Barb' me!" she snapped. "Just because you don't have the courage to face the truth doesn't mean I don't."

He closed his eyes briefly. "Barb, we've been over and over this. There's no proof Kelly was murdered. There's no motive, no nothing. It was an accident, honey. Why can't you accept it?"

"Because I know my daughter!"

The intensity of her words rang through my skin and into my bones, and my body shook with a sudden chill. Kelly had been dead for twenty years, but Barb had used the present tense. "I know my daughter." And so she did. Barb's knowledge wouldn't disappear because the flesh was gone. Her love for Kelly lived on; how could it not? The use of present tense made complete sense to me.

For the first time since I'd entered their house, I looked deep into their faces. Coward that I was, I'd skated over really looking at them. They'd had to endure the loss of a child and I didn't want to know what that looked like.

From what Maude had told me, I'd calculated the Engels to be in their early sixties. Maude had said they'd met at school, so I'd assumed the two were close in age. But either my assumption was wrong or their paces of aging had taken different routes. Much different.

John, dressed in casual slacks and a polo shirt, looked fit and trim enough to be featured on the cover of the AARP magazine.

Barb, however, had taken the harder road. Her skin already had the crepey look of advanced age, and her hair looked brittle enough that a rough combing would break off the strands an inch from her scalp. If her housedress was any indication, she hadn't bought new clothes in years. Each of her movements were choppy and disconnected, as if they'd been planned in advance, but had forgotten half the plan's steps.

"I knew her, too," John said quietly. "You seem to forget that."

"I don't forget anything." She pushed her chin into the air. "You're the one who forgets. You can't even remember her face without a picture, can you?"

John got to his feet and looked down at his wife. "No one murdered Kelly. She swam out too far and drowned. There's no bad guy, no conspiracy, and no stealthy figures running around in the night. It's time to stop being angry, Barb. It was an accident. An *accident*. You've held this too close for too long, and I don't care what Maude says, I'm not about to let this young woman take on your obsession." He looked at me. "Beth, thank you for coming, but there's really nothing you can do."

I glanced at Barb. She was perched on the edge of the chair, legs pressed tight together, fists on knees. Poised for action, waiting for . . . something. "Um," I said.

"Let me see you to the door." John waited politely as I maneuvered myself off the couch. I tried to make eye contact with Barb, but her head was down so all I could see was a mass of gray hair. "Thanks for the coffee," I said.

John opened the front door, ushered me onto the porch, and closed the door behind us. "I'd like to apologize for my wife."

"No need. Really."

"Before, she saw every day as an opportunity for fun. Now she spends her days reading biographies."

". . . Biographies?"

"She read though the entire biography section in the Rynwood Public Library in two years. Then she started driving to Madison, and somehow she got permission to check books out of the university's library. And now she has an eReader. Do you know how many biographies she's stuck onto that thing in the last year?"

"Well . . ."

"Five hundred! She reads all these books and a week later can't remember a thing about them. I used to ask questions, but when I asked her the names of Henry

VIII's wives two days after she finished a book on him and she could only come up with Catherine of Aragon and Anne Boleyn, I couldn't take it anymore." His voice trembled. "Just . . . couldn't."

I lifted a hand. To comfort him, to sympathize with him, I wasn't sure what, but he turned away from my touch.

"And now I need to apologize for my behavior." He was back to the patrician gentleman. "I am sorry. This isn't how you'd intended to spend your Sunday afternoon, I'm sure."

"My children are spending the weekend with their father," I said. "But they'll be home soon. It is . . ." I stopped.

"It's what?"

"Mother's Day," I whispered.

My steady gaze met his, and after a moment, he looked down. Blew out a light sigh. Shifted his feet. "Yes." He cleared his throat. "Well. It is, isn't it? I'm sure the girls will be calling Barb soon. That should perk her up a bit."

He nodded and retreated into the house.

I walked down the porch steps and over to the bicycle I'd parked on the side of the driveway. I turned it around and glanced over my shoulder at the classic Colonial home where Kelly had grown up.

Four rooms down, four rooms up, a basic white box with green shutters and darker green shrubbery in front. Once upon a time there may have been flowers softening the edges of the hard-trimmed shrubs. Once upon a time there may have been tiny pink bikes scattered across the yard. A playhouse in the back.

I faced forward, swung my leg over the back tire, hopped on the seat, and started pedaling for all I was worth. I suddenly wanted to get away from this house. A house was all it was; it wasn't a home any longer. There was no nurturing going on there, no happiness, and certainly no laughter. And without laughter, how could love survive? Laughter was a—

"Wait!" A woman stepped out from behind a massive lilac bush, waving her arms. She ran out across the sidewalk and into the street.

I braked as hard as I could as fast as I could and almost somersaulted over the handlebars. The back tire lifted up, then came back down with a thump. My feet slipped, and the pedals whacked my shins as my shoes hit the pavement. Hard.

"There wasn't any way to talk to you in the house. Not with him there," Barb said. "Come on. He might be looking for me." She walked over to the shade of the lilac bush without looking to see if I followed.

I looked at my shins. There'd be big, dark bruises tomorrow.

"Come on!"

I pushed the bike over to where Barb waited.

"Okay." Barb lowered her voice and put her head close to mine. "John won't listen to me, the police won't listen to me, even my own daughters won't listen to me anymore." She looked left and right, and moved even closer. "Kelly was murdered and I know who did it."

Somehow I'd had a feeling this was coming. "Um . . ."

"You have to listen to me." She gripped my arm. "Aunt Maude promised she'd find out what happened if it was the last thing she did. And now you're here. You're going to help, right?"

My arm was going to be bruised, too. Long pants and long sleeves for a week. Excellent. "Yes," I said. "I'll do my best to help."

"Okay, then." She released my arm, nodding. "Okay."

Her eyes were sharply focused. The sharpness was concentrated on my face and I didn't much care for the bug-stuck-on-a-pin feeling I was getting, but it was nice to see her face alive with expression. I watched the sun dapple lilac shadows across her skin and realized that, a long time ago, she'd been a very pretty woman.

"Is your aunt Maude doing okay?" I asked suddenly.

"What? She's fine. Better than fine, for her age. The thing that will help her best is finding out what happened to Kelly."

I murmured a vague agreement, but she wasn't paying any attention.

"Kelly was a smart girl," Barb said. "And I'm not saying that just because I'm her mother. She was book smart like crazy, but with lots of common sense, too. The only thing she didn't get was people."

But how many eighteen-year-olds did? At that age, it was so easy to be locked into the importance of your own universe. At that age, you were still a ways away from realizing that adults had feelings, too. "She was young."

Barb grimaced. "You say that, but at eighteen my mother was married with a baby on the way. I had my first job when I was twelve. Kelly started saving money for medical school the day after we had to take her sister to the emergency room for stitches. Sliced open her finger washing a knife. Kelly was too young to leave alone, so she came in with me, watching when the doctor sewed up her sister. And there sat Kelly in the corner, all big blue eyes and not saying a word."

It was an easy scene to picture. The white hospital room, the shiny tools, the mixed smells of cleanliness and pain, and the little girl on a rolling stool, feet tucked up under her.

"When we walked out, Kelly asked if girls could be doctors. Girls could do anything, I told her. 'Then I'm going to be one,' she said. 'I want to sew people up and put them back together again.'"

The Humpty Dumpty rhyme sang through my head. "You told her how expensive medical school would be?"

"And how many years it would take, and in how much debt she'd be at the end of it. She didn't care." Barb almost smiled. "All she wanted was to be a doctor. Surgeon, later. She was trying to decide between cardiac and orthopedic when . . ."

"Yes," I said.

Barb blinked fast a few times. She didn't apologize, and I was glad for that. Apologizing for the sorrow of a child's death was ludicrous. "I ask you," she said, "how could she commit suicide? A girl so focused on medical school that she saved nine out of ten dollars she made? How?"

"Um, your husband thinks it was an accident."

She made a fist, swinging it down to hit herself hard on the thigh. "My husband is an idiot. Kelly was swimming at two years old. Two! Winning swim team trophies when she was six. She could have swam for miles and been fine. Just fine."

"So you think it was murder?"

"Of course it was," she snapped, sounding as irked at me as she'd been earlier at her husband. "Wasn't suicide, wasn't accident. It's the only thing left."

I squinted at the clouds and tried to come up with another option. Didn't have any luck. "So you . . ." Did I want to take this path? Not really. But the only other choice was to turn and run away. "So you know who did it?"

The answer came fast and furious. "Faye Lowery." She practically flung the words out of her mouth. "Faye was always jealous of Kelly. Always, always, always. From kindergarten on up, that little Lowery girl hated my Kelly. She thinks she's safe now, starting up that flower shop. But I know what she did and someday she'll get what she deserves."

So the perfect Kelly had an enemy. Interesting. But if jealous hatred in a teenage girl was enough to incite murder, there'd be a lot more early deaths in the world. "Um . . ."

"It's proof you want, I can see it. Just like the police. But you're a mother, aren't you? The burden of proof for us isn't the same. Listen to this." Barb held up a bony index finger. "First grade. Kelly got the role of Cinderella. Faye was one of the ugly stepsisters. Third grade, Kelly beat her out in the school spelling bee. Sixth grade, Faye came in second place to Kelly in Field Day. Hundred-meter dash."

The lines in her face deepened as she frowned. "Or was it the hundred-yard dash back then?" She put her hands to her forehead. "Why can't I remember? I should know these things. I used to know, why don't I remember?"

Her wild-eyed look tore at me, and I knew better than to say it wasn't important. "I'll look it up for you," I offered, "if you want. The school will have records." Or not. If schools had retention schedules, names of field day races probably didn't rate a twenty-year life span. But someone would know, and if Barb wanted, I'd find out.

"No." Her hands dropped to her sides, a small flop of noise against soft fabric. "It doesn't matter. What matters is that Faye lost to Kelly. Again. It happened over and over. Swim team. Band. Kelly played flute, you know. Track team. And the final blow was when Kelly was picked as valedictorian." She nodded fiercely. "That's what finally did it, don't you see?"

Kind of. "The police and your husband say it was an accident, and I've heard talk it was ..." The word wouldn't come.

"Suicide?" She scoffed. "Please. We've already gone over that. Anyone who thinks Kelly could take her own life didn't know Kelly. She was a good Catholic girl, and she had too much to live for."

"Does anyone else agree with your theory about Faye?" I asked.

"It's not a theory." Barb leaned close and I flinched away. "It's fact, I'm sure of it. And I'm not the only one who thinks so. My oldest daughter knows it was Faye." She straightened and gave a sharp nod. "She won't talk about it, but she knows."

Mom and a sister. Character witnesses par excellence. Outstanding. "You can't think of—"

"And Amy, of course."

I blinked. "Amy? Amy who?"

"Amy Jacobson." Barb held up her hand, her fingers crossed tight around each other. "Senior year, she and Kelly were like this."

Chapter 12

Halfway home, my lungs decided they'd had enough of the fast pace I'd set after leaving Barb Engel. My thighs had given up the fight a quarter mile earlier. I let the bike coast, then started rotating the pedals again, this time at a more sustainable rate.

Amy and Kelly knew each other. Amy and Kelly were good friends. Best friends, if Barb was right. Kelly had died twenty years ago; Amy died a little more than twenty days ago. One had died too young at eighteen, the other had died at—

My brain made a belated little click.

"We're the same age," I said out loud. "The exact same age." It was hard to believe. The Amy I'd known had acted like an old woman. Had mostly gray hair. Talked like someone from an earlier generation.

"Who's the same age?"

I jumped, jerking the handlebars, and sent the bike hard right. The front tire banged into the curb and I caromed back left.

"Hey, there." A hand steadied my shoulder, gently but firmly. "You all right?"

I braked to a hard stop. Put my hand to my chest to make sure my heart was still working properly, then looked at the man on the bike next to me, the man who was both instigator-of-near-death and savior-from-great-pain. "Officer Zimmerman."

"Oh, geez, call me Sean. It's not like I'm on duty or anything."

His easy smile relaxed me, but I made an internal cluck over the state of his gray T-shirt and denim shorts. The boy was obviously not married or living with his mother. Neither would have let him loose in public with that combination of paint-pocked shirt and dirt-encrusted shorts.

"Do you often talk to yourself?" He was still smiling.

"When you hear people say that talking to yourself is the first sign of insanity, don't believe a word of it."

"Yes, ma'am."

"And it's Amy who was my age," I said. "Amy Jacobson."

He nodded. "The lady who was really, really allergic to bees. I was on that call. But I'd never have guessed you were the same age."

"I'm forty-one." Almost forty-two, but why age yourself more rapidly than necessary?

"No kidding." Sean squinted at me. "I would have said early thirties, max."

I wanted to reach out and pat his cheek in gratitude. "I wonder if Amy was sick in some way. Illness can make you age fast."

He nodded. "My grandparents were like that. Same age, but Gramps got Parkinson's and looked twenty years older. Ms. Jacobson, though, I don't remember anything about her being sick."

Illness aged a person. So did pain. And unhappiness. "Remember when I was in your office the other day, asking about Kelly Engel?"

"Sure. Report said accident, but the notes said . . . something else."

"Do the notes say anything about the possibility of murder?"

His gaze slid away. "There was a mention, but that's about it."

The boy hadn't been in law enforcement long enough to develop that bland yes-ma'am look. He had the words almost down, but the body language needed work. "The notes mention Barb Engel, I suppose. And her theory that Faye Lowery killed her daughter."

He shifted from one foot to another. "The possibility was investigated thoroughly, Mrs. Kennedy. There's no way Ms. Lowery could have killed Ms. Jacobson. Mrs. Engel was told that, more than once."

"You mean there was an alibi?"

"Ms. Lowery was attending a sleepover party with a number of other girls. All of those girls gave statements that Ms. Lowery did not leave the party during any portion of the evening."

A slumber party didn't seem like such a great alibi to me. Get a bunch of teenage girls talking and which of them is going to notice that one of them was gone for half an hour?

On the other hand, girls usually had slumber parties with their closest friends, and it could be very easy to get your friends to lie for you. "I know I went out for a little," she could have whispered, "but it was to meet my boyfriend. Don't tell, okay?" Ten out of ten girlfriends would go along.

"Mrs. Engel said that it'd be easy to slip away from a party like that," Sean said. "And really easy to get your friends to lie for you, but none of the girls ever said anything different. Even years later, none of them changed their stories."

I looked at him curiously. "All that was in the notes?"

"Oh. Well, no, not really." He picked at a piece of dried paint on his shirt. "The chief told me."

My chin went up. "And did Chief Eiseley also tell you that I was an interfering busybody who should keep to her books and not mess around in things she has no business messing around in?"

Sean flicked a glance at me. "No, ma'am. He said Kelly Engel died a long time ago and it was too bad her mother couldn't let her rest."

The starch went out of my upper vertebrae. True enough. Barb was old before her time thanks to the anger she was nurturing so close. But did she have a choice? Do any of us have a choice about our feelings?

"It was nice to see you again, Mrs. Kennedy." Sean dipped his head and pedaled off.

As I watched him speed away, his legs whirling in small circles, I wondered why Gus could so easily recall so many of the details from a death from so long ago.

Maybe Barb Engel wasn't the only one keeping Kelly close.

"Mom! Mom!"

The kids bounced out of Richard's SUV and ran across the yard to where I was pulling the first weeds of summer. How was it that I positively enjoyed the task in May, was bored by it in July, and had to force myself to get out the gardening gloves from mid-August on?

But that guilt was months from now. Today I was happy with the way the shadows were reaching across the lawn, happy with the pile of weeds in my bushel basket, and even happier to greet the children rushing toward me.

"Look, Mom, we brought you a Mother's Day present. I get to tell you, but he gets to give it." Jenna elbowed her brother. "Now, Oliver."

Oliver's gallop had been hampered by his hands being behind his back. Now he handed me his offering. Offerings, actually, because he had two handfuls of the yellowest daffodils I'd ever seen. "Happy Mother's Day!" he shouted.

I stared at the flowers. "Why . . . why . . ." Had they ever given me a Mother's Day present? The construction paper bouquets they'd made in Sunday school counted to some extent, but not like this. I looked up at Richard with my eyebrows raised. He shook his head.

"Do you like them?" Jenna asked. "I wanted to get you roses, but Dad said these would be better. He said they'd last longer, that you'd have more time to enjoy these."

"Your dad was exactly right." I took the flowers and reached out to hug my children tight. "This is a wonderful present and I can't imagine anything I would have liked more." I tipped my head down to smell their hair, to breathe in their scents, to make the moment last forever.

It didn't, of course. Oliver was the first one to start squirming, then Jenna. I gave them both one last squeeze and, heart full to bursting, I let them go.

"The only thing that could make this a better Mother's Day," I said, "is if you two get your bags into your rooms without leaving them in the kitchen, or the family room, or on the stairs. And," I added, "it would be a perfect Mother's Day if you could do that in complete silence, except perhaps for a few rousing verses of 'Seventy-six Trombones.'"

Oliver frowned. "I don't know that song."

"Come on." Jenna pulled at his shirt. "Let's get our stuff. She knows we don't know it."

"But . . ."

Jenna started off and Oliver followed. "What Mom wants," she said, "is us to take our stuff upstairs without her having to bug us about it."

Oliver's plaintive voice drifted across the grass. "Why didn't she say so?"

"She was trying to be funny, I think."

"Oh." The SUV's doors opened. "No one laughed."

"That's because she wasn't very funny."

I glanced at Richard.

"The original idea was a new cell phone," he said, "until it became clear that Jenna assumed she'd get your old one."

"Not until she's fourteen." I caressed a yellow petal. So soft, it felt almost like a feather. "I thought we agreed on that."

"We do. Unless you want to consider waiting until she turns sixteen, when she starts driving."

Driving. Someday I'd be waving good-bye to my daughter as she backed out of the garage. The first time Marina's oldest drove into Madison for a concert with a carload of friends, she'd cleaned the kitchen from top to bottom. "I'd have gone nuts if I hadn't done something," she'd said. "The DH read a book about the history of the paper clip. At least that's what he said. Then I noticed that he'd been reading the same page for half an hour. After that I got some help with the highest shelves."

"Or eighteen," Richard said, "when she leaves for college."

In a few short years Jenna would be eighteen. Where was the time going? I suddenly wanted to rush inside

and hug the kids hard enough to keep them from growing up. Of course, if they never got older, they'd never
have any kids of their own and I was already anticipating
all the ways I'd spoil my grandchildren. Lots of books, of
course, but also trips to Chicago. We'd spend the morning in the Field Museum, have lunch in what I still
thought of as Marshall Field's, then—

"Beth?"

"Hmm?" It was hard to leave my future grandchildren.

"There's a problem with Jenna."

The grandkids vanished. "What kind of problem?"

"Don't look like that," he said. "It's not that important. Just a little affair of the heart, I'd say." He smiled,
chuckling.

How had I not noticed what was going on with Jenna?
What kind of mother was I that I didn't know she was
interested in a boy? What else had I missed? "What happened?" I asked, keeping my knee-jerk reaction of *how
can you say affairs of the heart aren't important? Maybe
Jenna's only eleven, but that doesn't mean her feelings
aren't real!* tucked safe inside my head.

"I think it must have happened at her hockey class."
Richard put his hands into his pockets, jingling his loose
change. "When I picked her up afterward, she was very
quiet. Wasn't even interested in helping to choose the
pizza toppings for dinner."

After Jenna's course of Thursday hockey lessons
ended, Coach Sweeney had called me and recommended that she sign up for Saturday morning lessons,
mixed boys and girls. "She might go far," he'd said. "My
assistant is a goalie, but he can only be there on Saturdays."

I'd basked in the "she might go far" for days. Richard

allowed that more coaching would help her and agreed to pay half.

"She didn't insist on pepperoni and sausage?" I asked. Jenna, the meat eater.

"Ate ham and mushrooms without blinking."

"Something's really wrong." I glanced toward the house.

"Maybe, but she was almost normal this morning and when there was a television ad about Mother's Day, she was the one who said we needed to get you something."

Jenna. My daughter, my love, my life. "Did you ask her about it?"

"Certainly." He sounded affronted. What kind of a father did I think he was? "She said there wasn't anything wrong. I asked her again, a few minutes later, and again she said she was fine. What else could I have done?"

Men. I knew it was time to change the subject. I'd talk to Jenna and find out for myself what was troubling her. "How is your new job going?"

"Fine. I've restructured the workflow for sixty percent of the staff already. Office efficiency has increased by nine percent. Corporate headquarters is very pleased."

"I'm sorry you have to drive so far," I said. "Thank you for taking it on. I know you did it for the sake of the kids."

"On the contrary, it's given me a substantial amount of time to study."

"... Study?"

"I'm taking a trip to Italy this fall."

"... Italy?"

"Yes. The commute allows me to play language CDs. I've already gone through half of the first Berlitz course. At this rate I should reach a conversational level by August. I don't expect to be fluent, of course, but I'll have a firm grasp of the language and that should suffice."

Richard was going to Italy? The Richard I'd known had always said there was no reason to travel overseas when there was so much to see in the United States.

"Travel expands your horizons," he said. "You should consider going abroad. It would do you good."

I gaped at him. Every time we'd celebrated a milestone anniversary, I'd tried to convince him to go on a trip. Fifth anniversary, he'd declined to go to Mexico. Tenth anniversary, he'd rejected a Norwegian cruise. Fifteenth anniversary, he wouldn't even discuss my suggestion of a trip to the Holy Lands.

"Yes," he said, nodding, "you should travel. You're getting a little provincial, don't you think? When's the last time you went anywhere out of the Midwest? When's the last time you really stretched your mind?"

I quit listening. Stopping Richard once he got up onto a soapbox wasn't worth the effort. Travel? Hah. He'd obviously forgotten how little money a children's bookstore owner made. My budget barely stretched to trips up to Mom's, let alone trips in an airplane. And my mind was being stretched quite nicely, not that it was any of his business.

He blathered on about all the things I should be doing. While he talked about taking classes that would count toward a master's degree, I stretched my mind even further by planning the next day.

"That will work," I murmured. "That will work nicely."

"Really?" Richard's eyebrows went up. "I never thought you'd be interested in a class on decision theory."

I smiled. "You never know, do you?"

That evening, after I'd kissed a sleepy Oliver good night, I shut his door and went into Jenna's room. She was sitting up with her arms wrapped around her knees, her Christmas-present copy of *Brodeur: Beyond the Crease* turned facedown on the bed. I wasn't certain that she would read a three-hundred-twenty-page biography, but once she'd opened the cover she'd become fascinated by the former NHL goalie's story.

I sat at the foot of the bed, picked up the book, slipped in a bookmark, and laid it on my lap. "What's wrong, sweetie?"

She shrugged. "Nothing."

Right. And I was the Queen of Wisconsin. "You didn't want chocolate on your ice cream tonight."

She sighed. "I just didn't feel like it."

"Thanks for the flowers. Your dad said it was your idea."

A slight smile, a head dip, and a shrug. "You're welcome. You do a lot for us."

My body almost went into convulsions from the multiple points of view it suddenly had. Shock, that my daughter was growing up. Gratitude, that she was growing up to be considerate and thoughtful. Surprise, that she was, in fact, growing up. When had this happened? "I love you," I said softly.

You have no idea how much. And until you have a daughter of your own, you never will.

"Um," she said, pulling her knees closer to her chest. "I love you, too."

We sat there a quiet moment. I listened to the sweet sound of her breathing, then asked, "So what's wrong?"

For a long time, she said nothing. I didn't want to ask a third time, but knew I would if I had to. Maybe not tonight, but tomorrow. Or the tomorrow after that. On and on until I found out what was wrong and did my best to help.

She picked at the comforter cover. "Coach Sweeney," she said. "He called me 'kiddo' yesterday."

"I call you kiddo."

"That's what I mean. He's not my mom or my dad. He's not nearly as old as you are. And he missed seeing this really good save I made during scrimmage and he didn't care. At all." She slid down in the bed. "All he said was, 'I'll catch your next one, kiddo.'"

I made a noise that I hoped communicated sympathy.

"He cooks, did you know? He knows how to put a salmon on a board and cook it on the grill."

"Planked, you mean?"

"Yeah." She rambled on about Coach Sweeney and the more she talked, the more animated she grew.

She might be feeling better, but I was not, because I knew exactly what was wrong with her. I didn't want it to be true. Didn't want it to happen. Not yet. Not ever, if I had any choice. Certainly not now. Not this minute. Some other minute, far off in the future.

Jenna was in the throes of her first crush. And it was destined to end badly.

I'd had grand plans to wake up early the next morning, get some work done on the story project, make a nourishing breakfast for my children, pack their lunches, and get us out the door with time to spare. That had been the plan. The reality had been waking up with a scratchy throat, rain whipping against the windows, and a black cat on my head. I thumped off the alarm, moved George off my pillow, and went back to sleep.

The next time I woke up, it was still raining, but my scratchy throat was gone, Spot was sitting on the floor looking at me with a hopeful expression. I glanced at the clock. So much for getting up early. I hated when I did this: make lovely get-things-done plans and then jettison them at the first sign of indecision. I ended up being mad at myself all day, and for what? For want of a little self-discipline.

"Never going to beat Claudia this way," I told Spot.

He wagged his tail and grinned, clearly agreeing with me. Of course, at this point he'd agree with anything I said in hopes that it would get him outside.

"You know," I told him, "it isn't supposed to be like this. You're the responsibility of the children. Why don't you ask them to let you out?"

His tail thumped against the carpet and he squirmed an inch closer to the side of the bed. Another half inch and I'd be getting dog breath on my face.

"All right, you've convinced me." I tossed back the covers and got up. Ten minutes later, I was toweling off a wet dog and fending off questions I couldn't answer.

"Does it rain more on Mondays than any other day?" Oliver dragged over a kitchen chair, turned it around, and kneeled on it, letting his arms hang long over the back. "This girl at school says there's this song about it."

" 'Rainy Days and Mondays,' " I sang to Spot. "They don't get you down, do they pup? It's just a song, Oliver. I don't think it's a commentary on the weather."

"What's a commentary?"

"It's like a comma, only it has a tary at the end." Jenna slid into the kitchen in stocking feet. "Look, Mom, I went all the way from the stairs to here in one slide!"

I looked from one child to the other. "Where were you two when Spot needed to go out?"

They both shrugged.

"What's a tary?" Oliver asked.

"Jenna's being silly," I said. Either that, or she was hanging around Marina too much. "A commentary is a bunch of reasons." Sort of. "Here, Jenna." I held out the towel. "He's your dog, remember?"

She backed away. "Only half mine. He's half Oliver's, too. It's his turn to dry."

I closed my eyes and prayed for strength. "You two can negotiate later. I want someone else to dry so I can make your breakfast."

"It's just cereal and juice," Jenna said. "That's not like a real breakfast. You know Alexis? Her mom cooks real food every morning."

Her mom didn't have to go to work every morning, either. "One of you take this towel in the next five seconds or there won't be any allowances this week. Five. Four. Three—"

Jenna broke first. "Fine." She whipped the towel out of my hand. "I'll do it." She glared at her brother. "Again."

Oliver looked from the dog to his sister to me. "Why doesn't dog hair keep growing like people hair does?"

My irritation over my children's behavior had been replaced with amusement by the time I got to the bookstore.

"It is a good question," Paoze said. "Why does not dog hair keep growing?"

The university's semester had ended and Paoze was back to working full time. He was also working a thirty-hour week as a waiter at a Madison restaurant. I'd been steeling myself for his resignation, but when I girded up the courage to talk to him about it, he said that working at the store wasn't work at all, so could he please continue as a staff member?

Lois turned away from him, her head down as she rifled through a box of board books. I was the only one who could see her evil grin.

"Dog hair," she said, "is one of the most unusual substances on earth. Did you know that dog hair, all by itself, reproduces? Even off the dog, it has a life of its own. One little hair can multiply by the thousands. For years no one understood how the backseat of a station wagon could get covered by dog hair during a ten-minute drive. It took groundbreaking research by a group of scientists in Newfoundland — that's in Canada, you know — to find out what really happens."

"Really?" Paoze sounded as if he was falling for the story, but when he caught my eye, he shook his head.

"You bet." Lois winked at me. "And what's more, they proved that light-colored dog hairs reproduce faster on dark fabric."

"And vice versa?" Paoze asked.

"Absolutely. And you know why this all came about? Because the scientists were from Labrador. You know, like the dog? That's where all those dogs come from, see, and the dog hair was multiplying so fast that this one scientist was almost smothered to death. They had to find a way to stop it from multiplying, so — "

"You can stop now," Paoze said. "I do not believe any of this. You are going to have to try harder, I think." He gave Lois a sweet smile and walked away.

"Rats." Lois let the board books drop to the bottom of the box. "Thought I had him. There really is a Labrador, you know."

"What goes around comes around," I said.

"What?"

"Nothing." I nodded at the wall clock. "Cookie time. And I have an errand to run. I'll be back in a little bit."

I stopped at the antiques store and bought half a dozen chocolate chip with raisins and half a dozen Amazingly Awesomes. White bag in hand, I walked down the side-

walk. The dark red paver stones that made up the sidewalk were still wet from the rain on this shady side of the
street. I stooped to move a wriggling worm to the safety
of a flower planter. "Stay there, little guy," I told him,
brushing my fingers on my pants. "You'll live a much longer worm life if you do, okay?"

On the next block, I noticed another sidewalk-stuck
worm, walked past, then felt guilty. I made an abrupt
turn to go back and take care of him. Half a step on my
reverse journey, there was a great *Crash!*

I catapulted forward, trying to escape whatever it was
behind me.

"Good heavens!" Debra O'Conner, my friend and
one of the local bank's vice presidents, hurried toward
me. "Beth, are you all right? That nearly hit you!" She
gave me a quick hug, then we both looked at the sidewalk.

Sharp shards of brick lay spattered in a large circle,
the center of which I had almost been walking through
at the instant of impact. My head felt light and I blinked
away the dizziness.

"Saved by a worm," I said shakily.

"A . . . what?" Debra frowned. "Are you sure you're
all right? Maybe you should lie down for a while. I can
call Evan." She reached into her purse for her cell phone.

"No. Don't." Quickly, I reassured her of my hale and
heartiness. "I don't want to bother him about an accident. See?" I pointed up at the crumbling brick. "Half of
those others are ready to go, too." We peered at the walls
of the old barber shop. Its owner had retired to Florida
five years ago and a faded For Sale sign was taped to the
inside of the glass door.

"Well," Debra said briskly, "Rod should be maintain-
ing his building, even if he hasn't had an offer in three

years. And no wonder, if the interior is in this same shape."

She made one last attempt to mother me, but I put on a smile and waved good-bye. I had things to do and being taken care of wasn't on the list.

A faint electronic "ding" announced my arrival at Faye's Flowers. I stood inside the front door, eyes closed, breathing in the lush scents. I had no idea what any of them were, of course, but that didn't stop me from enjoying them.

"Ma'am, are you all right?"

My eyes snapped open to see a very tall and very blond woman roughly my own age looking at me. "Yes, fine. Thanks. I was just, um, well, I just like how your store smells." An embarrassed Beth had entered babble mode. Beware! "And I was wondering if all florist's smell the same way. I haven't been to many, you see, so I was just . . . wondering." I ran out of words. Fortunately.

She smiled. "No one has ever asked me that question before."

Somehow I wasn't surprised.

"But you're right. The basic scents are the same. Any differences are probably in the gifts." She opened her palm toward an antique chest of drawers, each drawer pulled out slightly to reveal a selection of specialty soaps. "Lavender, ginger, jasmine. This is a favorite." She picked up a bar wrapped in a pale green ribbon, sniffed, smiled, and held it out.

I leaned forward. Eucalyptus. That's what I'd been smelling. Lovely. Without even looking at the price, I said, "I'd like two, please." Making them the only two things I'd ever bought in my adult life without a consideration of how the budget would deal with the purchase.

"Is there anything else?"

The woman wore the polite shopkeeper's expression. Trying to please, trying to be all things to all people, and trying not to be a weasel about it. I'd seen the same look on my own face in the reflection of the bookstore's windows.

"Are you the Faye in Faye's Flowers?" I asked. "Faye Lowery?"

"Not Lowery." She held a bar of soap in each hand. "I've been a Lewis for almost fifteen years."

Barb hadn't mentioned that detail. She also hadn't mentioned that Faye was six feet tall, blonder than a beach lifeguard, and gorgeous enough to turn George Clooney's head. The combination made it hard to believe that she'd ever been jealous of Kelly, but maybe she'd been a late bloomer.

I introduced myself as the owner of the Children's Bookshelf and secretary of the Tarver Elementary PTA. "Do you have children?" I asked.

"Three cats, no kids," she said cheerfully.

"Well, the Tarver PTA believes that anyone can contribute." At least I was pretty sure we believed that, even if it wasn't exactly spelled out anywhere. "For years our treasurer has been Randy Jarvis, and he doesn't have children, either." Or even a wife. "We've found," I said, "that business owners are highly qualified volunteers." It was a recent discovery, made in the last thirty seconds, but she didn't need to know that.

"Thanks," Faye said, backing away, "but I'm really busy with the store right now. Would you like these wrapped?" She bumped into the counter and twirled around to stand behind it. Safe.

"Let me tell you about some of the projects the PTA is doing."

She got the classic glazed look somewhere between my description of a museum field trip and our hopes to raise money for new library computers. "But the most exciting thing we're doing right now is the senior story project."

"Stories?" She sounded almost interested. As in, interested enough in pleasing her customer to keep the conversation going, but not interested enough to continue the topic any longer than necessary. I knew the tone of voice very well. Just recently I'd used it when a customer was going on at length about the wonderful carpet in her new doghouse.

"We have a group of children interviewing residents at Sunny Rest." I said. "In a few weeks we'll have a book of stories bound and ready to sell. Would you be interested in taking a few books? All profits go to educational projects of the Tarver PTA."

She placed the soap in the middle of a piece of tissue paper. "Let me think about it, okay?"

"You should read some of these stories," I pressed, watching her closely. "My son is interviewing Maude Hoffman."

"Oh?" She folded the tissue paper around the soaps in a tidy little package. "How old is Mrs. Hoffman?"

"Eighty-three. Her story is sad, really. No children, and then her favorite great-niece died at only eighteen."

"That's too bad." The soap disappeared into a flat-bottomed bag with handles of twisted paper. "And much too young to die. Car accident?"

"She drowned."

Faye's hands, which had been steadily moving, went still. "When was this?"

"About twenty years ago."

She flicked a glance to my face, then to the cash I was

holding. "That's a long time ago." She took the money and started making change.

Sometimes. Sometimes not. "She was from Rynwood, and Maude said if she'd lived, she would have been about my age."

Faye counted out my change and said nothing.

"We look about the same age, too," I said. "Are you from here? Maybe you knew her. Kelly Engel?"

"Of her." Faye shut the cash drawer. "Wouldn't say I knew her."

"No? Rynwood's not that big. I would have thought . . . well. Did you know there's some question about how she died?"

"The police said it was an accident." Faye pushed my bag across the counter.

"I hear some people think it was suicide."

"Not Kelly." She took a step backward, retreating toward an open doorway through which I could see green tissue paper, white plastic buckets, and shelves of ceramic vases. "She thought too much of herself for that. She'd have assumed Keith would come back. It had to be an accident. Hope you enjoy the soap."

And she was gone.

I went back out into the halfhearted sunshine with three thoughts. One, that Barb had been right: Faye did indeed have a wicked temper. Two, that she'd learned to control it, mostly.

And three, that she was hiding something.

Chapter 13

"How do you know Faye was lying?" Marina asked. "And lying about what, pray tell?"

I glanced at her expression, but it was one of open interest. I breathed a quiet sigh of relief. Last fall Marina had ventured into Shakespearean territory to add interest to her remarks and I'd spent a few tense weeks trying to sort out true quotes from Marina-manufactured quotes.

"It wasn't so much lying, as that she wasn't telling the whole truth," I said. "A mom knows this kind of stuff. Do you know when Zach is lying?"

"Talks to his shoes," she said promptly.

"How do you know when the DH is lying?"

"He mumbles. So you're saying Faye what's-her-name was lying because she did what?" She fluttered her fingers in a "come on, tell" gesture.

"Looks like it's going to be a big one," I said idly, watching our offspring. We were in Marina's spacious backyard and Jenna, Oliver, and Zach were waving their arms at the maple tree, making plans for a tree house. Their grandiose gestures didn't worry me; Marina's DH was an engineer who would go to great—and probably expensive—lengths to make sure the structure was safe and sound. "She started off by saying she barely knew Kelly, which I know isn't true, then made a cruel comment that Kelly wouldn't have committed suicide because she was too much of a narcissist."

Marina put on her Junior Birdman glasses, making a circle of finger and thumb, extending the other fingers, and placing the circles upside down around her eyes with her fingers along her jaw line. "And this is proof of murder?"

"Stop that. Of course it's not proof. But the two statements are inconsistent, and—" My cell phone trilled. I fished it out of my purse. "Oh, bother. This will only take a second." I hoped. "Hello, this is Beth."

"Bethie, you figured out whodunit yet?"

I closed my eyes. Why had I ever given Auntie May my cell phone number? I ran through a quick mental list of what a hassle it would be to get it changed and decided to let it go. After all, Auntie May was ninety-one. She couldn't possibly live to more than a hundred and twenty.

"You haven't, have you?" Her voice, always piercing, now penetrated my skull as thoroughly as a toddler's shrieks rattled my molars. "What you been doing, girl? Don't tell me you're spending all your time on that story project."

I had, in fact, spent more hours than I'd guessed possible on the project, and in the car was another stack of papers I'd gathered from Tarver a bare hour earlier. But it was truly a labor of love and I couldn't wait to unveil the end product. "These things take time, Auntie May."

She made a scoffing noise. Either that, or she was choking. "Time is what you don't have."

So, not choking. Which was good news, but a little

bout of coughing might have been nice. Not a big one, of course. Just enough to tire her to the point of having to hang up. I sighed. Bad Beth, for thinking such a thing. "How does time enter into this?" I asked. "Kelly has been dead for years."

"And every one has taken a year and a half away from Maudie."

I tried to do the math, but gave up quickly. "She isn't sick, is she?"

"Sick?" May shrieked. "She's eighty-three years old, with a poor excuse for a heart and a piece of crap blood pressure. Of course she's sick! Not that you'd know about her health, with your prancing about town. Oh, I saw you with that pretty Evan Garrett, don't think I didn't. Shame on you for waltzing around having a good time when Maudie is suffering so."

The unfairness took my breath away. But this happened often to anyone in the presence of Auntie May, so I tried not to take it personally. I'd once heard her lay into the mayor after he'd accidentally dropped a plastic coffee cup cover onto the sidewalk. And not long ago I'd eavesdropped as she flayed the verbal hide off a teenaged girl for wearing clothes more suited to a lingerie show than a public street.

Her words still hurt, though, more than sticks and more than stones. "I'm trying, Auntie May."

"Gritting your teeth, aren't you?" She chuckled. "I know the sound. Hear it regular."

"How sick is Maude?" I asked. "She's not . . ." I fumbled for the words. "Not in any real danger, is she?"

"Stop by and see for yourself," Auntie May snapped. The phone went silent.

"Wipe that look off your face," Marina said.

I glanced over. She had slid down in her chair and was

tilting her face up to the sun, eyes closed. "Your eyes are shut," I said. "How do you know?"

She made a rude noise in the back of her throat and I had a sudden flash of the future starring Marina as the Auntie May of the 2050s. Auntie Marina? Or maybe Grandma Marina? No, I had it: Mammy Marina.

"The problem with you, mah deah," Mammy drawled in her best Southern belle accent, "you ah a product of your fe-ahs."

"My fears?"

"Why, yea-ess." She slid down another inch, looking as relaxed as a cat. "For some reason, you're afraid that Maude is going to die before you figure out what happened to Kelly and you're already feeling guilty as all get out. So there's guilt and worry and the teensiest bit"—she put her thumb and index finger half an inch apart—"the teensiest bit of speculation about what you're going to do next. But, wait, that bit is growing rapidly, you can see it unfurling as we speak." Her palms were a foot apart, then two, then her arms were outstretched as far as they could go. "And by now, Beth has a plan. Next thing you know, she'll be making a list. If we're lucky she won't put a title on it, but will we be that lucky? I think not."

But I'd stopped paying attention when she'd made the unfurling remark. I leaned over and dug through my purse for a pad of paper and a working pen. I had a list to make. Title: Amy/Kelly Connections.

The next morning I dropped the kids off at school and drove downtown, parking in my normal spot in the alley behind the Children's Bookshelf. But instead of walking into the store and getting to work, I slung my purse over my shoulder. "Hi ho," I said. "It's off to my former employer I go."

Three blocks later, I walked in the door of the Ryn-wood *Gazette*. Though the old wooden desks and type-writers of yore had been replaced by cubicled computers decades ago, I liked to think a faint scent of ink ribbon and carbon paper lingered, impregnated into the walls and floor and ceiling.

"Hi." The young receptionist smiled. "What can I do for you?"

An instantaneous loss of fifteen pounds from my hip area would have been nice, but instead I asked if I could have a few minutes of Jean McKenna's time.

"I can ask, but she's pretty busy."

"Tell her it's Beth Kennedy."

The girl picked up the phone. "Jean? It's Lana. There's a Beth Kennedy here to see you."

Jean's strong voice came through the receiver loud enough for me to hear it without straining. "What the heck is she doing here? I have a paper to get out, for cry-ing out loud."

Lana swung her apologetic gaze up to me. "Okay, I'll tell her you're too busy."

"Hey!" Jean shouted. "I didn't say anything of the kind. Tell her to come on back. But ten minutes is all she gets."

I told Lana I knew the way and skirted the cubicle maze to get to the rear of the building. The sole window in her office faced north, keeping the room dark and cavelike. I'd said so once, and Jean had blinked, looked at her surroundings, and shrugged.

I knocked on the door and went on in. "Morning, Jean."

"Yeah, yeah." She was typing furiously at her com-puter and didn't look up. All I could see was her graying hair. "You know better than to show up this time of day. What's wrong with you?"

I plopped down in the guest chair. "Do you want the list?"

She glanced up at me over the top of her reading glasses, but didn't stop typing. "You don't really have a list of your faults, do you?"

"Not on paper."

She grunted and went back to the computer. "Let me get this paragraph done. Would you believe what they're doing in the township? At their board meeting last night I thought the trustees were going to start swinging."

"For real, or is that wishful thinking?"

"Wouldn't that make a great front page? ELECTED OFFICIALS IN FISTICUFFS OVER STREET LIGHTS. Think of the papers that would sell."

She whacked at the keyboard hard enough to make it bounce off the desktop at each whack. Jean still hadn't learned that computer keyboards didn't require the same impact of a manual typewriter. She went through keyboards like most people went through a roll of paper towels. A few more thumps, a pause while she reread her copy, a muttered "Save, Jean. Don't forget to save," then she leaned back, putting her hands behind her head.

"So what's up? Please tell me you have a great story. If not, you only have five minutes."

"I'm looking for information."

"Go to Google, that's what everybody else does."

"I don't want information from a search engine. I want real information."

She sat back, tossing her head to get her too-long bangs off her face. "Two sentences that are music to my ears. What do you want?"

"Everything you know about Kelly Engel."

"Kelly, Kelly, Kelly . . ."

I let her flip through her mental filing cabinets. She'd

get there eventually. Besides, she'd bite my head off if I gave her hints.

After muttering the name a dozen times, she snapped her fingers. "Kelly Engel. Fair-haired girl wonder. Drowned in Blue Lake twenty years ago. No, a little more than that. Cops said accident, everyone else said suicide. Except her mom, who swore up and down it was murder. She was the only one, though. Well, almost the only one." Her sardonic gaze went briefly heavenward, then came back down. "You go to church. Is it some kind of sin to speak ill of the dead? Bad luck? Anything?"

"I just sing in the choir. Someone other than Barb thought Kelly was murdered?"

She grunted and put her feet up on the edge of the desk. "Woman was obsessed. I hated to see her coming in with that scrapbook."

"Scrapbook?"

"Yeah, a great big thing. One of those monster three-ring binders with those awful photo album pages. You know, that clear peel-back plastic? Put a photo down on that sticky white cardboard and it's either stuck there forever or it doesn't stick at all and it slides out onto the floor of your closet behind the shoes you haven't worn in three years."

I nodded.

"Anyway, she had it filled with newspaper articles of anything even close to what happened to Kelly."

"Drownings, you mean?"

Jean shook her head. "No. Anything called accidental that Amy could figure out a way to be murder."

I sat up straight. "Amy? Amy Jacobson?"

"Well, yeah." Jean lifted her eyebrows. "Who did you think I was talking about? It was a running joke around here, Amy and her scrapbook. The crime book, she called it. You really didn't know? Amy talked about you, like you were really good friends. I figured you must have known about it."

Now I was the one shaking my head. "I'd never even heard Kelly's name until after Amy died."

"Huh."

We sat there, each pondering different things. At least I assumed so, because it was unlikely that Jean was wondering how much longer she could stay in this office without my staff mutinying from want of Alice's cookies.

"Amy was a weird one," Jean mused.

"She seemed normal enough to me. Other than the not going out during the day thing."

Jean scrunched her fifty-five-year-old nose. "And the scrapbook and how she took off for fifteen years without telling even her parents where she was and the goofy way she made a living and that she never cut her hair and how she wouldn't eat anything that ever swam and that she hated almost everyone in this town and, oh yeah, not going out during the day. But you mentioned that already, didn't you?"

I held up two fingers. "Questions."

Jean flicked a glance at the wall clock that was ticking away time. "Fast ones."

"I thought Amy was scared of everyone, not that she hated them."

"Hah. It was Kelly's death that twisted her up inside. She felt guilty, somehow. I never knew why, but there you go. Turned her mad at all of Rynwood that Kelly was dead and people saying she took her own life. Ate Amy up something fierce, so she left until she had to come back to take care of her parents."

I nodded, filing the information away in my mental pocket to pull out for later perusal and cogitation. I folded my middle finger down, leaving my index finger standing.

Jean turned back to her keyboard. "Better hurry."

"What did Amy do for a living?"

"Wow, you really didn't know her very well, did you?"

"No, and no deducting your kibitzing from my answer time."

"Yeah, yeah." She started whacking keyboard keys. "Amy was a graphic novelist. Can't believe you didn't know. Your store carries all her books. The author Jake? The Aqua City series?"

There were so many questions bouncing around in my head it was amazing that I was able to walk back to the store.

Amy was Jake?

Why had she never said?

Amy kept a scrapbook?

Why hadn't I ever seen it?

Why hadn't I known?

Amy hated most of Rynwood?

And on and on. After a while, the questions took on a circular route. I'd wonder about her Jake-ness for a while, wonder where she'd come up with the idea for a Victorian urban fantasy set at the bottom of the Atlantic Ocean, wonder why she'd never said a word to me about her massively successful series, wonder if Kelly's drowning death had anything to do with Jake's fantasy world, then I'd circle around to wondering about the scrapbook.

What, exactly, was in it? Jean had said newspaper articles, but I wondered if Amy had found a pattern that meant anything, wondered if something could be found if someone with a mind open to all possibilities went through it, wondered when she'd started keeping it, wondered where it was, and wondered if she'd kept it up until she died. Which sent me around to thinking about Rynwood.

If Amy had truly hated the people of Rynwood, I wondered, was that explanation enough for her disinclination to go outside during the day? That way she couldn't see people and people couldn't see her. Maybe she'd made up the whole being allergic to sun thing. It didn't make any rational sense, but my fear of snakes wasn't exactly rational, either.

It all jumbled together in my fuzzy brain, thoughts and questions banging into and bouncing off each other. The harder I thought, the faster the banging, and I spent the next couple of days responding to questions with answers that didn't necessarily fit.

On Wednesday afternoon, I sat at my desk, trying to work through a stack of returns. Lois had poked her head in and asked a question. I'd given an absent answer and assumed she'd go away, but instead she came in, moved a stack of publisher catalogs from chair to floor, and sat down.

I glanced at her, saw the serious expression, and pushed away the keyboard. "What's up?"

She reached forward and tapped my desk with her index finger. As she was wearing a new-to-her charm bracelet, this made a cheerful jingling noise. She'd found the bracelet at a flea market and I'd been treated to a charm-by-charm recital of each dangling object. Hammer, pliers, saw. Wrench, screwdriver, drill. Why Lois was enchanted by it, I did not know, but the bracelet had inspired a new outfit of denim jumper modified to have front pockets similar to a pair of overalls. She'd belted it with a tape measure, added a pendant plumb bob necklace, and completed her attire with wide-strapped sandals.

Now, she jingled her charm bracelet with a few more finger taps. "The question is, what's up with you? And what are you doing back here, anyway?"

I clicked the computer's mouse. "Returns."

"Now, now. There's no fooling me. I'm a mother, too, you know. What are you really doing?"

Though Lois was my manager and friend, she sometimes forgot who signed her paychecks. Not that they were very big ones, and I certainly didn't want to play overbearing owner, but still. "Why is it you're not afraid of me? I have the power of hiring and firing, you know."

"You have the power to force Jenna to wear dresses to church, too." She shrugged. "Paoze and Yvonne are worried that you're worried. Yvonne thinks store sales are down and we're going to close."

The concept that my preoccupation could affect my staff hadn't entered my head. "Oh. But they're not. We're not. We're doing quite well, really."

Lois nodded. "And Paoze thinks you're going to marry that Evan Garrett, hand the store over to me, and sail off into the sunset."

"That's ridiculous."

She looked at me with a sarcastic "Really?" expression all over her face. "How long have you been dating? A year? Time to fish or cut bait, I'd say."

"I'm not . . . I mean the kids aren't . . ." The papers on my desk were suddenly in dire need of straightening. "The last couple of days I've been catching up on the story project stories, that's all. I got behind a little bit and had to play catch-up." I was repeating myself, always a sign that I was uncomfortable. But maybe Lois didn't know that, maybe—

"You're repeating yourself," Lois said. "You only do that when you're feeling itchy about something."

Why, why, couldn't I learn to lie? Even the ability to hold back on the truth would be good. But, no, I had to have the compulsion to tell the whole truth and nothing but the truth, especially to any woman older than myself. I blamed my lack of control on growing up with two sisters who would sit on me and tickle me until I screamed if I didn't tell them whatever they wanted to know. The experience had given me full sympathy with torture victims who confessed to sins they didn't commit.

"Did you know," I asked, "that Amy Jacobson was Jake?"

Her hand went to her plumb bob. "No kidding?"

"Nope."

"No kidding." Her eyes went distant. "That's just . . . wild."

"And did you know that Amy and Kelly were good friends their senior year of high school and Amy hated most of Rynwood because everyone said Kelly took her own life?"

For once, Lois didn't say anything. She toyed with the plumb bob, stared into space, and didn't make a single sound. The bells to the front door of the store jangled, and she didn't move. The phone rang and she didn't twitch.

I took the small mental leap the situation required. "Is that what you think? That Kelly committed suicide?"

She tugged on the plumb bob, making the cord dig deep into the skin at her neck. "It seemed so obvious."

"Seemed? You don't think so now?"

"It's all your fault, you know," she said vaguely. "I was okay thinking that she was just a depressed teenager who didn't give herself enough time to get over a breakup. It made sense and it was sad, but I was okay with it. All of us were. But then you come along and ask questions."

I couldn't decide if that was compliment or criticism, so I left it alone.

"Which means it's up to you to get answers." Her attention swung to me. "Find out what really happened. Find out if Amy was right. Find out if Kelly was murdered. If Amy was murdered. Murder . . ." Her shoulders sagged a little. "I don't want there to be a killer in town," she said. "I don't want to find out that I've been selling books to a murderer. I don't want . . ."

Suddenly Lois straightened up. "Find out," she said. "You've done it before, you can do it again. Find out what happened that night."

"Okay," I said soothingly.

"Don't use that everything-will-be-fine tone with me, young lady. Promise to find out. Promise!"

This had the eerie feel of déjà vu. "I promise."

"Good." Lois nodded sharply. "I love getting promises out of you. Get one from Beth and you know the job's done. So what's your next step?"

"I have no idea."

"Oh, you." She poked my upper arm. "Such a jokester. Bet you're working on a plan already."

And, of course, I was. Before she was out of the room, I'd pulled out the phone book and dialed the Engels. Of course Barb knew where Keith Mathieson was; how could she not? She gave me the name of his business. "You tell me if you find out anything, you tell me right away."

I assured her that I would, pulled out the big fat Madison phone book, and found the listing for the insurance agency where Keith worked. The woman who answered

the phone transferred me to Keith without asking any
questions, and before I was quite ready, he was saying,
"Hello, this is Keith. How can I help you?"

Um. Well.

"Hello?" he asked, a little louder

"Hi, my name is Beth Kennedy," I said in a rush. "I've
been talking to Barb Engel, she gave me the name of
your company, and I just wondered if you'd give me a
few minutes of your time."

"I'm sorry, what was your name?"

I told him again. "It's Barb Engel that told me where
you work."

There was a long beat of silence, then, "Mrs. Engel?"

"Yes," I said. "Barb Engel. Kelly's mother."

"Kelly." He breathed the name. "I haven't heard anyone talk about her in a long time."

"I'm sorry to bring up such a sad episode in your life,
but I'd like to talk to you about her. About the night she
died."

More silence. This time it went on so long and was so
deep that I began to hear the background noises in his
office. A radio played a news broadcast, a copy machine
was copying, a telephone was ringing.

Finally, he said, "No. I'm sorry. I can't talk about Kelly.
Please give Mrs. Engel my regards. Tell her . . . tell
her . . ." There was a click, and then a dial tone.

Slowly and silently, I hung up the phone. Of all the
things I'd thought to hear in Keith's voice, I hadn't expected this. I hadn't expected tears.

Wednesday twilight in mid-May lasted long into the evening. It lasted past packing up the kids and sending them
off with their father and his Speak Italian in Two Hours
CDs, lasted past a quick vacuum of the house, and even

lasted past a PTA meeting during which I mollified my fellow PTA board members with a stack of edited stories. Claudia, however, was a whole other kettle of stinky fish.

She suffered through the presentation by Millie Jefferson, the school psychologist, with her toes tapping and eyes darting in my direction. Millie spoke about summer projects parents could do with their children and handed out packets full of enticing information.

But before Millie was all the way out of the room, Claudia flipped through the inch-high pile of story project papers. "Where are the rest?"

I stifled a bad word. Not that I'd expected a pat on the back, but it would have been nice to get at least a grudging nod of acknowledgment for my work. "The kids who want to do one last interview are handing them in to me on Monday. I'll have them edited and to the printer by Thursday morning and the books will be printed the week after Memorial Day."

"Hmm." Claudia turned a page, read a few words, made a short snorting noise, then turned another page. "What if some of the kids don't turn in their stories?"

"Then their stories don't get in the book."

Randy grunted. "Simple. I like simple."

But Claudia wasn't done. "What if the printer doesn't get the books printed up in time? If anything goes wrong they won't be ready for the assembly."

That part was true. The schedule was a little tight and there wasn't any leeway for disasters. Maybe Claudia was right. Maybe we would wind up looking like an incompetent organization that shouldn't be allowed to bake cupcakes, let alone tackle a project with this kind of scope. Maybe—

"Well, Beth?" Erica asked, eyebrows raised.

I didn't like the way her eyebrows were arching, I didn't like the way she was toying with her reading glasses, and I really didn't like the way she was accusing me, albeit in a backhanded way, of managing the story project poorly. I had safeguards in place, it would all work out. Why didn't they trust me?

"Why—" I bit off rest of the question. It would come across as unprofessional at best and whiney at worst. I fished around for words, found a few that might do the job, and started over again. "Why, it's all taken care of." I smiled and hoped my high school grammar teacher would forgive me for ending a sentence with a preposition. Saying "Care of everything has been taken" just wouldn't have been the same.

"Taken care of how?" Claudia asked.

I patted the old diaper bag I used as a briefcase. "The printer gave me a guarantee, double our money back if not delivered at least two days before the school assembly. He said if he can't get it done here in Rynwood, he'll send it to a shop in Madison." And he wouldn't do that because the printer in Madison was a cousin and the competition between the two was of outrageous proportions.

Claudia was still frowning. "Why is the printer doing all this?"

I kept the smug smile off my face. Mostly. "Because he's Sydney Stillwell's brand-new stepfather."

Enlightened nods went all around the room. Even Randy instantly grasped the implication: New stepfathers were top candidates for PTA projects. New boyfriends and girlfriends were good for donating money, but it took the commitment of marriage to get the hands up when it was time to sign up volunteers.

"Fine." Erica used her engraved gold pen to draw a

line across an item on her legal pad. "Anything else? Claudia?"

The meeting moved on, and I tried to forget the expression I'd read on Erica's face. She'd looked bizarrely like my mother, back when I was young. They both wore that "Are you about to disappoint me?" expression very, very well.

I hurried out of the room as soon as Erica banged the gavel, not looking back. It was getting dark, and I had somewhere to go.

Chapter 14

Blue Lake was quiet in the twilight. Gentle waves lapped up against the shore, a rhythmic sound I'd heard every night for years, growing up next to water. The sound comforted me as much as it made me long for what was gone.

The beach sand was cold against my bare feet. The sign on the lifeguard's chair read No GUARD ON DUTY, SWIM AT YOUR OWN RISK. Of course not, not this late. Almost dark, and nearing the time Kelly drowned. On almost the same day. Creepy didn't begin to cover what I was feeling.

"Breathe," I whispered, trying to relax into myself, trying to go back into the past. Trying to be young again, trying to be eighteen, trying to be blond, to be slim, to be valedictorian, to have just lost the boy I'd always thought I'd marry.

Everything was in my head—except the being blond part; even the wildest of my imaginings didn't get me that far into fantasy—and I was ready as I'd ever be. I took my sweatpants off, laid my purse on top of them, and pulled my sweatshirt over my head and dropped it on the pile. Before I could stop to think, I ran fast as I could, feet thudding onto the sand, into water that was ankle-deep, then knee-deep, then I hurled my body headlong into a shallow racing dive straight into the cold darkness of the lake.

The water was shockingly cold. The warm temperatures of the last weeks may have heated up the air nicely, but they hadn't budged the water much above freaking freezing.

I surfaced, gasping with deep hoarse breaths, kicking hard, arms whirling, trying to work hard enough to keep from turning into an ice cube. The raft materialized in front of me and I swam around it twice, then three times, before my body stopped screaming at me to *get out of the water now, you moron!*

By the fourth time around, my fingers had turned numb, but the rest of me had adjusted. I rolled onto my back and floated, kicking lazily and looking up at the stars.

The night lights of Madison crowded out the Milky Way and dimmed the smaller pinpoints of light, but the Big Dipper was there, rotating around the North Star just like it always had.

I kicked once more, sending a "kerplunk" of water high into the air, and slid into a sidestroke. Not too far away, two hundred yards at most, was the point of land where Kelly had been found.

All around me was the peace of a mid-May night. Too early for summer revelers, the evening was punctuated only by the chirps of spring peepers and the far away noises of televisions and quiet conversation on patios and decks.

I swam silently by unseen voices, an unwilling voyeur to vacation plans, casserole recipes, and lamentations about the baseball standings.

All of that slid past as I swam into the darkness, my senses tingling. I felt so alive, so free, so . . . young. Kelly had felt this way. She'd heard those same conversations, seen the same lights, felt the same water on her skin.

She'd followed the shore, just like I was, swinging wide around the docks and boats and heading to the county park, its point sticking far out into the lake. In the daytime there were too many boats to swim safely to the point from the beach, but at night the boats were home on their lifts. Why not succumb to the lure of the rising moon? Why not dive in and enjoy the wildness of black water? Why not live a little?

The point was close now. I changed my angle, wanting my feet to touch bottom on sand, not on the mucky grassy area that lurked to the left. I hated mucky and I hated water grass even more.

My breaths were coming a little too fast. Maybe I'd gone too hard, or maybe I'd gone too far. But the point was close and then I'd be able to rest. I'd be able to stop and think about Kelly. Maybe then I'd be able to—

Something touched me.

Brushed up against my ankle.

Flickered up the length of my thigh.

I shrieked. Or, rather, I tried to shriek. Tried to scream, tried to call for someone, anyone. Instead, water rushed into my mouth. I choked and sputtered, tried to suck down air, got more water.

Quit panicking.

I flailed my arms and legs, trying to find the lake bottom, but I was too far out. I opened my mouth for air, but the only thing that came in was more water. Everything was black, the sky, the water, the land, and I'd lost any sense of up and down.

You're making it worse, you know.

The voice in my head didn't sound like my own. It was young and self-assured. Once upon a time I'd been young, and these days I was occasionally self-assured, but I couldn't ever remember being both at the same time.

You're going to drown if you keep struggling like that. I should know.

Could that be . . . Kelly? A girl dead for more than twenty years was talking to me? Clearly, I was hallucinating.

This happened before, remember?

I did, but didn't want to. My conversations with the murdered Tarver principal had been a one-off and probably the result of an overactive imagination. My mother always said I'd come to grief because of it, and here I was, about to drown thanks to a remarkably dumb idea to re-create a death scene. Talk about stupid. How could I ever have thought this would help anything?

Keep still.

I wanted to point out that since I didn't have any air left in my lungs I'd sink to the bottom like a rock, but I didn't have any breath to talk.

Just do it!

Fine, I thought. If I drown it'll be your fault.

I stopped waving my arms around, stopped kicking, stopped everything. My body went quiet. I felt myself moving, but didn't know which direction I was going. Eyes wide open, but the only thing my eyes could see was darkness.

So badly did I want to open my mouth and breathe, that I almost didn't care if it was water instead of air. My chest hurt, my heart hurt, all of me ached for the loss my children would be facing. I couldn't let them grow up motherless. I couldn't let them down. I couldn't . . .

couldn't . . . but I wanted so badly to breathe . . . Jenna . . . Oliver . . . I'm so sorry. . . .

And then my fingertips brushed sand.

Go!

Instinctively, I curled my legs up underneath me, placed my feet firm against the ground, and shoved with all my might.

All was darkness, but now I knew which way was up. I kicked and clawed my way to the surface, pulling myself higher, stretching my spine long. My head burst through the surface and I turned my face up, sucking in great heaving gulps of air.

Now get dry and warm before you catch a cold.

"Wait," I gasped. "What happened that night?" I treaded water, searching all through my head for the voice. "Please tell me. Please?"

But she was gone.

Evan looked down at me. Large beads of water hung off the ends of my hair, and my sweatpants and sweatshirt were stained wet from the moisture of my bathing suit. I stood on his front porch, and the light he'd switched on was far too bright for my eyes.

"Beth, what on earth? Come on in, you're dripping wet. What happened? No, stay right there on the tile, I'll get a towel." He kept talking as he ducked into the guest bathroom. "Are you okay? What's wrong? The kids are all right, aren't they? Here, let me dry your hair." He put the towel on my head and scrubbed, guaranteeing snarls. "You're shivering. Soon as you get a little dryer, I'll get you some clothes."

Ten minutes later my wet stuff was rolling around in his dryer and we were settled in his study. The walls were lined with bookshelves that held a few books, a few diplomas, a few pictures of his grown daughters, and a large number of golfing trophies.

He'd turned on the gas fire and I pulled a chair directly in front of it. Holding my hands out to the warmth, I prepared myself for the questions I knew were coming. But I might as well delay the inevitable as long as possible.

I plucked at the sweatshirt I now wore. I'd pushed the sleeves up toward my elbow; if I'd let them hang, they'd have hung over the ends of my fingertips with six inches to spare. "Is this yours or one of your daughters'?"

"Mine." He turned a wing chair to face me.

"These too?" I pulled at the sweatpants, the waist bunched up, as I'd had to pull the drawstring tight to keep the pants from sliding off.

He sat, putting one foot up on the fireplace hearth, leaving the other on the floor. "Are you going to explain, or am I going to have to ask what happened?"

I smiled. "You know I don't like talking about the stupid things I do."

"Basic questions, then," he said. I nodded assent. "In what body of water did you come to be submerged?"

"Blue Lake."

"On what day and hour?"

"Tonight." I looked at the grandfather clock in the corner of the room. "Just half an hour ago."

"Did you intentionally go into the water?"

"Yes."

"Ah." He propped his elbows on the chair arms and placed his palms together. "Swimming in the dark. I see. And you came here for . . . what?"

What I'd wanted was a hug, but I supposed dry clothes weren't such a bad substitute. "When I was out swimming, a piece of lake grass wrapped around my ankle." I flashed back to the panic that had engulfed me so completely. I, who'd learned to swim before I learned my ABCs, had panicked. I shook away the fear. "I got a little scared and I . . . I just wanted to see you."

His face lost the attorney look and he became Evan again. He leaned forward and took my hands in his. "You're still cold. Come here." He pulled me up into his arms and sat us down again, this time with me on his lap.

I laid my forehead against his, taking care to keep my wet hair away from him.

"Now," he said. "Are you going to tell me why you were out swimming all alone in the dark?"

"I'd rather not."

He chuckled. "Is this when we start deciding how stupid you were?"

"How about later?" His skin smelled of man-soap, a delicious scent that was doing quivery things to my insides. I kissed his temple, just where his blond hair was going white.

"Was Marina involved in this?" he asked. "Don't tell me it was some sort of dare."

"Okay, I won't tell you." Marina hadn't the least idea I'd gone out to the lake. I hadn't told her for the simple reason that she'd have insisted on going with me. She too would have wanted an explanation, and saying that I wanted to commune with a dead teenager would have earned me a burst of laughter and an elbow in the ribs. "Funny," she'd have said. "Now tell me the real reason."

"Ah," Evan was saying. "I thought so."

He'd misinterpreted my answer. I started to correct him, then let it go. He would have taken my protestations not as truth, but as a defense of friendship. Which it would have been. Truth, too, though.

Evan kissed my forehead. I loved it when he did that.

Loved the feeling of being taken care of, being close, being cherished. I watched his blood beat through the veins in his neck, counting the beats, mesmerized by the feel of this wonderful, handsome man. What did I ever do to deserve him? He was kind, he was thoughtful, he—

"Don't you think," he said, "that it's time to move on from Marina?"

—he could be more than a little overbearing. I drew back a little. Watching his pulse wasn't that interesting. "What do you mean, move on?"

He stroked my damp hair. "Just a thought, Beth, that's all. Don't you think she holds you back? You have so much potential."

"Have you been talking to my mother?" I slid off his lap and sat on the hearth, fluffing my hair in front of the fire's heat. "She used to say the same thing about my best friend in high school."

"And was she right?"

I stopped, midfluff. "No, she wasn't." Though I spoke quietly, I spoke with a "no questions allowed" tone of voice.

Evan shifted so that both his legs were on the hearth, crossed at the ankles. His position effectively trapped me—legs on one side of me, chair on the other. I pushed away the feeling of claustrophobia and concentrated on drying my hair. He wasn't trapping me on purpose, he was just getting comfortable, that was all.

"Don't you think," he asked, "that our friends are one of the ways by which we're measured?"

"Yes." My breaths started to come short and fast. I didn't like enclosed spaces, I didn't like not being able to move when I wanted to, and I really didn't like being kept from moving by another human being. I hated crowds, even when the crowd was only two people.

I glanced at him. He was sitting with his elbow propped up on one arm of the chair, his chin resting on his thumb, middle finger laid just below his very kissable lower lip. His index finger, however, was tap tap tapping his cheek.

I was not going to start a defense campaign for Marina. Of all the people in the world who didn't need defending, it was Marina Neff. Sure, she could try the patience of a veteran nursery school teacher with her fake accents and constant wordplay games, but her virtues were as obvious as her faults.

If Mr. Garrett thought he could dictate who my friends were, he was gravely mistaken. Matter of fact — I yanked my fingers through my hair too hard and winced with pain — if Mr. Evan Garrett thought he had any right whatsoever to tell me what to do about anything, he was mistaken. One more comment about Marina and —

"May I ask you something?" Evan sat up, put his feet on the floor, and faced me.

The intensity of his gaze made me nervous. "Um, sure." As long as the question didn't involve anything about ending a friendship, a change in staffing at the bookstore, or a lifetime commitment, I was good.

"If I asked you to take Spot with you when you go out, would you do it?"

"Take . . . Spot?" His request made no sense. "But . . ."

"I know that Spot is certainly no protection against a real assailant, but just the presence of a dog could give you a small measure of safety. An attacker wouldn't know that Spot is more likely to lick him to death than to bite him."

I gaped at him. "You're worried about my safety?"

His smile was crooked. "You'd rather I didn't?"

"Well, no. I mean of course I don't want you to worry,

but it's just I didn't expect . . . I didn't . . . what I mean is . . ." I had no idea what I meant. I'd dived into babble mode, where every word I uttered was bound to be stupid.

"Beth." Evan took my hands. "We've danced around this for months. I know you're not sure the kids are ready, but I want to marry you. I love you. I want to take care of you and make sure you're safe and warm and happy. You deserve all I can give you and more."

I wanted to say something eloquent, something we'd both remember, something worth writing down. "Oh."

He smiled. "You don't have to answer right now. I've waited for this moment for a long time and I'll wait as long as it takes. But will you do one thing for me? Promise that you won't go out alone without your dog?"

His light blue gaze rested on my face. A caress. No, more than that. A claim. I was being laid claim to, even if I hadn't yet acknowledged the ownership.

"I'd be much happier about your safety," he said, "if you at least had Spot with you."

The idea that this attractive, fit, intelligent, semirich man had just proposed to me was going to take some getting used to. There were a number of questions to be considered. Would he be a suitable stepfather for Jenna and Oliver? Was he the man with whom I wanted to spend the rest of my life? I'd thought that, once, about Richard, and had wept long tears when I'd pulled the rings off my left hand.

Then, softly, in almost a whisper, he asked, "Please?"

The thoughts in my head fuzzed together and I said the worst thing possible. "I promise."

Chapter 15

Marina's voice roared out of my cell phone and into my poor, defenseless ear. "He what?"

"You heard me the first time," I said.

"Sure, but I can't believe Mr. Evan Garrett would propose like that. On a weeknight? I'd have thought he'd have witnesses and a string quartet at the very least."

"There was a fire in the fireplace." Gas fire, but still.

She grunted. "Point. But I am seriously bummed my guess was so wrong."

I put my hand over the phone. "Jenna! Oliver! Stay on the trail, okay? And make sure Spot doesn't get into anything stinky." Vague assents wafted backward. The section of the park where we were hiking was so thick with maple trees that darkness seemed imminent, even though it was only seven o'clock. After dinner the kids had been so full of energy that I'd suggested a walk.

I took my hand off the phone. "So how wrong were you?"

"Very," Marina said, "since there was no moonlight, no horse and carriage, no flowers, no ring in a robin's egg blue box, and no obscenely sized bouquet of roses. And I must say I'm not happy that it took almost twenty-four hours for me to get this news."

"I was swamped at the store. And I was trying to edit the story session stories, and the phone hardly stopped ringing all day."

"Mmm."

Why, exactly, I hadn't told Marina right away I wasn't quite sure myself. I hadn't told the kids yet, either. Maybe tonight, after we got home from this walk. Or Sunday might be good. I could ease into it over the weekend. Drop some hints. Jenna would pick up on those right away, though Oliver might need it spelled out a little more. As in, "How would you feel if Evan lived here all the time?"

But would he? He owned a perfectly nice home. Not kid-proof, with its off-white upholstery and objects of art placed on pedestals, but nice enough.

"So," Marina said. "I hear you went for a swim last night."

I blinked. "How did you know that?"

"I am all knowing and all powerful."

"Of course you are," I murmured.

"Plus, I can't believe you forgot that Debra-don't-call-me-Debbie O'Conner lives across the street from the beach."

I had forgotten. The O'Conners used to live not far from Marina, but last summer they'd moved. "Debra spies on people who go swimming?" I asked.

Once upon a time, Debra had had ambitions to be much more than a small-town bank vice president. Plus, she'd had her hair cut in Chicago, worn spiky high heels, and made all other mothers feel inadequate by doing all her baking from scratch.

In the last year or so, however, she'd shifted her goals from business to enjoying life as much as possible. Which, since I was lucky if I had time to enjoy my children's kiss at bedtime, also made me feel inadequate.

"No, Debra takes her dogs for a walk just before going to bed." Marina clucked at me. "What were you doing out there, oh silly one? Trying to re-create the scene of Kelly's death?"

"Something like that."

I expected her to berate me for doing something so stupid without her coming along to take notes, but she said, "Well, did you figure out anything?"

A cloud went over the sun, and the tree-induced gloom through which we were walking darkened a little more. Jenna and Oliver kept on, paying no attention to the sky, but Spot cast a doggy look upward.

And there I was in the water, arching my head back, trying to find up, trying to find air, hearing Kelly's voice in my head.

I'd never told anyone, not even Marina, that I once thought I'd heard the voice of a dead woman. But it was only a stress-induced hallucination, that's all. My own projection of what she would have said. My own wish to believe that the dead lived on in another place and might, under the right circumstances, have something to tell us.

Then again, I'd been in extremely stressful circumstances last fall, when trying to help the family of a dead man, and I hadn't heard his voice.

Maybe you only hear women.

"What?" I asked.

"Didn't say a word," Marina said. "I'm waiting for you, remember? For the answer to life, the universe, and everything? And don't tell me forty-two."

"You'd have a better sense of humor if you read more books."

"And you'd be less of a know-it-all if you didn't read as much. And no sticking your tongue out at me."

I grinned. She knew me too well, and I was about to tell her so when my mom instincts went "twang." The hiking path in front of me split and the kids were starting down the wrong trail; there wasn't time on a school night to walk that long route. "Hey, you two!" But they'd already disappeared into the gloom. "Sorry, Marina, gotta go fetch my offspring." I clicked the phone off and hopped into a slow trot.

"Jenna?" I called. "Oliver? Come back!"

Nothing.

I started to run a little faster. "Jenna?" Her name came out in a pant. "Oliver?"

Nothing. Why didn't I see them? How had they gone so far so quickly? How could they just vanish like that?

Faster, faster, faster.

They'd be around the next bend in the trail, wouldn't they? They'd be close by, waiting for me, of course they would.

Nothing.

Time spun out slowly and I lived an agonized life in which Jenna and Oliver never came home, never found their way back. All my fault, all of it. I'd never forgive myself. Jenna . . . Oliver . . .

Then I heard voices. My children! But who else . . . ? A man's voice.

My mouth suddenly tasted of bright adrenaline. A medium-sized woman versus a grown man in a secluded part of a very large park. Spot would be no help; why hadn't we adopted a Rottweiler?

I put on a burst of speed, coming around a curve in the trail with fast, pounding feet.

If I could get there first, head him off, maybe I could distract him, maybe by attacking him I'd give the kids time to get free, maybe I could—

"Hey, Mom." Jenna looked at me. "Why are you running?"

—and maybe if I stopped leaping to the most extreme conclusions possible there'd be one less way to look like an idiot. My immediate drop from terror-induced run to embarrassed walk made my feet trip over themselves. Pete Peterson leapt forward, grabbed my arm, and held me upright.

"Whoopsy daisy," he said. "All you all right?"

"Fine." I brushed the sweat off my forehead. "Thanks. How are you doing these days?"

"Oh, you know. Busy."

"Mr. Peterson likes Spot," Oliver said.

"Well, who wouldn't?" Pete said. He squatted and held out his hand for a doggy lick. "Not sure you'd make much of a guard dog," he said, ruffling the floppy ears, "but you're a pretty good dog for a dog."

"A pretty good dog for a dog," Oliver repeated, frowning slightly. Then he smiled. "That's funny."

"Only on the third Thursday in May." Pete gave Spot one last pat and stood. "Well, I'll see you three around."

"Mr. Peterson plays disc golf," Jenna said. "You know, they put a course in last year. Over there." She pointed, glanced at Pete's half smile, and frowned slightly. "Or is over there?" She pointed in the opposite direction.

"I can throw a Frisbee." Oliver went through the motions with an invisible disc. "Can we play, Mom?"

I looked from one child to the other, sensing a conspiracy. "Not tonight. It's much too late."

The instant chorus of "But, Mom—" died out when I put my fingers in my mouth and started to take a deep breath. For years the threat of my whistle had been an excellent behavior modifier. It wouldn't work much longer and it was already losing its effectiveness with Jenna, but I might as well take advantage while I could.

"Not tonight," I said firmly. "Besides, we don't have any Frisbees with us."

"Tomorrow?" Jenna asked.

"Yeah, how about tomorrow?" Oliver bounced up and down on the balls of his feet. "Please please please?"

"Tomorrow night we're having dinner with Evan."

Their long faces told me that dining at the country club compared badly to the adventure of disc golf.

"I'm not busy Saturday afternoon," Pete said. "We could do a round or two. If you want."

"Can we, Mom?" "Pretty please?"

I looked at my children, then at Pete. "Are you sure you don't have anything better to do?"

"Sure, but playing Frisbee sounds like a lot more fun than cleaning my garage."

He grinned, and since he had one of those contagious kinds of smiles, I grinned back at him.

"Cool," he said. "Then it's a date." He gave Spot a pat and bumped knuckles with the kids. "Two o'clock? See you guys on Saturday," he said, and strolled off.

"Time for us to get home." I herded dog and children together and we set off in the direction from whence we'd come, dog first, then kids, then me. After a few steps I looked over my shoulder. Pete was still in view, just turning away.

"Caught you," I said softly.

Oliver started walking backward. "What?"

"Nothing." I skipped forward a step, took his hand, and spun him around. "No walking backward unless you can say the alphabet backward, too."

"Z," he said. "Y, X . . . um . . ."

"W," Jenna said.

Oliver pulled away from me and started skipping ahead. "Z, Y, X, W," he sang. "Z, Y, X, W . . . V!"

I felt Jenna's hand steal into mine. Here, in the park, in the dusk, where no one could see us, she wanted to hold my hand. A warmth rushed through me and I squeezed lightly. "So," I said, oh-so-casually. "Is Coach Sweeney still calling you kiddo?"

"Probably," she said. "He calls everybody that. Even his girlfriend."

Uh-oh. "Girlfriend?"

"Yeah, she came to the last lesson. Her name's Roma and she's a vet. Isn't that cool? Don't you just love her name? She lives in Minnesota and has this really neat haircut. She said my hair might look good with that kind of a cut, too."

I relaxed. Crisis averted; the crush was officially over. Bless Roma, whoever she was. "What kind of a cut is it?"

Jenna talked on, and we walked down the trail, our feet in step, our hands and hearts together.

On Saturday morning I dropped the kids off at Marina's, whereupon she interrogated me with the ruthless efficiency of a four-time mother.

"Vhat," she said in a horrible German accent, "are you doing about Amy Yaycobson?"

"Not enough."

She nodded as if she'd expected my answer. "Und Kelly Engel?"

I jingled my car keys. "Same thing."

"I see." She tapped her index finger against her front teeth. "Are Amy's death and Kelly's drowning connected?"

Marina's game suddenly didn't seem at all amusing. "I don't know, okay? I just don't know."

"Hey, Beth, I didn't mean—"

I waved off her apology. "Sorry. There are so many different versions of what happened that I can't figure it out. Does a mother have the better idea of what her eighteen-year-old daughter is doing, or does the daughter's friends? Is a police report the best answer to what happened to Amy, or . . ." I sighed.

"Or," Marina said, "should you trust your own instincts?"

"My instincts aren't worth a thin dime," I muttered.

"Hey, hey." Marina grabbed me by the shoulders. "What's with that crappy attitude? I thought I fixed all that."

"You did?"

"Well, sure. It was the day I convinced you to become PTA secretary. Every good thing that has happened to you since then is a direct result of that action."

"Really."

She held up her hand and starting holding up fingers. "Proof point number one. You haven't called and asked me what you should cook for dinner in months. Number two, last fall you stood up to that horrible Marcia and fired her. Number three, you've helped bring not one, but two, killers to justice."

I waited, but it seemed she was done. "All this is because you browbeat me into being PTA secretary?" The connection seemed tenuous, at best.

"Well, sure. Way down deep inside you've craved a position of authority. Now that you're on the PTA board, you're becoming the person you were always supposed to be. You've learned to talk to people you don't want to, and you've learned to put yourself forward. It's been good for you, see?"

She went on, but my thoughts were jogging in place,

back at where she'd said I'd learned to talk to people I didn't want to.

It wasn't true, of course. If I had, I'd have confronted Gus long ago and found a way to a reconciliation. I would have put my foot down with Auntie May, and I would have had a long, firm chat with Claudia Wolff.

No, I still had a definite tendency to retreat from confrontation. Bad Beth, who shied away from the hard things in life. Bad Beth, setting a poor example for her children.

As Marina kept finding more positive outcomes of my secretarial role—which apparently included helping Debra O'Conner become human, firing Paoze's ambition to write the Great American Novel, and my new recipe for macaroni and cheese—I realized there was someone I did want to talk to.

"No confrontation required," I murmured.

Marina paused in the middle of trying to include Oliver's story-writing ability as a part of the argument proving how much being PTA secretary had improved my life. "What's that?"

"Nothing," I said. "And it's past time for me to get going." I called out a good-bye to the kids. Lame "See ya's," came back from the family room. I collected my purse and headed for the back door.

"Hey, Beth? There's one little thing left for you to work on improving."

Just one? That was good to know.

"Quit with the being afraid thing, okay? It's a waste of time, you know."

I tried to lift one eyebrow. Failed. "Am I your project today?"

"This day and all days." She grinned. "Forever and ever. Aren't you lucky?"

I stuck my tongue out at her and left, shutting the door with a bang.

Due to a young girl and her father waiting outside the front door, I opened the bookstore ten minutes early.

Lois shook her head and watched as the child flew past on her way to the picture book section. "I can't believe you did that. Time on the sign says we open at ten o'clock. This is like breaking a promise."

"If we'd made that kid wait ten minutes, she'd have convinced her dad to drive to the mall and gone to the toy store instead."

"Huh." She looked at me approvingly. "And here I thought you were being a pushover."

I wasn't about to tell her that it had been the beseeching look in the large brown eyes that had convinced me to open the deadbolt. The businesslike reason had come to me just in time.

Paoze poked his head around an endcap of middle grade books featuring the latest big new thing—mermaid vampires. "The water is now hot. Mrs. Kennedy, would you care for tea?"

"Hello? Am I invisible today?" Lois put her fists on her hips. "Don't I get an offer?"

"Thanks, Paoze," I said. "But I have some errands to run. That's assuming you two can manage to work together without someone having to call law enforcement."

"Hey, we're the best of friends." Lois stepped next to Paoze. She slung her arm around his shoulders and clunked her head against his. "Right, kid? Butch and Sundance. Holmes and Watson. Batman and Robin."

"Robert Parker and Harry Longabaugh," Paoze said, "were thieves. I do not wish to be associated with the Sundance Kid."

"Fine," Lois snapped, pulling her arm away. "You can be Bert and I'll be Ernie."

"I prefer to be Laurel," Paoze said.

"Meaning I'm Hardy?" Lois's voice went up. "Are you calling me fat?"

"You can be Eddie, if you wish."

"Who's Eddie?"

Paoze turned away from her and toward me. Dropped his eyelid—the one out of sight of Lois—in a slow wink. "Eddie is the partner of Vince." He looked at her askance. "You have not heard of them? I thought everyone knows."

She tipped her head to one side. "Those names are kind of familiar. Are they guys from some TV show?"

"It is very popular with young people," he said. "Eddie is a woman, of course. Vince is her partner. Together they solve many crimes."

Lois nodded. "Okay, I think I've heard of it. Takes place in California, doesn't it?"

He let her have that one. "They are based in Los Angeles, yes, but they travel all over the world. The interesting thing about this partnership is that Vince is much younger than Edwina. Eddie."

"Yeah? Sounds like a great show."

"Vince and Eddie work for a shadowy organization of which we know little. When they are undercover many people think she's his mother, which they use to their advantage. Older women are often underestimated, and mothers even more so, especially by men. They use this knowledge to entrap many criminals. In one episode, she pretends to be in the hospital on her deathbed while Vince finds proof that medications are being stolen by a group including a doctor, an administrator, and a janitor. In another episode, Vince pretends to be lost in the Florida Everglades, which enables Eddie to infiltrate a human trafficking ring."

Lois kept nodding until he started talking about an episode that had Eddie and Vince hang gliding in North Dakota. He really should have known better.

"Wait a minute," Lois said. "Hang gliding? In North Dakota? There's no Eddie, is there? And there's no Vince. You fooled me. You actually fooled me. I can't believe it!"

Her howl of outrage was a thing of beauty. Paoze had, at last, suckered her.

I walked out, grinning broadly.

This time I barely heard the electronic "ding" as I walked into Faye's Flowers. The shop, already crowded with plants and greeting cards and adorable ceramic objects that would be horrendous to dust, was so packed with people that my claustrophobia kicked into high gear.

I stood a moment, looking at the pine ceiling, breathing in the eucalyptus scent, willing my panic to ebb, and slowly realized that the mass of humanity in the shop was really only three women, that they were shopping together, and that they were on their way out the door, purchases in hand.

They passed me by, chatting as they went. "My sister is going to just fall in love with this frog." "These soaps smell divine." "We'll have to remember to come back at Christmas."

I waited until the door closed, then moved forward through the store.

Do not be distracted by that shelf of gardening books. Do not allow yourself more than a glance at the scented candles. Do not stop, do not even slow down at the greeting card rack.

I reached the counter without picking up a single item—victory!— but Faye was nowhere to be seen. The counter was cluttered with point of sale items ranging from pens with daisies popping out their tops to appointment calendars, I averted my gaze from a selection of miniature picture frames. "Hello? Faye?"

Her voice came from somewhere in the back. "Be right with you."

While I waited, I kept my hands in my pockets and my eyes focused on the view out the window. Which wasn't very inspiring since it looked directly on to the beige vinyl siding of the building next door, but being bored was distinctly better than being lured into purchasing things I didn't need and couldn't really afford.

Faye bustled in. "Sorry about the wait. How can I—oh."

"Hi." Smiling, I held out my hand. "Beth Kennedy. I was in the other day."

"I remember." She used the quick "I suppose shaking your hand is required, but I'd really rather not touch you" grip. "You were asking about Kelly Engel."

"Yes. But—"

"So what is it today?" Faye put her hands on the counter and leaned forward. She was using all six feet of her height to intimidate, and the technique was working well. "A bouquet of carnations along with ferns, baby's breath, and what I really thought about Kelly?"

I made an open-palmed gesture, inviting her opinion.

"That girl," she said tightly, "was a hoity-toity little you-know-what who thought she was better than everybody else."

Her venom rushed out and hit me with the force of anger held in too long.

"You should have seen how the town turned out for her funeral. All the tears and the sobbing and the wailing." Faye rolled her eyes. "What a crock. Most of the people didn't know her and most of the ones who did had been talking behind her back the week before."

She stopped, and looked at her hands. She made fists, then released them.

"Talking about what?" I asked.

"Oh, all the horrible things girls talk about at that age." She shook her head, leaving her high school years behind. "How she deserved being dumped by her boyfriend, how she didn't deserve valedictorian, how she wasn't that pretty, not really, and why couldn't the boys see that?"

All very interesting, but not surprising. I remembered my high school years too well, sometimes. "I was wondering about the slumber party. Were you there?"

"Oh, for crying out loud." She tossed her head back, exposing her slender neck, then brought her head forward so fast that her hair fell in front of her eyes. She shoved at it roughly. "How many times am I going to be asked about that stupid party? Yes, I was there. No, I never left. No, I never saw anyone else leave. Are you satisfied, Miss Nosey Pants?"

Nosey Pants? I briefly wondered if I'd missed a new children's cartoon. Because thinking about cartoons was preferable by far to dealing with the emotions that were rolling over me with enough speed to pull me down. The ship is in danger, Cap'n! What should we do? Steady yourselves, men. This could be a rough ride.

Faye made shooing motions at me. "Now go away and tell Mrs. Engel that her daughter's death was an accident. Axe. Ih. Dent." She enunciated crisply and cleanly. "There's no mystery to any of it, okay?" Her gaze skittered over the top of me.

"That wasn't," I said, "what I was wondering about.

What I'm curious about is who else was at the slumber party."

Her face went quiet for an instant, then started up again. "Who else? You want to know who else?" Her voice went loud. "What I want to know, is what business is it of yours?"

Large parts of me wanted to flee the scene, but a growing, glowing, and heretofore unknown portion of me was ready to face up to the famed Lowery anger. Let her rant and rave, I could take it. Let her smite me with her words, I would not fall back from the blow.

I stood tall. Which put the top of my head at least six inches below hers, but if I tipped my chin up I could look her full in the face without hurting my neck too badly.

"Maude Hoffman made it my business," I said evenly. "Barb Engel made it my business. Why, after all this time, are you still so angry? Why do you still care so much?"

"Because you're wasting my time!" She slapped the countertop, sending a slap of piercing sound straight into my ears. "And because you're still here. Why are you still in my store? Get out!" She charged around the end of the counter, arms pumping, blond hair flying. "If I have to tell you one more time, I'm calling the cops."

She stood in front of me and crossed her arms, an Amazon handing down a command. "I'll give you until the count of three to get going."

If she called the Rynwood Police Department and Gus came over, I'd probably get tossed in jail. If Officer Sean caught the call, I might get off with a disappointed look. Which was a hard thing to take from someone half my age. Either way, I'd be removed from the premises without getting any answers.

"Thank you for your assistance," I said politely, and

threaded my way through the retail maze to the front door, thinking furiously all the way.

Because there was one other thing I knew. It wasn't a fact, but it was real enough, and it was learned thanks to years of motherhood, PTA meetings, bookstore owner-ship, and forty-one years of living among human beings.

Faye was lying.

When I walked into the bookstore, Lois looked at me and frowned. "What's the matter?"

"Nothing." I made a beeline for the back of the store, doing my best to send off "Leave me alone" signals.

"Don't believe you." Lois dogged my footsteps, fol-lowed me into my office, and shut the door behind us. "You're white as the skin on my legs in April. What's wrong? And don't you dare tell me nothing."

I sat in my chair. Stared at my computer. Saw a blank screen. Didn't care.

"Um," Lois said. "Beth, are you okay?"

Her soft voice of concern almost undid me. Maybe I could keep a stiff upper lip against anger, and maybe I could turn my cheek away from a personal attack, but how could I keep from responding to kindness? And if I reacted to her kindness, a reaction to Faye's hatred would come right after, and I didn't have time for that.

"I have an idea," Lois said briskly. "Why don't you go out for a walk? Clear your head of whatever fuzziness is in there. We need you to be bright-eyed and bushy-tailed and right now you're dull-eyed, slack-jawed, and near to drooling."

I swiped at my mouth with the back of my wrist. Dry. Whew.

"A walk will be perfect." Lois tugged at my hand. "Go

to that park you're always talking about. Get some fresh air, and don't come back until you've walked off those cookies." She squinted. "Of course, since it's already ten thirty, there probably aren't enough hours in the day for that. But you could get a good start on one of them, yes?"

She shoved my purse at me and I clutched it to my chest. "Lois," I said, then stopped. What could I say next? That a few harsh words from someone I barely knew were making my hands shake? Or worse than that; I'd almost drowned two nights ago and had been saved by a ghost I didn't believe in?

"Go." She gave me a gentle shove. "No coming back until you can put together a complete sentence."

Since there was no possible way I could do that, I left.

Outside, the light breeze that had followed me to Faye's and back had grown into a stiff wind. I'd been afraid of wind for years thanks to a legendary storm in my childhood, complete with hail and falling trees. Today, though, the gust that blew into my face was invigorating me. Intrepid Beth, going out for a walk in weather that would keep most people inside.

I drove home and ran into the house for a jacket. Spot looked up from his dog-hair-covered dog bed.

"Oh, bugger." I'd promised Evan I'd take Spot with me whenever I went out alone.

It was broad daylight. What could possibly happen?

Most likely nothing.

But I'd promised.

If I took Spot, though, I'd have to bring him back home, and there was a To Do list at the store that needed some serious crossings-off. Taking even this much time away was an indulgence. If I had to bring Spot back, I'd get that much less done.

But I'd promised.

Muttering small annoying thoughts about men, I grabbed the leash from the hook in the laundry room. "Come on, boy. Let's go for a walk."

Ten minutes later, we were deep in the park. Dabs of light filtered down through the leaves, dappling Spot with spots of sunlight. "You're the oddest looking leopard ever," I told him.

His tongue hung half out of his mouth and he gave me a doggy grin. Clearly, he was agreeing with me.

"Yep," I said. "For a leopard, you make a pretty good-looking dog. And for a—" A large wasp buzzed close to my face. I swatted it away. "Be a good wasp and go home, okay? I'm sure it's not far and . . . oh."

Half a dozen yards in front of me, in the middle of the trail, lay the scattered bits of a fallen wasp nest. Around the light gray papery chunks buzzed hundreds of homeless insects.

I stopped dead and pulled Spot close to my side. If we didn't advance on their angry sorrow, we'd be fine. If we backed away from the complex remnants that had once been a community, we wouldn't be targeted.

Slowly, oh so slowly, I edged backward, quickly learning that Spot didn't like moving that way. He whined, and I looked sharp at the circling wasps. Did they hear? Could they? Hadn't I read that insects didn't really hear? Or was it that they heard differently? If they did, would they interpret Spot's whine as a threat and zoom after us?

"Come on, boy." I started to spin around, giving the wasps one last glance . . . and the world stopped.

I stood still, one thought and one thought only running around in my head.

Could it be?

Was it possible?

I stared at the nest, thinking, wanting to know the answer, yet not wanting to know. Unfortunately, there was only one way to find out.

"Let's go, Spot."

Chapter 16

The grass on Amy's lawn was past knee high. If it didn't get cut soon, the city would be sending a polite yet firm "mow your lawn soon or you'll get fined" letter.

A fleeting thought to mow it myself wormed its silly way into my brain and I shook my head to send it back out again. No. Not my responsibility. Not even close.

Spot and I plunged into the green mass. We waded up the drive, around the side of the house, and into the backyard.

Here, where overgrown bushes shaded much of the grass, the lawn looked not so much abandoned as merely unkempt. Which was a good thing, because I needed to take a close look at . . . well, at all of it.

Spot and I stood in the middle of the yard. I turned all the way around, trying to remember if I'd ever heard the details. All I knew was that she'd been found here with an EpiPen and a can of bee killer.

Spot bumped his head up against me and I rested my palm on the soft fur over his eyes. "We'll do a grid pattern," I said. "Start over there"—I pointed to the right—"go to the opposite side of the yard, then come back across. If we don't find anything, we'll start there"—I nodded at the far back of the yard—"and work back and forth toward the house. See? That way we'll cover everything at least twice."

The dog seemed as interested in a leaf tumbling across the grass as in anything I'd said.

"You could at least pretend to listen," I muttered.

We started in the lilac bushes next to Thurman and Lillian's house. Their windows were shut and the shades down. I hoped Thurman was doing well and that they were off on an adventure somewhere.

I studied the ground. Leaves, twigs, dried-up pieces of flowers, and nothing else. The over-warm weather had pushed the lilacs to bloom early and their light scent was almost gone.

"We'll start here," I told Spot. "Ready, set, go."

Every few steps I glanced up and re-aimed myself at the garage. Walking, head down, I saw grass, grass, more grass, then the fading white paint of the garage.

Sidestepping two feet, I called, "About face!" I spun in place, moving the leash from one hand to the other. "Forward march!"

Back across the yard we went, marching into the lilacs, looking hard, finding nothing, then back to the garage. Back and forth, going deeper into the dark, overgrown backyard, bushes closing in from all sides. Amy had died in here, it was right here that she'd gasped her last breath, right here. . . .

Suddenly, Spot's warm and panting presence was a great comfort. I went down on my knees and hugged him tight, then pulled back and looked into his face. His big brown eyes gazed into mine, then he lunged at my cheek with his wet tongue. Smiling, I wiped my face and gave him another hug. "I love you, too."

Then I stood up and started walking again.

Back and forth, back and forth, searching for something, searching for anything, finding nothing.

Back and forth.

Back and forth.

It was on approximately the forty-second trek across the yard, which was about fifteen minutes into the sinking feeling that this was a complete waste of time and that I should have gone back to the store long ago, that I looked at the largest bush, a thick thorny mass whose branches grew low to the ground. "It's going to be in there, isn't it?"

Spot looked up at me and didn't say anything.

"Of course it will be," I said, sighing. If forty-one years of life on planet Earth had taught me anything, it was that answers weren't usually found by seeking the easy way out. Which was too bad, really, because it sure would be nice, at least once in a while, to learn something without great pain and agony.

I put my arms over my head and plunged into the darkness.

Sharp scraping of skin, tuggings at hair and clothes, a sudden black panic thanks to a long-ago TV nature show about snakes living in trees, pushing branches back over my head, fighting through, on my knees, looking down, looking, looking . . . and there it was. What I'd hoped to find. What I'd wanted to find.

But now that I'd found the evidence, I realized that I hadn't really wanted to find it at all.

The entire weekend I thought about what I'd seen. Throughout dinner with Evan, throughout the romantic happy-ending movie colored warm by a lush score, and throughout our hand-in-hand walk in the warm evening,

I kept thinking about Amy. Amy and her killer. Because I now knew, without a single doubt, that she had been murdered. The question was, what did I do with the knowledge?

The obvious answer was to go to the police. But the local police were satisfied that Amy's death had been accidental.

And who else could I talk to? I knew a deputy with the sheriff's department, but she'd defer to local jurisdiction for something like this. "This happened in Rynwood?" she'd ask. "Then I'm sorry, but you need to talk with your own police department. Have a nice day and don't hesitate to call if you need anything."

"Beth?" Evan pushed back a strand of my hair. "Are you feeling okay?"

"Mmm." No, I wasn't. I was heartsick that Amy had been murdered, and conflicted about my next course of action. Talking to Sean would be easy, but it wouldn't create the results Amy deserved. Talking to Gus would be harder than telling my daughter that she couldn't go to the mall with her friends until she was older. Once upon a time he'd understood. Once upon a time he'd believed in my instincts. And listened.

"What do you say we head back home?" Evan asked, swinging my hand. "I have a nice bottle of wine just waiting to be uncorked."

"Mmm."

So all I had to do was get Gus to listen. Of course, the last time I saw Gus, he'd as good as thrown me out of his office and told me to never come back, not in a million years. Or words to that effect.

"A nice Malbec," Evan said. "And I found a new brand of organic dark chocolate to try. How does that sound?"

"Um . . . nice."

It would be appalling to face the man who used to be my friend. It would make my stomach hurt and tangle up my tongue so that my words would come out silly or stupid, or both.

So easy to let it go. So easy to disregard what I'd found. So easy to pretend that it didn't matter.

But it did. Amy had mattered, and her death should be—even in my head I hesitated to say avenged; melodrama was more Marina's style than mine—should be shown for what it was. Murder couldn't be swept under the rug. If you tried, it would sit and fester and grow until it filled the room, the house, the whole world.

So I had to talk to Gus.

I had to try.

The next morning I prepared for church with a trepidation I hadn't felt since I'd been selected to sing a solo in junior choir. With even a little bit of luck, my upcoming talk with Gus would turn out better than my singing had.

Choosing to talk to Gus at church was, of course, a seriously weenielike decision. I'd wait until after the service when he had coffee in his hand and his wife at his side. The social programming of generations would insist that he answer my questions politely. Perfect.

The plan should have cheered me, but it didn't. The drive though the morning sunshine should have perked me up, but that didn't help, either. And when Gus didn't show up, my spirits drooped even further.

"No Gus?" I asked the choir director.

Kay shrugged and shook her head. "Scale of C please," she said, and raised her arms.

Milling around in the lounge afterward, I tried to find anyone who knew anything about Gus's whereabouts.

"Nope, haven't heard." "Sorry." "No, and I haven't seen Winnie lately, either."

It was true; I hadn't seen either Gus or Winnie at church . . . well, since Gus and I had fallen out.

"What's the matter, Beth?" The gentleman I'd asked was frowning. "Have you heard something about the Eiseleys?"

I hadn't heard a thing. Didn't know anything, didn't want to know anything, especially if it had to do with me being the reason Gus and Winnie had left the church.

No. It couldn't be. I was taking my tiff with Gus much too seriously. Families didn't leave a church they'd attended for decades because of a minor argument with a fellow church member.

But they did. I'd seen it happen with wretched regularity.

I magicked a smile onto my face, reassuring the man with whom I was talking, but it wasn't doing anything for me. Because now that I couldn't talk to Gus at this congenial location, I'd have to do it tomorrow. On his turf.

Monday morning was so busy that it wasn't until after lunch that I could take time to slip out. Usually I enjoyed walking through downtown, drinking in the sights and smells of Rynwood, waving at the ever present Cindy Irving and complimenting her on the lush landscaping. Today, however, the sun had heated the world past the point of happiness. August temperatures in May? Ick.

I gave Cindy a limp wave and walked in as much shade as I could find. Trees, awnings; I even slowed for a moment in the shadow of a parking meter. Even using all the precautionary measures I could find, my forehead was still damp with sweat when I opened the front door of the police department.

"Oh . . ." I'd expected to be immersed in a bath of air-conditioning, and what I was got instead was a stuffy and slightly warmer version of outside. My face, already hot, flushed a little hotter.

All the windows were open in an unfulfilled attempt to bring in a cross breeze. No wind, no air, nothing but stifling heat that wanted to knock me to my knees. How could anyone work like this? I peered over the edge of the counter. Maybe Sean had fainted and was lying on the floor, near death from heatstroke. Or would it be heat exhaustion? One was worse, but I could never remember which.

"Be right with you." The voice was polite, male, and headed my way. It was also the voice of Gus.

I backed up, putting one hand behind me, looking for the door handle, finding it with my hip. I turned in preparation for a quick exit, but I wasn't quick enough.

"Sorry about the broken air conditioner, and the wait." Gus and his footsteps came into the room. "We're short-staffed today and—oh. Hello, Beth."

The top half of my body turned around, but the bottom half remained pointed in the outward direction. "Um, is Officer Zimmerman around?"

"No."

That was too bad. I'd convinced myself that I could get Sean to listen to me. Now I had no choice. I hated when I didn't have choices. Of course, I didn't always like having choices, either, especially in the grocery store. Was I a horrible mother if I didn't take the time to study the numerous brands of paper towel? Was I neglecting my children if I didn't research the pros and cons of the newest variety of peanut butter? Grocery stores were full of temptation and guilt and wouldn't it be nice if you could just order groceries online?

"Do you have a question?" Gus asked.

"Sean's okay, isn't he?" I glanced at the counter. I hadn't seen him down on the floor, but maybe he was behind the desk where I couldn't see him.

"Vacation. Do you have a question?" Gus asked again. The consonants came out clear and strong. "A real crime to report?"

I searched for something to say. Surely there was a topic the two of us could discuss that would establish some common ground. Get a firm base first, then move on to more troublesome topics. At least that's what the management articles said.

"Didn't see you in church yesterday," I said. "We missed you and Winnie both. How is she these days? I haven't seen her in weeks, it seems."

"Winnie's fine! Leave her out of this."

I blinked. Gus rarely raised his voice, not even when doggedly running after miscreants and ne'er-do-wells. "Um, I'm glad Winnie's doing okay." And what a dumb thing to say that was.

Gus glared at me and I began to take a serious interest in my shoes. Which, now that I looked at them, were in dire need of polishing. It was rarely a good idea to look at your own shoes.

"Since you don't seem to have anything to say," Gus said, "I need to get back to work. Have a good—"

Then it all came blurting out. "I went back to Amy's. I found something. Proof that she was murdered."

"Amy Jacobson's death was an accident."

"How sure are you?" I edged forward, but still kept one hand on the doorknob. "Absolutely positively one hundred percent sure? Sure way deep down inside?"

Gus's shoulders rose and fell. "What, exactly, did you see?"

He was using the patient voice. I'd hated that voice when my brother used it, hated when my former husband used it, and now I was hating it all over again.

"A broken wasp nest."

Gus gave me a look. Not the one I'd been hoping for, the aha-that's-the-missing-piece look, but more a what-is-she-talking-about expression accompanied by a side order of slipping tolerance.

"A wasp's nest," he said.

"And it was broken." I waited for him to arrive at the inevitable conclusion, but he didn't seem to go anywhere. "Don't you see? Someone tossed that nest into Amy's backyard with the intent of having the wasps sting Amy. This proves it was murder."

Gus didn't move. Didn't blink, didn't even breathe, as far as I could tell. "It proves nothing," he said, "except that there's a wasp nest in the yard, much like every other yard in town. Why are you so intent on murder?"

"Because she was so allergic to stings that she would have had any wasp, bee, or hornet's nest removed as soon as it got started."

"New or old nest?"

A question! He'd asked a question! Maybe he was listening to me, maybe he was taking this seriously. "I'm not exactly an expert on wasp nests."

"Me, either. No one here is, if you can believe it." Gus spread out his arms to include the entire building.

"Maybe you could call the university and talk to an entomologist. Get him to come take a look?" I felt around in my purse for my notebook and pulled it out. "I've been taking notes and—"

"This isn't a TV show," Gus said, his voice going loud. "And the answers aren't always what we want them to be. It was an accident."

"And why are you so insistent that it's not murder?" My voice was getting loud, too. "Why can't you see another point of view? Are you always so right that you can't take a second look at your conclusions?"

"You have no right to question this police department."

I was suddenly glad I was gripping the door handle. At least this way I knew which way was up. "I have every right," I said, more quietly. "If I see a wrong, it's my duty to see that it's corrected."

"Beth Kennedy, fighter of evil."

He smiled, but it was more a smirk than a proper smile, and it looked all wrong. Where had the real Gus gone? Who was this unkind stranger who had taken over his body?

"All that is necessary for evil to triumph," I said, quoting somebody or other, "is for good men to do nothing."

"And you're the good man in this case?" Gus asked.

"I'm certainly not the bad one."

"You're implying that I am?"

"I'm trying to get you to do your job."

The words hung in the air between us, dry and bony and ugly. We stared at each other through the invisible letters. I saw a lined and weary face, one that I loved like a brother. What he saw I did not know.

I took a small step forward, hand out. "Gus, I didn't—"

"Yes, you did." His shoulders rearranged themselves inside his uniform, under the Armor Express vest all on-duty officers wore. "You meant every word of it." He nodded. "Thank you for your comments. I'll study the file. If I have any questions, I'll let you know."

He spun around and marched off. Three seconds later, his office door shut. Firmly, but not loudly.

I opened the front door. Cell phones and cordless

handsets had taken away the satisfaction of ending a phone call with a bang, but at least there were still doors to fill the gap.

Slam!

"I knew he wouldn't be any help." All the way back to the bookstore, I had my head down, muttering to myself. "Amy was murdered, I know she was. And so was Kelly." But the proof of that was even more ephemeral than a wasp's nest. Gee, Chief Eiseley, how do I know Kelly was murdered, Chief Eiseley? Because, that's why.

"Faye was lying," I told the sidewalk. "Maybe Barb was right, maybe Faye did kill Kelly. Maybe Amy found out, somehow." The idea took hold and I started to run with it.

"Sure. That makes a lot of sense." I almost stumbled into Cindy Irving, who was backing out of a planter bed. Some atavistic instinct made me dance out of the way of her garden cart. I waved at her absently, and carried on with my monologue.

"Yes, Amy found out. Faye had to keep Amy quiet. Everybody knew about Amy's allergies, so all Faye had to do was find a wasp nest and lure Amy outside."

My words were coming out clipped and my breaths were puffing out in short bursts.

"Amy found out and Faye found out that Amy had found out. . . ."

I slowed from a fast, arm-pumping walk to a slow and lethargic saunter. Because my logic had just fallen apart. How would Faye have known what Amy was doing? More to the point, how would reclusive Amy have known what Faye was doing?

There was something I was missing. A big fat piece of the puzzle wasn't in the box.

"Think, Beth," I told myself. "Think."

"About what?" Al from the antique store was out in front, sweeping the sidewalk clean.

I jerked out of my daze. "Um, about the likelihood of Alice making a calorie-free cookie that tastes just as good as the real ones."

He laughed, shook his head, and kept on sweeping.

"Think," I said, putting one foot in front of the other, working on movement, hoping for momentum, praying for any thought that might help.

But nothing came.

The next few days zoomed past in a blur of final story session editing, signing permission slips for end-of-school field trips, and covering for Lois at the store. "It's my youngest," she'd said on the phone. "You know, the daughter with multiple college degrees and a successful career as a Chicago computer geek? Well, not only hasn't she had time to get married or provide me with a few more grandchildren, but it turns out none of those cooking lessons I gave her stuck in her pointed head. Especially the one about leaving potato salad out in the sun."

"You mean . . . ?"

"Yup. Food poisoning." Lois made a gagging noise. "She'll be better in a couple three days, but right now she needs some TLC."

"She needs her mommy."

"She needs some common sense." Lois snorted. "I'll be back by Friday. If I'm lucky, Thursday."

"You're a good mom, Lois."

"That and a buck might get me a cup of coffee. If I can talk Ruthie into a senior discount, that is."

She'd hung up and I wondered if a grown-up Jenna would ever call me and ask for help. I tried to imagine my tomboy, my don't-make-me-wear-pink daughter picking up the phone and saying, "Mom? Can you come over? I don't feel good."

No, that image didn't work at all. I'd go to her, of course I would, no matter if she lived in Rynwood, in California, or in Siberia. I'd get to her as fast as I could and mop her fevered brow, murmuring terms of endearment that would make her smile despite her illness.

But Jenna hardly ever got sick, and she was starting to realize that I couldn't fix all of her problems. When she grew to adulthood, what would she call me about?

I considered it all week, and by Thursday afternoon, I thought she might call if she had to go to the hospital. I'd just decided that though a sliced thumb wasn't nearly enough to warrant a call to me, a broken leg would be, when the phone rang. Though I was only two feet away, I couldn't make myself pick up the receiver. Only stared at it.

After two rings, Paoze reached across the counter and took up the receiver. "Good afternoon, Children's Bookshelf. How may I help you?"

Feigning unconcern, I straightened a pile of bookmarks.

"Beth Kennedy?" Paoze turned to look at me. "One moment, please."

He leaned forward to pass me the phone over the counter, but I was already there, snatching the receiver out of his hand. I listened for a very short minute. "I'll be right there." I dropped the phone, ran to grab my purse, and shot out the door.

I rushed into Maude's room. Her frail form lay under thick layers of blankets. Auntie May was sitting bedside, stroking her friend's limp hand.

"How is she?" I whispered, kneeling on the floor.

Auntie May shook her head. "The doctor won't say." She sniffed. "They won't tell me anything. Just look at her, though. Just look at her!"

Maude's face was even paler than normal. Her hair, usually brushed into a tidy do, hung on her head in flat strands. In spite of the blankets, her body was quaking with shivers.

"Is she running a fever?"

"What part of 'they won't tell me anything' didn't you hear?" Auntie May whispered. Or as much of a whisper as she could manage.

I reached out to feel Maude's forehead, but Auntie May knocked my hand away. "Don't wake her up," she said. "First time she's slept in two days and now you want to take that away from her?"

Guilt spewed into the air and came down over me like a net, wrapping tight. "Why didn't you call me sooner?"

"Now Miss I'm-So-Busy says she's not really that busy? Sure, with Maudie here close to death you'll make time, but when she needs—"

"Nooo." Maude flung her head to the side.

"There, there." Auntie May patted her hand. "I'm here. Beth's here. She'll tell you all about Kelly." She sent me a look filled with broken glass and razor wire. "Won't she?"

"Well, I . . ." What I had was nothing. Not really. The buckets of speculation didn't count; neither did the tubs of conjecture. My notebook was filling up, but it was filling up with unanswered questions. None of it would comfort Maude.

"Kelly." Maude lifted her head off the pillow, neck cords straining. "Kelly? Are you there?"

The skin on the back of my neck tingled. I listened,

keeping completely still, waiting, trying to hear. But all I heard was my own short breaths and the jangle of Auntie May's bracelets as she comforted her friend.

I closed my eyes, searching deep, but there was no Kelly anywhere near. I swallowed down my relief. It was always a good thing when you were the only one in your own brain.

"Kelly?" Maude struggled to sit up. "I'll find out, I promise. If it's the last thing I do." She looked at me, but showed no sign of recognition. "I won't die until I find out, my Kelly. I won't. . . ." She fell back against the pillow, groaning.

That did it. I reached for the call light and pushed the button firmly.

"Hey, now." Auntie May grabbed at it with her clawlike hands. "What are you doing?"

I held it out of her reach and made sure the red bulb on the console above the bed went on and stayed on. "Maude is sick. She needs help and I'm making sure she gets it."

"Aw, she'll be fine." Auntie May patted Maude's cheek. "See, she's looking better already."

Maude turned her head from side to side, moaning things I couldn't make out. Something about justice, something about murder. It sounded like a bad made-for-TV movie, but maybe those movies were more realistic than I'd given them credit for.

"She needs a nurse," I said.

"Pills." Auntie May made a gagging noise. "All they want to do is give you pills."

"Better than needles," Maude said weakly.

Auntie May shot me a startled glance. "Maudie? Was that you? How are you feeling? Is your fever gone?"

But Maude had descended back to nonsensical

ramblings. A picnic, now, with deviled eggs and ham sandwiches and stale potato chips.

"All right, ladies." Tracy, the nurse's aide, came bustling into the room. "What's the problem here?"

Maude fluttered her eyelashes. "Tracy? Is that you?" she asked in a quavery voice.

"All day and half the night." Tracy stood at the foot of the bed, hands in the pockets of her scrub pants, and surveyed her patient. "Hmm." She flicked a practiced eye over Auntie May and, finally, looked at me. "Beth, can we talk?"

"Well, sure, but don't you . . ." I nodded at Maude.

"I'll tend to her in a minute." She gave Auntie May a hard look. "And after that I'll be taking care of you."

We walked a few steps away from Maude's doorway. Tracy looked over my shoulder. "That woman will drive me batty," she muttered. "Come on in here." Across the hall was a door labeled LINENS. The lock was a keyless entry and the buttons made fast electronic beeps as Tracy entered the code and nodded me inside.

Surrounded by white sheets, white pillowcases, and white towels, Tracy gave a deep sigh. "I started to tell you this once before and I never got to finish."

Which was what I preferred, really, because there were things I didn't want to know, but she seemed intent on talking.

"It's about Maude." Tracy leaned back against the concrete block wall.

"You're not going to tell me anything that will violate the privacy laws, are you? I wouldn't want to put you at risk."

She nodded. "Okay. Thanks. But what I'm going to say doesn't have anything to do with privacy. It's common knowledge and I'm surprised you don't know already."

There was an awful lot I didn't know, including the temperature of the sun's surface, the size of a hockey puck, and what we were going to have for dinner that night. "Don't know what?"

She shoved her hands in the pockets of her scrub top. "She was in the papers and everything, but it was so long ago that maybe it was before you moved here. See, for years Maude was in the—"

Her beeper went off, loud in the small space. "Hang on, okay?" She unclipped the beeper and scrolled through the numbers. "Rats. I have to go." The beeper went back onto her pocket. "I get off at three. Could you stay until then? I'd really like to talk to you."

I glanced at my watch. Two forty-five. "Sure."

She hurried off to whoever it was that needed tending to, and I went back to Maude's room.

"What did Tracy want?" Auntie May demanded.

Maude's eyes were shut and her breathing was even. I gestured toward the sleeping woman and spoke quietly. "Tracy was called away. I don't know what she wanted."

Auntie May grunted. "That girl likes to talk more than she should. Just like her mother. Grandmother, too. Yep, Eunice was a corker for talking. Told her once that she'd talk to a post if it had ears. So I painted ears on a fencepost and introduced her to it." Auntie May snorted out a laugh. "Eunice didn't find it funny. No sense of humor, that one."

I picked up my purse, made my good-byes, and went to the nurse's station.

"Tracy's working an extra half shift," said a harried man with a clipboard in one hand and three-ring binder in the other. "Someone called in sick."

"Is there any chance I could talk to her for a minute?"

"She'll have a break in two hours."

I couldn't possibly wait around that long. However . . . "Could I borrow a phone book, please?"

He thumped it on the counter. "Just leave it there when you're done," he said, and strode down the hall.

I flipped pages until I came to Tracy's last name, but there was no Tracy. And no entry for her husband. Frustrated, I flipped the book shut. Tracy must be one of those people who'd canceled her landline. How was I going to call her at home tonight if I didn't know her phone number?

I walked the halls for a few minutes, looking for Tracy. A CNA finally took pity on me and told me that Tracy was giving Mrs. Johnson a bath. "She'll be half an hour, at least," she said cheerfully.

After thanking her, I started my walk back to the store.

Maude wasn't going to rest peacefully until I found out once and for all what happened to Kelly. Plus, I wouldn't rest easy until I satisfied myself that I'd done all I could.

Ever since that night at the lake I hadn't been sleeping well, I wasn't able to concentrate for beans, and now I was sick with guilt over Maude.

Think, Beth. Think.

If only I could.

That night I made a quick dinner of boneless chicken breasts, bread from the bakery, and coleslaw from the grocery store. We went to the park with Spot and met up with Pete for another lesson in disc golf.

"They're catching on fast," Pete said, and got big grins from both kids.

The bike ride home was punctuated by bursts of laughter and short stretches of silence. A happy way to travel, and one that made me want to sing made-up songs of spontaneous joy. If I did, however, Jenna would roll her eyes and push ahead, which would have spoiled the mood, so I kept my music inside. *It doesn't get,* I sang silently, *any better than this. I will bet, that this is bliss.*

The three of us held together as a group throughout the final evening chores of emptying the dishwasher, packing up backpacks for the long Memorial Day weekend with their father, getting into pajamas, and brushing teeth.

When I knocked on Jenna's bedroom door, she was sitting up in bed, reading *The Lightning Thief*.

"How many times have you read that?" I asked.

"Not enough." She turned the page and didn't look up.

"Another half hour," I said, "then it's lights out."

"Mmm-hmm."

I went into Oliver's room for his bedtime routine of a lullaby and a kiss good night.

"Mom?" Oliver held his stuffed dog, Big Nose, up in the air.

"What, honey?"

"I like Mr. Peterson. He's nice."

"Yes, he is."

"Sometimes he makes me laugh so much my face hurts."

I smiled. Pete had the gift of relating to children as if they were real people and not a slightly different species that just might turn into something human if everyone was very, very lucky. He also had a gift of making people see the funny side of almost everything.

"Do you think I could make people laugh like that?" Oliver asked.

"You"—I kissed him on the forehead—"can do anything you put your mind to."

"Like getting good grades even in math?"

"Yup."

"And like writing Mrs. Hoffman's story? Parts of it are really sad, but maybe I can make it turn out good."

For a moment I couldn't speak.

Oh, Maude. I want to write you a happier story. I want you to have danced at Kelly's wedding, I want you to be babysitting her children, I want you to be surrounded by love and laughter, I want you to go gently into the good night that waits for us all.

The lullaby of choice that week was "All Through the Night." I sang it through, twice, then kissed him again. "Sleep tight, Ollster."

"No bedbugs, Mommy," he said, already half asleep.

I tapped on Jenna's door and poked my head in. "Twenty minutes."

"Mmm."

Smiling, I went downstairs. If staying up too late reading was the worst habit she picked up from me, maybe I wasn't doing such a rotten job as a mother.

But the time I reached the first floor, my smile had dropped away. Maybe I was doing okay as Mom this week, but I'd been neglecting my store in favor of looking for answers to Kelly's and Amy's deaths, and that wasn't a good way to run a business.

With the lullaby still humming in my head, I went into the study and hunted through my purse. An empty sandwich bag, a small toy truck, and a pen that didn't work, but I couldn't find what I wanted.

I plopped the purse down on the computer chair and looked around. Where, oh where, had it gone? Could I have slid it into one of the bookcases?

Not in with the thrillers, not with the mysteries, not with the historicals, not with the parenting books or the biographies or anywhere else in the study.

In the next half hour, I ransacked the kitchen, the laundry room, the family room, the living room, the dining room, and my bedroom. I went out to the garage and looked there. I climbed into the car, looked under seats and in the trunk.

Nothing, nothing, nothing. I couldn't find it and panic was setting in. The notebook. The spiral notebook with all my Amy notes and my Kelly notes and my lists and thoughts and questions and finger-pointing.

It was gone.

Chapter 17

The next morning I woke up with a cat on my stomach. For a moment I lay there, sleepily petting George's black fur, happy to know my children were just down the hall, content with my life, and ...

"Oh, no! It's gone!"

I pushed a protesting feline aside and jumped out of bed. Finding that notebook was priority one. Well, two, after I got the kids up, dressed, fed, and off to school, but it was a two that was very close to a one.

Morning records were broken as I rushed about like a mad thing, assembling lunches and pouring orange juice. Once I caught the kids exchanging surprised looks. Jenna shrugged and went back to her cereal. Oliver frowned, then blew bubbles in his juice until I told him to stop.

"Are we late?" he asked.

"No, honey. I just need to get to the store as soon as I can."

"Why?"

Because your mother is an addle-brained idiot who can't be trusted to keep track of something as simple as a notebook. "I have work to do, that's all."

"Oh." He drank some juice. "Dad says he's going to

take us to a parade this weekend. Why is the parade on Monday? I thought parades were on Saturdays."

I looked up from the kitchen counter where I was slapping strawberry jam onto peanut buttered bread. Now, he wants an explanation of Memorial Day? I didn't have time to do this, but I didn't want to miss a teaching opportunity, either. "Well . . ."

"Because Monday is the holiday," Jenna said. "Not Saturday."

"Oh." More juice went down. "Okay."

Sometimes the easy explanation really is the best answer. Why did I make things so hard for myself? I flashed Jenna a grateful smile, but she was busy drinking the milk out of her cereal bowl.

Fifteen minutes later, I waved good-bye to my beloved children. Ten minutes after that, I was in my office, searching for the notebook.

All night long I'd tamped down my panic by telling myself I'd left the dratted thing at the store. It was in my office. Of course it was. In a drawer or on the desk or on a chair or on the floor. No need to worry. Or, no need to worry that much. It'll be fine. It'll all work out.

But things weren't working out. The notebook wasn't in my office and there was no way I would have left it up front.

Knowing that, however, didn't stop me from inspecting the books behind the counter to see if the notebook had gotten mixed up with them. Didn't stop me from shoving aside the wrapping paper to see if it had wandered back behind.

"What are you doing?"

I heard Lois, but since I was on my hands and knees, head tilted at a funny angle, my right eyeball peering at the small gap between the counter and the wall, I couldn't see her. "Looking for something. How's your daughter?"

"Into applesauce and chicken soup,"

"That's good," I said absently. No notebook down there. No room, really, but you never knew. "Beyond soda crackers?" I stood up, brushed off my hands, and looked around. If it wasn't at home, wasn't in the car, and wasn't here, where was it?

"What on earth is so important that you're getting all dirty first thing in the morning?"

"Oh . . . nothing."

Lois made a noise, and I knew she was going to launch into a diatribe about my penchant for understatement.

"Look," I said, "there's something I need to do. I'll be right back." Without waiting for a response, I hurried out the front door.

Half walking, half trotting, I covered the short blocks to Sunny Rest with the hope that I'd dropped it underneath Maude's bed. Or maybe it fell out of my purse in that linen closet and slipped between the pillowcases and washcloths.

I tried not to think about my future if the notebook had been found by someone with an average sense of curiosity. Who could resist reading a notebook filled with handwriting? Who wouldn't want to read someone else's private thoughts?

By the time I reached Sunny Rest, I'd worked myself up to a near panic.

"Hi, Beth." The receptionist smiled at me. "Are you here to see Maude? She's in the solarium."

"She . . . is?" I blinked. "So she's feeling a little better. That's good."

The receptionist's smile turned into a vague frown, but I didn't have time to discuss Maude, not right now. "Say, has anyone turned in a spiral notebook? About so by so." With my hands I made a rectangle about four inches on one side, six inches on the other.

"Let me look." Her head disappeared while she ducked behind the counter. "No, sorry, I don't see anything. Did you lose it . . . ?"

But I was already pushing open the door, headed back outside.

Where could it be? Had it even been in my purse that day I was at Sunny Rest?

I thumped my forehead with the heels of my hands. What was the point of having a brain if you couldn't get it to work when you needed it? What was the point of trying to learn the names of all the U.S. Supreme Court justices if you couldn't find the one thing that might help you track down a killer? What was I going to forget next, my children's middle names?

"Jenna Elizabeth, Oliver Richard," I said out loud. "Jenna Elizabeth, Oliver Richard." After repeating their names a few more times, the clutch of anxiety that had seized me started to release its hot grip.

There. I wasn't losing it, not completely. And as long as I could find that notebook, everything would work out just fine.

But then the very real possibility of *not* finding it pushed me along the sidewalk a little faster. I looked under trees and under shrubs. I looked under the edge of fence lines and around petunias planted at the curb. I peered under cars.

Don't panic. It's around here somewhere. All you have to do is find it. You're good at finding things, remember? And you're good at figuring things out. Link up Kelly and Amy in the right way and you'll find the truth. You're close, so close.

My pep talk worked fine until my stupid imagination chose to play a video of Claudia and Tina out for a power walk yesterday evening. "What's that?" Tina would have pointed.

"Looks like a notebook." Claudia stooped to pick it up. "One of those cheap spiral jobs no one but college kids uses."

"Maybe there's a name inside?" Tina asked, standing back. Touching anything that had touched the ground had her running for antibacterial soap and warm water.

"Just like in grade school?" Claudia asked. "No one does that anymore. If you lost it it'd be an invitation to invade your privacy, and . . . well, would you look at that. Beth Kennedy." She laughed loud and long. "Such a surprise. Wonder what's in this little gem?"

"Shouldn't we return it?" Tina edged closer.

"Of course we should. And we will." Claudia grinned. "Right after we read it." She flipped through the first few pages. "Geez, what kind of chicken scratches are these?" She thrust the notebook at Tina. "Can you read this?"

Tina kept her hands behind her back, but peered at the open page. "Well, sure. She writes like my sister. Kinda."

"What's that say?" Claudia pointed to a titled list. "There, at the top."

"Um . . ." Tina squinted, opened her eyes wide, then squinted again. "It says potential suspects in Amy Jacobson's death."

I shook away the image. That hadn't happened. It couldn't happen. Wouldn't happen. Claudia would not read that list and see her name sitting high at number six. She would not read the other names, and she would not read my ramblings that included far more than questions about Amy and Kelly. If Claudia got her hands on what had turned into a stream of consciousness litany of my deepest thoughts, I'd be the laughingstock of not only the Rynwood PTA, but the whole town of Rynwood. And, thanks to e-mail and Facebook, the entire cyberworld would soon be giggling at me.

What idiotic impulse had made me write—in pen!— that the summer after my sisters had forced me to watch *Jaws* at age eight, I'd been afraid to swim in the lake? And I must have been feverish the night I wrote that Claudia Wolff frightened me.

My steps went faster and faster. If Claudia read that, I'd have to resign as PTA secretary. I'd leave the PTA altogether, and I'd close the store. Move the kids to a place where no once had ever heard of Facebook.

I slowed, trying to think if such a place still existed. Slowed a little more when I realized that there probably wasn't a place like that. Not any longer.

"But maybe," I said out loud, "there are places still on dial-up. No one on dial-up would be on Facebook, would they?"

There had to be pockets of dial-up everywhere. We might not have to leave the country. Maybe not even the state.

Cheered, I refocused on the task at hand. Outside a small apartment building a flat piece of cardboard sent my heart racing, but it was only a piece of packaging. I picked it, a candy wrapper, and the cap from a soda bottle up off the ground to toss and looked around for a garbage can. There.

I crossed the street into the official downtown blocks and dumped the litter in. Took two steps away, then went back. I pushed back the garbage can's lid—please, don't let it be full—and, one eye shut, looked inside. "Hello?" I called quietly. "Are you in there?"

My voice echoed around the plastic liner and came back at me. I remembered that the city emptied garbage cans on Monday and Friday mornings. If someone had dumped my notebook in, it was on its way to the landfill and no way was I going to work that hard to find it. Claudia-sponsored embarrassment would fade. Eventually.

"What are you looking for?"

I looked up. "Oh, hi, Alan. Um, it's not that important."

He leaned on his broom. "Do you feel okay? You look a little odd."

No, I wasn't okay. The new scuffs on my shoes, the dirt on my pants, and the scratch on my hand were mere outward manifestations of the mess on the inside. Frustration that I couldn't help Maude, anger that I couldn't manage to keep track of a simple notebook, confusion over the tangles between the past and the present, and always, always, sorrow and longing for those who had died before their time.

Why couldn't I figure this out?

"Beth . . . ?" Alan, concern all over his kindly face, reached out to touch my arm.

I jerked away. "Thanks, Alan. I'm fine. Really, I am." Ignoring his frown, I started walking backward. "Just looking for something, that's all. I'm sure it's here somewhere. Probably dropped it yesterday. . . ." Just outside Alan's store was a planter filled with holly bushes. I pushed the branches aside, looking deep into the dark green thickness.

Nothing.

Nothing in the next planter of daylilies, nothing in the garbage can, nothing under the garbage can.

Where, where, *where?*

"Beth Kennedy, what on earth are you doing?" Flossie stood outside of her grocery store, hands fisted on her hips.

I brushed past her, intent on looking in the flower box attached to the hair salon next door. "Looking for something." Nothing in the red geraniums, nothing in the sweet alyssum, nothing in the ivy dangling over the edge.

"Beth ... ?" Denise hung out the door of the salon. "If it's weeds you want, I have plenty at home."

I gave her a blank look. Weeds? What was she talking about? Maude needed me and I needed to find what I'd so stupidly lost. I blinked at Denise a few times. She was asking that question again; did I feel okay? Why did people keep asking that?

She was still talking when I turned away. There were lots of places left to look. Another whole block of downtown was ahead of me, and I hadn't even touched the alleys and side alleys.

Nothing under the teak benches next to the dentist's office, and nothing tucked into the table of seventy percent off items outside the gift shop.

Where was it?

"Beth, honey? What are you doing?"

I hurried past Ruthie. Nothing behind the newspaper racks outside the pharmacy. It wasn't in the container of dried grasses by the accountant's front door and no one had left it on the window ledge outside the Green Tractor.

Where was it?

No one had put it in the rack of brochures outside the chamber of commerce.

Where?

I pulled at my hair. *Where?!*

"Beth!" Strong hands gripped my upper arms. "What is the matter with you?"

I tried to yank myself free, but he was too strong. "Let me go!"

"Not until you calm down and tell me what's going on."

"Nothing!" I glared up at Evan. "Leave me alone!"

He put his hands on my shoulders. "Beth, you're traipsing all over downtown with dirt all over your face, blood on your hands, the hem of one pant leg torn out, and a rip in the neck of your shirt deep enough to show more cleavage than you see at the Academy Awards. Everyone's looking at you and it's a little embarrassing." He tipped my chin up. "What is going on?"

I jerked my chin away and twisted out of his grasp. "Nothing." I did not like having my chin tipped up against my will and I did not like my shoulders being clamped down upon. With his size and strength advantage he could twist me into a pretzel if he wanted, but I would not go willingly. "I'm fine, why do . . ."

My voice trailed off as I looked down the street. Almost every downtown business owner and half their staff was out on the sidewalk, staring at me. Most had their mouths open.

I looked down at myself. Evan hadn't been exaggerating. Dirt was ground into the knees of my pants in large round splotches. My ragged fingernails looked as if I'd been digging in the garden with my bare hands. Blood streaked my arm and the back of my wrist—a scratch from something, I didn't remember what. And my shirt . . . I hitched it up, hoping my feminine undergarment was now under cover.

"Beth?" Evan's tone was turning harder. "I think I deserve an explanation."

Deep down inside me, down below the ever present

concerns about my children, below the misty grief that was hovering over me, underneath my fears of early onset Alzheimer's because what other reason could there be for imagining the voices of dead people in my head, down in the darkest part of my hidden self, I suddenly realized something very important.

I wasn't in love with Evan.

At all.

If I was really in love, I would have been more considerate of his wishes. If I truly loved him, I wouldn't have kept my investigating to myself. I would have talked about what I was doing and asked for his opinion. I wouldn't have kept a bland smile on my face and said, "Oh, nothing," when he asked what I was thinking about.

And if he truly loved me, he would be taking me into his arms, murmuring things like, "It'll be all right. Don't worry, whatever it is, we'll get through it." He wouldn't be worrying about my appearance and his primary question wouldn't be about himself. No, it would be something like, "How can I help?"

He reached for me, but I backed away.

"Beth." He let his arms drop to his sides. "Let's go inside and get you cleaned up. Then we can talk."

"Hide me away from the prying eyes, you mean?"

"I mean you should get inside and get cleaned up."

He said it with a smile, but even dull-witted me could sense the hardness inside.

And it was a hard truth to realize that I'd been fooling myself—and Evan—for all these months. I'd been so blinded by Evan's good looks, his charm, and the way he didn't have to tally up the month's budget in his head before going out to dinner, that I hadn't stopped to take stock of how I really felt.

I rubbed the back of my hand, thinking.

"Beth," he said. "Let's go inside."

"I don't think so, Evan."

"Don't be ridiculous. You can't go around town looking like that."

He reached out to take my hand, but I took another step backward. He hadn't asked me if I was okay. Sure, he'd asked, "What's the matter with you?" but that wasn't anywhere near the same. And he hadn't asked me if a child-oriented emergency was what had sent me staggering down the street in dishabille. That was more than I could forgive.

"Good-bye, Evan." My voice was calm and even. There wasn't a chance I could keep that up, so I nodded and turned away.

"What are you doing? Beth?"

His voice tugged strong at me. I shook my head and kept walking. Ten feet distant, I stopped. I hadn't said I was sorry.

But, then again, what was there to be sorry about? Besides everything.

I walked away and didn't look back.

Chapter 18

Marina drained the tea mug and bumped it onto my desk. "That's all you said? Good-bye? A perfect moment for an exit line, and you blew it completely. Why did I know that was going to happen? You should have come to me, I would have prepped you with a dozen possibilities."

"Like what? 'Frankly, my dear, I don't give a—'"

She waved off the end of my sentence. "Little pitchers," she said, wagging her index finger at me and nodding at my office doorway. Outside of it, in the small kitchenette, Paoze and Lois were in a competitive conversation about the merits of green tea over black tea, with Paoze taking the firm lead due to his Asian heritage. I knew for a fact that he hated the green stuff, but Lois didn't. I smiled. It was going to be an entertaining summer.

"You're worried about a college student overhearing a quote from a classic movie?" I asked.

"When I waltzed in, and I do mean waltz, dahling." She blew an imaginary smoke ring and tapped the end of her invisible cigarette onto a pile of shipping notices. Considerate person that she was, she picked up the nonexistent ash and brushed it into the wastebasket. "A short minute ago, there were at least three young children perusing the volumes on your lowest shelves."

I pushed my chair back and propped my feet up on an open drawer. It was Friday afternoon before a holiday weekend, and I'd decided not to enter the store from the time I left today until Tuesday morning. The knowledge was giving me a taste of that summer vacation feeling, and I was enjoying the faint flavor. "Neither Lois or Paoze would be back here if anyone was in the store."

Marina switched from Greta Garbo to Cowgirl. It was a new persona and she hadn't gotten it quite right. "Well, whistle me pink and call me honey. Ah didn't know you had such surefire instincts. And if Ah may say one other thang, Ah'd like to say you don't sound real busted up about your bust-up with that pretty boy."

I'd been thinking the same thing. How could so many months of romance end with so little emotion? Right now, I was most concerned about telling Jenna and Oliver. Their father was picking them up straight from school, so when would I tell them they wouldn't be seeing Evan ever again? It wasn't news I wanted to break over the phone; I needed to be there to read their faces and give them the hugs and kisses they'd need.

And what had I been thinking, bringing a man into their lives who wouldn't be there forever? They'd already lost their father being in their daily lives—which wasn't strictly true, since Richard's former job had taken him on the road four days out of five, but still—and now I was yanking Evan away from them.

Last night I'd called him. He came over after the kids had gone to bed and we'd talked and talked, but the end result was still the same.

We'd sat on the couch and he'd held my hands in his large ones. "Beth, please say you'll think this over. I love you. I want to marry you. We can work this out, I know we can."

It had been so tempting to fall into his arms, tempting to let myself be taken care of, tempting to convince myself that this was meant to be. All so very attractive, just like he was. Why didn't I love him? I wanted to; I'd wanted to for months. But I was finally seeing that I didn't love him, and if I didn't now, after this long, why would I ever start?

I sighed. Why had I begun seeing Evan in the first place? Why hadn't I trusted my instincts and stayed away from men until the kids were older, say, in their forties?

"Uh-oh." Marina was back to being Marina. "I know that look. You're feeling guilty about something. Let me guess. Hmm." She lined the tips of her fingers over her eyebrows. "Hmm. I say Beth feels guilty about . . . her children. Yes, that's it!" She held out her hand, palm up. "Prize for the winner, please."

I gave her a bookmark.

"Thank you, thank you." She waved it above her head like a trophy. "Now, don't you feel guilty about ending it with Evan. He wasn't right for you and I'm glad you finally saw the truth of it before I had to show it to you."

I looked at her. "You never did like him, did you?"

Her new bookmark became an airplane. It flew high and then low as she said, "What I didn't like is how you were around him. You weren't yourself, my sweet. You were the person he wanted you to be."

And that, in a nutshell, was why I wasn't going to weep into my pillow that night.

We sat there for a moment, quiet with our own thoughts, until Marina sailed the bookmark into her purse and snapped her fingers. "Say, did you know Richard is going to Italy this fall?"

"Yes, can you believe it? All those years I wanted to go abroad, now he decides to get up and go."

"Did he say who he's going with?"

I frowned. I hadn't once thought about that.

"Aha. I see he didn't. He's going with"—she leaned forward—"with a friend." When my expression didn't change significantly, she added, "You know, a *friend*. A girlfriend. From his new office."

My emotions tumbled around in a tangling whirl. Anger, pain, sorrow ... but once the tumbling slowed, I found the that primary emotion was surprise. And pleasure. Because now I didn't have to suffer any guilt about his long commute.

"So, a good thing, yes?" Marina asked. "Yes. I see it. Now, what were you thinking about back there a minute ago when you got the long face?"

"Actually, I was thinking about relationships. About ..." If I hemmed and hawed for the right amount of time, she might believe I was trying to come up with the right words, not that I was trying to slide out of her question. "About how they can end in such different ways. About Kelly and her boyfriend. Remember? Everybody said they were the perfect couple. Made for each other. And then he dumps her, and she dies."

"Worst ending of all." Marina went away somewhere, so far that I had no idea where she'd gone. Before I could pose a gentle question, she shook her head, tossing a pink scrunchie to the floor and setting her hair loose. "What do you know about him? Kelly's boyfriend, what's-his-name."

"Keith Mathieson."

She made rolling motions with her hands. "More. I know you have more."

"Are you saying I hold back?" She just looked at me. "Okay, okay. He's part owner of an insurance company on the other side of Madison. Lives in Madison, too."

"Married?" Marina asked. "Kids?"

I shook my head. "That's all I know." When I'd called Barb to ask, she was eager enough, but when it came down to facts, she hadn't known much. She'd gone on and on about how he hadn't even had the decency to show up to Kelly's funeral, how the bouquet of four dozen roses had been nice, but why hadn't he at least come to the visitation?

Since the answer to that was easy—fear—I was sure she'd been asking a rhetorical question. Most of the town thought Kelly had killed herself because of Keith; facing the accusing eyes must have seemed an impossibility to an eighteen-year-old.

Poor kid. Who among us would have that kind of moral fiber? Although . . . I closed my eyes for a moment, trying to think of Oliver as Keith. Would I have made Oliver go to his dead girlfriend's funeral? If he'd begged me, tears streaming down his face, would I have relented and let him stay home?

Not a chance.

"This has got to be your shortest list ever." Marina held up an imaginary pad of paper. "The title of this list is, Beth's Minimalist Information About the Boyfriend."

"It's all I have." I'd talked to a few other people about Keith, but he seemed to have dropped out of life in Rynwood altogether. His parents had retired to Florida a few years ago, and his only sibling, a brother, had lived in Colorado since college.

Odd, to think that a family could have been raised in this town and then moved off, no traces left behind. How easy it was to be washed away from a place you'd lived. So easy to be forgotten after you were gone.

"Quit that," Marina said. "You're getting that sad-looking face again and it's just too nice a day. Come on." She jumped out of her chair.

I stayed put. "Where?"

"You know where Keith Mathieson works, don't you?"

"Why?"

She gave a martyred sigh. "For a smart woman, sometimes you can be dumb as a box of rocks."

"Marina, I am not going to barge into that man's office and start asking him questions about Kelly."

"Why not?"

I gaped at her. There were so many answers to that question that they jammed up the speech center of my brain.

"First off," she said, "you've been asking the wrong questions of the wrong people. You should have started with the boyfriend." She shook her head sadly. "Why you didn't get me in on this earlier, I do not know."

I did, but I didn't want to say why. Because it was all wrapped up with Gus. Because I hadn't wanted to push at that pain and Marina would have insisted on helping me clear up whatever it was, and what if even Marina couldn't find the old Gus? Maybe he was gone forever, and I really, really, didn't want to think about that.

"Are you stuck?" Marina grinned and held out her hand. "Because I can help you up out of that chair."

I grabbed hold of her wrist and let her pull me upright. "Maybe I was stuck, just a little."

"That's all right." She thumped me on the back. "What are friends for?"

Unexpected tears blurred my vision. I reached down to open the desk drawer that held my purse and rubbed the wetness away. "Apparently they're for making me do things that I don't want to do."

"Exactly!" Marina stuck her finger in the air. "You make me write thank you notes and I get you out of your chair. Even trade, yes?"

Once again she'd summarized our relationship in twenty-five words or less. "Even trade," I agreed.

"Well, then." She jingled her car keys. "No time like the present. Shall I drive?"

"Let's take two cars."

She lifted her eyebrows, but I got out my own car keys and ignored her look of reproach.

Because I had a plan.

Keith Mathieson's office was in one of those soulless strip malls. Someone had done their best to add character to the space, but no matter how many planters you placed around the doors and no matter how tidily you trimmed the shrubs, a strip mall was a strip mall and there was no disguising the fact.

Marina and I parked out of sight along a side street. As we'd arranged, she stayed put while I got out and scoped out the businesses all in a row. Party store, dollar store, pharmacy, Keith's insurance office, Chinese restaurant.

I walked into the party store, rummaged in a cooler for a couple of sodas, grabbed some chips, and surreptitiously studied the staff. Behind the counter, a thirtysomething manager-type chatted with a kid who must have been eighteen to work in a store like this, even though he didn't look old enough to have taken driver's training.

When I'd almost memorized the brand names of beef jerky hanging on a rack, the teenager went to the back of the store and I went up to the counter.

"This it?" the manager asked, ringing up my purchases, no movement wasted.

I upgraded his status from manager to owner. "All set," I said. "Say"—I pointed out the plate glass window in a very vague direction—"is that Keith Mathieson's car?"

"Piece of crap silver Toyota? Yeah, that's Keith's. Must be twenty years old if it's a day." He asked if I wanted a bag. "Told him five years ago to get something a man wouldn't be embarrassed to be seen driving. A pickup, or an SUV even, but he said he'd drive that Toyota until it couldn't be saved. Rust bucket city, you know? Hey, lady! Don't forget your change!"

I retraced my steps and pointed out Keith's car to Marina.

"Huh," she said. "You'd think an insurance agent would make enough money to buy himself a new car at least every decade. Ready?" She started her car, grinning. "Can't believe you came up with this idea all by yourself."

Marina drove into the lot's first entrance. I took the second entrance, enacting the plan I'd formulated after spending five minutes with Google's satellite imagery. The parking lot was big enough to have a row of parking spaces down the middle, and I'd leapt to the conclusion that a store owner would park in that row. Spaces against the building for customers, farthest spaces for staff, spaces in the middle for owners. And there was Keith's car, smack dab in the middle of the lot.

I stopped my car next to his rear bumper; Marina parked hers next to his front bumper. I turned off the ignition with satisfaction. He'd have to talk to me now.

Two minutes ticked past. Marina leaned out her car window. "Is it five o'clock yet?"

"Almost."

Thirty seconds later, she asked, "Is it five o'clock yet?"

"Patience is a virtue."

"Says you." She turned her car radio to an oldies station, pushed back her seat, and put her feet up on the steering wheel. We sat through "Paperback Writer," "Time for Me to Fly," "Build Me Up Buttercup," and were halfway through "Stairway to Heaven" when the front door of the insurance company opened.

"Is that him?" Marina asked.

"Shhh!"

We watched as a man about my age turned around to lock the door, apparently oblivious to the car situation in front of him. Maybe that wasn't Keith, maybe it was his partner or—

The man tugged the handle on the front door then turned to face us. He stood stock-still for an instant, then headed our way.

"That's him." Marina grinned. "This should be fun."

I watched Keith walk toward us with a fast, stiff-legged gait. He wore his hair just a little longer than any other male insurance agent I'd ever met. His khaki pants, white shirt, and navy blue blazer were so classic that they were almost trendy again.

Fun? I wasn't so sure. Marina, with her inherent longings for excitement in her life, was in her element, watching the oncoming stranger with gleeful anticipation. I was watching him with the stomach-twisting dread of incipient confrontation.

He reached Marina first. "Excuse me, but that's my car you're blocking."

"Keith Mathieson?" She arched an eyebrow.

"Yeah." He looked at her, at me, then back at her. "What do you think you're doing?"

"Ask her." Marina nodded in my direction. "This is all her idea."

Every hair on my arms stood up. Was this what it felt like to be tossed under a bus?

Keith marched over to my car and stood with his arms crossed. "And you are?" he asked, looking down at me.

I'm nobody, who are you? "Beth Kennedy. Remember a while back? I called and asked you about Kelly Engel."

"And?"

His posture didn't indicate a softening of his can't-make-me-talk attitude. How on earth was I going to convince him to confide in me? What could I possibly say to make him want to open up?

"Do you remember Maude Hoffman?" I asked. "Kelly's great-aunt?"

"No, I don't."

For the first time, I looked directly at him. Before, I'd been looking at his shoulder, or at his forehead, or at his neck. Now I looked him straight in the eyes. "Aunt Maude is the most lovable human being ever born." I said flatly, stating it as pure fact. "If you say you don't remember her, you're lying."

He rearranged his arm-crossing stance. "Okay, maybe I remember. What does that have to do with blocking my car? I can call 911, you know." But he didn't reach for the smart phone clipped to his belt.

"Maude asked me to find out what really happened to Kelly that night. Auntie May says . . . you know Auntie May, don't you? She says Maude won't rest easy until she knows for certain what happened."

Keith's shoulders slumped to an angle that suited the creases of his jacket. "Kelly's death was an accident."

I looked at him. "Lots of people say she killed herself."

"Lots of people have their heads . . ." He stepped back and raked at his hair with his fingers. It settled back in the exact same position as it had been before. "Look,

Kelly didn't commit suicide. There was no reason for her to do a thing like that."

"That's not what I hear."

He tipped his head back, tightening the skin on his neck, and breathed in deep. "I'm sure not. Now, if you don't mind, I would like to go home. It's been a long day and—"

"People say she killed herself because you broke up with her."

For a moment he looked right at me. In the sloping set of his shoulders I saw grief worn red and raw and fresh. In the lines of his face I saw the sorrow of love lost forever. And in the wetness of his eyes I saw the truth.

"You didn't break up with her, did you?" I asked softly. "She broke up with you."

"It was time to move on, she said." His voice came at me so low I could barely hear it. "That we'd had a high school romance, but it was time to go our separate ways."

"I thought you two had a plan."

He shrugged, half shaking his head. "Turns out it was my plan, not hers."

I blinked as a sudden thought struck me.

"Oh, don't worry," he said. "The police checked me out left, right, and center for an alibi. I was working that night at the movie theater. It was still downtown then and I was there, selling popcorn from the first evening show at seven all through the midnight showing of *Rocky Horror*."

Marina made a noise—she was a huge fan—but I quieted her with a glare. "Did you tell the police she broke up with you? And not the other way around?"

"Every time they came to the door. Over and over. But once they were satisfied that I couldn't have done it, they went away." He stared off into the distance, looking back into the past with such a sad expression that I couldn't stand it any longer.

I opened the car door and got out. "Keith." I said, touching him on the arm. "Why didn't you want to talk to me, earlier?"

He glanced at me, then away. "Everyone assumes they know what happened and they all hate me for it. 'There goes the guy who made Kelly Engel want to kill herself.' 'That's the guy who practically killed Kelly. Why isn't he in jail?'" He shook his head. "I don't talk about it. And no one else has, not for years."

"Barb thinks Faye Lowery killed Kelly out of jealousy."

Keith nodded. "I know. She might be right, but I don't know. The only thing I know is Kelly's dead and a day doesn't go by that I wish she was still alive."

Poor Barb. Poor Keith. She was trying her best to keep Kelly alive by insisting on finding the truth. He was trying to keep her alive by staying in the past, driving the same car, wearing the same clothes, keeping the same haircut. Three tragedies, not one.

"Why don't you move away?" I asked impulsively. "Don't you think you should move on? Find someone to marry. Have kids. Move to Chicago. California. Anywhere but here."

"I tried," Keith said. "A couple of times. But . . . it didn't work out. Besides, Kelly's grave is here, you know."

For a moment I couldn't move. Couldn't talk. Finally, I nodded. Because, somehow, I did know.

Chapter 19

The next morning I woke and had absolutely no idea what day it was. Tuesday? No. Thursday? No. Still mostly asleep, I ran though almost every day of the week until I finally settled on Saturday.

And not just Saturday, but Saturday on a holiday weekend. A long weekend during which I was banned from the store, and in which I had no children to feed or clothe or clean. Or hug. Or kiss. Or—

The phone rang. I sighed and reached over to pick it up. "Hello?"

"Quit that," Marina said.

"What?"

"Whatever it is that you're doing."

"I'm not doing anything."

"Exactly! And that's your problem."

"Um . . ."

"I know how you get, moping around when the kids are gone. What did you plan for today? No, let me guess. Going around the house on your hands and knees and cleaning the baseboards? Scouring the shower grout with a toothbrush?"

My plans had included washing the kitchen floor and renting a carpet shampooer to clean Jenna's and Oliver's rooms, but she didn't need to know that. "It's sad, isn't it?" I mused. "How Keith's never got over Kelly."

"Yeah." Marina blew a sigh through the phone line and into my ear. "What a waste. Guy needs to buck up a little, don't you think? I mean, honestly. Blowing his entire life because his high school sweetheart died? Get a grip. Romance is nice and all, but this is carrying things too freaking far."

I thought about that. I knew what she meant, that Keith was wallowing in his misery beyond all sense, that he should snap out of it, get some help, and start living. But . . . was there really such a thing as a perfect match? A soul mate? I'd never thought so, but what if I was wrong? What if I'd been made for a particular man? And what if he died? After him, anyone else would be second best and it might be best to live alone. But . . . could being lonely ever be the right answer?

"Yo, Beth. Are you there?"

"Kind of. What are you doing today?"

"Trying to decide between making a cake for my neighbor's son's graduation party, entering a skydiving competition, and working on a cure for forgetfulness. How about you? And I don't want to hear about your list of chores. Tell me something fun."

"Is vacuuming the car considered fun?"

"Not on any planet in the solar system."

"Then I guess I'll have to solve a couple of murders."

I stood on the sidewalk opposite the police station, trying to assess the likelihood of Gus being on duty. The police car parked out front was the most obvious sign that at least one officer was in the building. It was Saturday, on a holiday weekend. Yes, he'd probably scheduled himself. So, no, I didn't want to go in.

"Coward," I muttered.

"What's that?" Cindy Irving was behind me, pushing a cart full of weeds and grass clippings.

"Just trying to convince myself to do something I don't want to."

"Beth, you are such a Goody Two-shoes. What are you going to do, turn yourself in for parking in a no parking zone?" She held her wrists together, in anticipation of the handcuffs. "Take me now, officer. I'm a menace to society." Laughing, she picked up the handles to her cart and trundled off.

"Don't be such a pansy," I told myself, then before I could change my mind about jumping off the high dive, crossed the street and barged into the Rynwood Police Department.

"Hey, Mrs. Kennedy." Officer Sean came to the counter, smiling. "What's up?"

I looked around. "No Gus?"

"The chief's out on a call. Fender bender at the mall entrance. Is it important? Because I can call him."

"No, no," I said quickly. "Just wondered, that's all. I, um . . ." Coward. "I lost a spiral notebook the other day. I don't suppose anyone turned one in?"

"Haven't seen one, but let me look." He crouched down behind the counter. "Gloves, mittens, hats, cell phones if you can believe it, and a boot. Look familiar?" He held a bright red child's boot up high. Left foot.

"Sorry."

"Makes you wonder where the other one is, doesn't it?" He stood up. "No notebook. Did you check at the stores? Maybe someone turned it in where you dropped it."

"Thanks, I'll do that." Or not. Cowards don't have to do such things. "I have another question. Remember I was asking about Amy Jacobson?"

"The lady who died a month or two ago. Sure, I re-member."

"Did you, did the police, take anything from her house?" He started to say something, so I hurried up to keep him from talking. "Because I was talking to Jean, the editor of the paper, and she said Amy was always carrying a three-ring binder."

"A . . . binder."

I blinked at Sean. He'd sounded just like Gus. Casual and interested, but also reserved. It was a lot to pack into two words, yet he'd managed it easily. Was this something they learned at the police academy? Or was it learned on the job, taught to you after a certain length of time in uniform? "Well, rookie," the chief would say. "You've been on the job six months. Tomorrow we teach you how to talk." "Yessir!"

"Yes," I said. "A binder. Jean says it was filled with newspaper articles about deaths like Kelly Engel's."

"And you think we might have it here?" Sean frowned. "Ms. Jacobson's death was ruled accidental. We didn't take anything from her home. Matter of fact . . ." He trailed off.

"What?"

He looked at the ceiling, at the doorway to Gus's office, down at the counter, and finally back at me. "Some relatives contacted us a couple of days ago. Cousins of some kind."

"And?"

The way he studied my face made me want to squirm. Not only had he picked up the law enforcement officer's tone, he'd also made the jump to the Cop Stare, the one that made you feel guilty even though you hadn't done anything wrong except for going three miles over the speed limit. Well, that and the time in college I was given an extra fifty cents in change at an expressway fast-food restaurant and didn't notice until I was a hundred miles away. I'd meant to send it back, I really had.

"And," Sean said, "Ms. Jacobson's cousins will be in town in the next couple of weeks to take care of things."

"Take care ... ?"

A breeze from an open window rattled some papers. He moved a coffee mug to act as paperweight. "Close up the house. Get it ready to sell, I guess. They called to say they'd be there, if any of the neighbors reported a break-in."

Amy was gone, I'd known that for weeks, but cleaning out her house seemed wrong. So permanent. Getting rid of her belongings as if she'd never existed. Life went on, of course it did, but why did cleaning out a house seem like such an ... an erasure?

"Mrs. Kennedy, are you all right?"

I put on an instant smile. "Fine, thanks."

"So what I'm saying is if you want to talk to Ms. Jacobson's relatives about her binder, just wait until next week. I took down their names. Would you like me to get it for you?"

Wait, wait, and wait some more. All I'd ever done in my entire life was wait. Waited to grow up and graduate from high school. Waited to get out of college and to get married and to get a real job, waited for my children to be born, waited for them to get older, and now I was still waiting.

I was tired of it.

The next morning the alarm woke me before dawn. I slapped it off and sat up. The windows were a medium shade of gray and it was too dark to tell if it was going to be a sunny day or a cloudy one.

I nudged the cat. "What do you think? Sunny?"

George opened his eyes a fraction of an inch. Stared at me—obviously telling me to leave him alone—and shut his eyes again.

I kissed the top of his head and was rewarded with a purr. I looked down at Spot, who was sitting on the floor next to the bed. "How about you?"

He put his chin on the edge of the mattress and looked at me with his big brown eyes, as easy to read as Oliver's when he watched the ice cream truck go past.

I patted Spot's furry head. "Don't worry, you can go with me." Because even though the Evan-induced promise to always take Spot with me had worn off with our breakup, I'd discovered that I liked having him along.

Half an hour later I was showered and breakfasted—if you consider a granola bar and a glass of orange juice breakfast, which I did—and Spot and I were on our way.

I parked the car a couple of blocks away and opened the back door. "Ready, boy?" Spot bounded out of the backseat with his tongue half out of his mouth. I clipped his leash onto his collar and we walked—oh, so casually—to Amy's house.

Halfway up the driveway, my cell phone rang.

"Bethie," Auntie May said, "Maudie wants to talk to you. Here, Maudie"—her voice went distant—"take the phone. What's that? It's too heavy? Okay, I'll hold it to your ear. Are you strong enough to talk? There you go, honey. Don't tire yourself out."

"Beth?" Maude's voice was thready. "Are you there, dear?"

"I'm here." My dry throat had a hard time with the words. "How are you feeling?"

"Fine, dear. Just—"

"Maudie," said Auntie May's faint voice. "Don't give the girl false hope. Remember what that doctor said."

"What?" I said loudly. "Maude, what's the matter?"

"It's just my heart," she said. "The doctor said . . ." She broke off and took a few panting breaths. "She said I shouldn't expect my little old heart to last forever, that's all."

"What does that mean, exactly?" The hairs on the back of my neck were tingling.

A few more panting breaths. "Well, honey, I'm not quite sure, but when I asked the doctor if I should crochet Christmas ornaments for the great-grandnieces and nephews, she shook her head."

"Oh, Maude." I wanted to sit down.

"Now, don't you worry about me, sweetie. I know you're doing your best to help me with Kelly. You . . . what's that May, dear? Yes, I—" She coughed. Once. Twice. Then a long jag during which my grip on the phone grew tighter and tighter. "I'm sorry, honey," she gasped out. "I'm just so tired. So . . . tired . . ."

"Maude?"

Short breaths punctuated the murmurings of Auntie May, murmurings that I couldn't quite make into words.

"Maude?" I called. "Maude!"

"She's asleep," Auntie May snapped. "No thanks to you. No respect for your elders, that's what's wrong with your generation. You don't care about anyone other than yourself, and sure not for a little old lady in a nursing home who asked for help."

"I'm trying," I said, pleading, begging for understanding. "I'm trying to do my best."

Auntie May sniffed. "Not good enough, is it?"

Her simple statement hit me hard. I bent forward as if I'd been slugged in the stomach. I wanted to say that

she was wrong, that I respected her generation very
much, that I spent so much time caring for other people
that I didn't know how to care for myself anymore, that
I wished I could spend more time at Sunny Rest. But she
didn't want to hear any of that, and wouldn't have believed me if I'd told her. "Auntie May . . ."

"*Do* something."

And she was gone.

I slid my cell phone back into my purse and looked
around at the day. Oddly, it was still morning. The sun
was just rising, shooting long lines of light through the
leaves of the trees. A beautiful morning, all fresh and
clean and unspoiled and decorated with dew. From the
long grass in Amy's backyard to the leaves of the trees
to the roof of Amy's house, bright drops of water caught
the sun and reflected it back.

Do something.

"What do you think, Spot?"

He looked up at me and wagged his tail.

"Ready for a little breaking and entering?"

I started my life of crime by knocking on the back door.
Maybe the cousins had showed up early. Maybe I'd be
able to borrow Amy's notebook. I'll bring it back tomorrow, I'd say. Thanks so much, see you then.

But no relatives came to the door. I knocked once
more, a third time, then took hold of the doorknob and
turned. Locked. "Rats." I tied Spot's leash to the white-
painted porch post, walked around to the front of the
house and tried that door. Also locked.

I blew out a breath and turned in a circle, thinking.
Somewhere I'd heard that over seventy percent of
suburban Americans hide a house key somewhere

outside. Of course, my source was probably Marina and therefore suspect, but I liked the statistic.

Under the flowerpot? . . . Nope, nothing there. In one of the window boxes? On top of the door trim? Tucked somewhere under the back porch? No, no, and no.

I brushed the dirt off my knees. Maybe she didn't have a key out here. After all, why would you need a key outside if you never left the house?

"Now what?" I asked no one in particular. "Auntie May doesn't expect me to break down the door, does she?"

Actually, she probably did.

I glanced at the garage. Would Amy have had tools out there? Maybe a crowbar would get the door open without too much damage. I could replace the trim easy enough. Maybe I could talk Evan into helping me and . . .

No. Not Evan.

I winced away from that topic. Took one step in the direction of the garage. Stopped.

Could I do it? Could I really break into Amy's house? What if one of the neighbors saw me and called the police? What if Gus drove out, siren blaring, and caught me?

Then again, what if Maude died today?

I turned back to the house. What if . . .

The first window I tried was securely locked. So were the second, third, and fourth windows. The fifth window—the smallest one—gave a small screech of protest, then went up.

I studied the size of the opened window. Looked at the width of my hips. Squinted at the window. It didn't look like a good fit.

Time to get inside before the neighbors heard me. I

looked around for something to climb on. I also wondered about the time and paperwork it took to get someone committed to a psychiatric hospital.

"A nice long rest might do me a lot of good," I told Spot.

He wagged his tail.

The porch stood sadly empty of ladders, chairs, and other devices upon which I could have clambered. But behind the garage I found exactly what I needed: milk crates.

I brushed off the detritus of a dozen autumns and lugged three of them to the side of the house. Two I stacked atop each other, the other I snugged up next to the pile of two. Up one step I went, then up the next, high enough to see into Amy's downstairs bathroom.

"Now what?" I muttered. It didn't sound so hard, climbing in through a window. Unfortunately, I had legs that didn't bend backward and a head on top of my shoulders.

One cramped calf muscle and two hard whacks on the back of my skull later, I was standing on the bathroom's linoleum floor. I turned around to shut the window and saw Thurman, pruners in hand, staring at me blankly.

"Hi!" I called, waving cheerily. "How are you? Say hello to Lillian for me." I slid the window shut and locked it. Just making sure the house was secure, Officer. I'll be going now, if that's all right with you. Bye-bye!

The dirt on my hands made me long to wash, but I couldn't bring myself to use Amy's towels. I dusted my hands on my pants, hoping my straightlaced and decades-gone grandmother couldn't see me, and, after peering through the lace curtain for any signs of Thurman, went to open the door for Spot.

"No getting on the furniture," I told him. "No chewing

of anything, no scratching on anything, and whatever you do, don't shed."

He trotted inside, ignoring everything I said, and stood in the middle of the kitchen, nose twitching as he sniffed the stale air.

Half a hope rose in me that he could smell Amy's crime book. "Good dog. Find it, boy."

He gave me a tilted-head look.

Sighing, I patted him. "Don't worry about it. You would if you could, I'm sure. Dogs always do their best." And unlike me, a dog's best was always good enough.

I shook off my self-pity, told Spot to stay, and started the search.

Working on the theory that Amy would keep a special book in a special place, I went to the dusty living room. Not on the round coffee table, not on the blond bookshelves, not on the end tables, not under the pale turquoise couch.

Methodically, I moved to the kitchen. No binder with the cookbooks. No binder in the junk drawer, no binder anywhere.

"I hate this," I muttered. This going-through of someone else's belongings made me feel icky. And it made me want to rush home and clean out my underwear drawer. It wouldn't do to have anyone else find that ratty pair in the back, not even Marina.

The binder wasn't in the guest room or the study where I gaped open-mouthed at Amy's artwork. Why hadn't she told me she was a graphic novelist? But before I even finished the thought, I knew the answer. I would have pestered her to do a signing at the store. To give a talk. To attend our author parties. All events that took place outside her house, most of which took place during the day.

Poor Amy.

I looked through the living room one last time—two last times—then looked up the narrow wooden stairs to where Amy's bedroom must be. I didn't want to go up there, didn't want to see that most private of places, didn't want to feel the sorrow that would surely stab at me.

But up the stairs I went, bleached pine step after bleached pine step. At the top, the white paneled door creaked as I pushed it open. "Oh . . ." I breathed, feeling not grief, but a happy surprise.

For Amy's bedroom was filled with light and filled with white. Tall windows facing east and south were welcoming in so much morning sun that turning on the light would have made no difference.

I blinked at the lush lace at the windows, the lace runner on the dresser, the lace draped over the dresser mirror, the lace-trimmed pillows on the bed, the comforter cover topped with lace, the lace lampshades. Feminine, yes, but more than that, sheer unadulterated gorgeousness.

Amy must have loved this room. She would have woken to this beauty every morning and fallen asleep in its embrace. No one who'd created this room could have been truly unhappy, no one who slept in this space could have left it without a smile on her face.

The binder was on the lower shelf of the white wicker nightstand. I removed it from its resting place and went silently down the stairs. I sat at the kitchen table, Spot sat at my feet, and I began to read.

When I finally looked up, my back hurt, my head ached, and my stomach was telling me that lunch would have been a good thing to have.

The notebook had ended up to be as much journal as crime-oriented notebook.

In the back were a number of empty notebook pages. I flipped to the back, hesitated, then unsnapped the binder, and removed the pages. "Sorry," I said out loud. "I'll replace them."

I dug into my purse for a pen and turned back to the first pages of Amy's notebook. There was the newspaper article that described Kelly's death. There was Kelly's obituary. There was the article about her funeral, complete with pictures of the crowd-lined street and the black banners hanging from every window in the high school.

It seemed a little overkill, perhaps, and my sympathy for Faye went up a small notch.

I made some notes. Factual ones, having to do with dates and times and places. None of this was more than remotely interesting, but it seemed like something that should be done.

Between the newspaper articles at the front and the articles at the back came pages and pages of scrawling adolescent script. I read it through a second time and this time I searched the angst for the kernels of information that lay beneath.

"It's all my fault," the young Amy wrote. "I'll blame myself forever and ever. She never would have died if I'd really been her best friend. I would have saved her, I never would have let her drown. It's all my fault, every single bit of it."

On and on for pages. I wrote, "Amy feels responsible," and kept going.

It wasn't until the twentieth page of frenzied journaling that I came across the reason for Amy's guilt.

"If only I hadn't gone out on that date. Why, *why*, did I think that seeing some stupid movie with some stupid guy was better than going to the slumber party?"

I wrote, "Amy out on date the night of Kelly's death." Tapping the pen point to the paper, I wondered if that was the reason Amy had never married. Would guilt have haunted her to that extreme? Could something that happened when you were eighteen cause you to make a decision you stuck to the rest of your life?

"Well?" I asked the air.

But there was, of course, no answer.

I paged through the loopy handwriting, hunting for the names I'd seen before. There. There. And there.

"Claudia Wolff is such a you-know-what," Amy had written. "She's the real reason I didn't go to the slumber party. Faye's okay. Tina isn't so bad, and all Cindy does is talk about either flowers or her chances with Keith now that he's ditched Kelly. She probably can't imagine how bad Kelly feels, so she probably called Kelly and asked if she wanted to get back with Keith and maybe that's why . . . No. I won't believe it. I won't *won't WON'T!!!*"

A tear-sized circle blurred the exclamation points, turning them into wavy lines of blue ink.

Four names went onto my list titled Slumber Party: Faye Lewis, Claudia Wolff, Tina Heller, and Cindy Irving.

I turned the names around in my head. Cindy, Tina, Claudia, Faye.

Faye.

Claudia.

Tina.

Cindy.

Faye, who was so obviously self-confident that the concept of murder to improve her chances of being valedictorian seemed as far-fetched as time travel.

Claudia, who committed her acts of violence via a poisoned tongue, was too passive-aggressive to dirty her hands with something as ugly as murder.

Tina, who formed her opinions via Claudia, might kill to stay in Claudia's good graces, by why would she have needed to? Had they had a fight?

I put a small star by Tina's name and considered Cindy. She landscaped the town of Rynwood until it looked like something from a movie set. She didn't have any children, wasn't married, and, as far back as I could remember, hadn't dated anyone. And yet she'd had a huge crush on Keith Mathieson back in high school. Which didn't mean anything by itself. But . . . ?

I licked my index finger and pushed Amy's pages backward, then forward, looking for what I was sure I'd seen on the initial read. Or had I? Maybe I'd dreamed it up, along with the voices of Amy and Kelly. Maybe I needed to find a good therapist and—

There!

"Cindy," Amy wrote, "scares me sometimes. She gets so she wants something so bad and she won't quit until she gets it. Look at how she got to be first chair clarinet in band. All she did all summer was practice. Then she wanted to be class president. Wonder how much money she spent buying French fries and Cokes for kids? She won, though. And then she decided she wanted Keith Mathieson."

I shut the book slowly. The rest of it was packed with newspaper clippings of accidental deaths from all over the country and I didn't see how a beer-infested man falling off a sailboat in Lake Erie had anything to do with Kelly.

Cindy, though. Could she have killed Kelly?

Closing my eyes, I summoned an image of her face, intent on yanking every last weed out of the large flower beds in front of City Hall. I heard the snick of her hand clippers as she trimmed an errant piece of grass next to a city sidewalk. I felt the lash of her tongue as she scolded me for letting a leaf stray into the flower box at the front of my store.

Yes. I could see Cindy killing Kelly for a better chance at Keith. It wouldn't have mattered, since Kelly was the one who did the dumping, but Cindy didn't know that. No one knew.

So . . . I looked at my notes and nudged Spot. "Say Cindy had killed Kelly. Just say." He made a groany noise and rolled onto my foot. "Why would she have killed Amy? Especially at this late date?"

He groaned again, but since I couldn't interpret dog speech, his suggestion wasn't helpful.

I stood and started to pace. "Why?" I asked Spot. "Why?" I asked the notebook. "Why?" I asked the kitchen at large, arms spread wide. "Why would . . ."

That's when I noticed the blinking light on Amy's answering machine. Without thinking it through, without thinking at all, I crossed the room and hit PLAY.

"Hi, Amy," said a male voice. "It's Keith. It was nice seeing you the other night. Are we still on for Friday at six? I might be a little late because I have to talk to our new landscaper about some plants she wants to try out. She's from Rynwood, actually. Do you remember a Cindy Irving? She was in our class at school . . ."

I pushed the OFF button. "Come on, Spot," I said quietly. "Let's go."

Chapter 20

The trees in the park gave shade from the sun, but no comfort. Spot's presence at my side gave companionship, but he provided no answers. We walked through the twisting trails, Spot looking up at me every so often to check on my mental status, me asking questions out loud. There weren't any answers, but who better to ask questions of me than me?

"What do I do now?" The trail underneath my feet was soft and quiet with its covering of brown pine needles. "If I go to the police, will they listen to me? More to the point, will they believe me? I don't see it, I just don't. They haven't listened to me yet, so why would they start now? It's all about proof and I don't have any."

Not yet.

I stopped. Looked around. I'd heard something. For real, that time. Hadn't I? I stretched out my ears and closed my eyes, trying to hear all around me. If I'd heard a voice, I should have heard footsteps. There might have been footsteps . . . but if I had, where were they now?

A creepy snaky feeling sniggled down the back of my neck, then Spot pushed his head up to my fingertips. He didn't seem to be worried, so why should I be? Back to the topic at hand.

"I need proof," I said firmly. "And how am I going to get some?" I flung out the hand that wasn't hanging on to Spot's leash. "You can't make it up, you know. It has to be real. It has to stand up in a court of law."

Again I heard a rustle that shouldn't have been there. I stopped. Looked. Listened. Didn't see anything, didn't hear anything.

Spot and I turned in a circle, me squinting into the shady murk, him dancing around my feet in anticipation of a new game. Nothing to see but trees, nothing to hear but the rustle of leaves. I shook my head to clear away the spookiness I'd conjured up and started walking again.

"All very well for you to say don't worry," I said, "but if I'm going to accomplish anything, I need to come up with something that will satisfy Gus, the prosecutor, and the judge. Cindy killed Kelly to clear the path to Keith. She killed Amy for the same reason. But how do I convince Gus? He's not going to question her based on a high schooler's diary and an answering machine message about landscaping."

Would he?

I thought for a while, head down, feet moving fast. No, he wouldn't. Even if I could get him or Sean over to the house, all they'd do was take notes, nod, and say this was all very interesting, but what did it prove? What I needed was—

My head jerked back as Spot yanked hard on the leash. When I started to scold him, he erupted into wild barking. "Spot!" I called. "Spot! Quiet!" He was barking and straining at the leash, staring down the trail, muscles quivering.

I squinted into the trees. Saw nothing. His sharp dog nose must be scenting a squirrel or a rabbit. We didn't have coyotes in the park, did we? "Calm down, boy." My hand went out to pet him. His back was rigid with tension. "Spot, what do—" I stopped, because I'd suddenly seen what my dog had seen some time ago.

Cindy Irving was rushing down the path, heading toward me with a shovel in her hands and a murderous look on her face. She said nothing at all, just ran toward me, raising the shovel high.

I stood, staring.

The open windows at the police station. She must have heard me talking. She's been following me, waiting, and now she's going to kill me.

Cindy came close, closer, and closer yet. Finally, panic grabbed hold of me and I was able to run.

Too little too late she's going to catch me she has too long a reach with that shovel she knows so well how to use it run don't let her get near you run *run RUN!*

I ran one way and Spot ran the other and the long dog leash pulled taut between us. Cindy, charging toward me, didn't see the strap and ran straight into it, catching it right at her knees.

Spot yelped and my head flung backward as Cindy's weight pulled us around. She fell headlong, keening out a long shriek, and crashed hard to the ground. There was a *crack!* as her head hit a tree root. She made a whimpering noise, then rolled to her side and lay still.

For two breaths, three, I stood quiet. When she hadn't moved after the fourth breath, I went to her. Knelt down. Saw that she was still breathing. "Spot? Come, boy." He came to me, tail wagging, and I unclipped the leash from his collar. "Good dog. Stay."

I wrapped the leash around one of Cindy's thick, powerful wrists. Around the second one. Tied as tight a knot as I could. Then I pulled my cell phone out of my purse and called 911.

An officer would arrive shortly, the efficient dispatcher told me.

"How long is shortly?" I asked. Pleaded, really. Cindy was too big and strong for me to take down a second time. The first had been sheer luck.

"As soon as possible," the dispatcher said. "Would you like me to stay on the line?"

"Beth?" called a male voice. "Beth!" Pete Peterson pounded into view. "It is you. I thought I heard Spot barking. Are you okay? What's the matter?"

I told the dispatcher, "No, thanks. I'm good," and flung myself into Pete's outstretched arms. Aid, when I thought it would be a half hour coming. Comfort, when I thought there was no hope of finding any. "I am so glad to see you," I half sobbed. "You wouldn't believe how glad."

He cupped the back of my head with his hand and pulled me close. "Don't worry," he murmured. "It'll be okay."

"Ohhh," Cindy groaned. "My head really hurts, it . . ." She blinked and looked down at the leash tying her wrists together. "Why am I tied up?"

I looked at her. Because you just tried to whack me on the head with a shovel, why do you think?

She blinked again, then looked up at me. "Why couldn't you leave well enough alone? Why did you have to go poking around, asking all those questions? It was none of your business!"

Pete stepped out of our embrace, but took firm hold of my hand. "I wouldn't answer," he said quietly. "Engaging someone like her is the worst thing you can do."

I nodded. He was right, and I should have taken his advice, but I couldn't stop myself from asking Cindy, "Does Keith know how you feel about him?"

Fear, anger, apprehension, and craftiness all flashed over her face. A slippery smile came and went. "He will," she said slyly. "Sometimes these things take time, that's all. Eventually he'll see I'm the best thing that could ever happen to him. Eventually he'll see how much I love him. Once he sees that, it'll all be okay."

Her smile, laced with dreams and fantasy, made her look almost beautiful. It was the look of a bride on her wedding day. Today, everything will come true. Today, everything will be perfect.

I swallowed. Obsession didn't look anything like I'd imagined.

Cindy strained against the leash that bound her wrists together. "But every time I got close to getting close to him, someone would mess it up for me. First Kelly, then that girl in college, then Amy."

Suddenly I couldn't breathe. I put my hand to my neck. Yes, there it was. My pulse. Strong and steady. "What girl?" I asked.

Cindy's gaze fastened on mine and I realized I was looking into the eyes of a killer. Revulsion rose in me, so strong that I almost choked.

"It was that Kelly that ruined it," she said. "They were always together, always! How was I going to get a chance with her there all the time? And then after she died, I thought, now. Now is my time. Now he'll see. But people started saying she committed suicide and he was never the same after that."

I started to move forward, to ask the question quietly, to whisper it in her ear, but Pete held me back. I tugged, and he held me firm. "Please," he said. "Please stay back."

He'd said "please." Twice. I stayed back. But I did crouch low, putting myself closer to Cindy's level. "Kelly didn't commit suicide, did she?"

"What makes you say that?" Her crafty look had returned.

Lots of things, but none of them carried any serious weight, so I didn't say anything.

Cindy smiled. "You don't know. No one does. Except me. It really was an accident. Just like the police report says."

I rocked back on my heels and would have fallen over except for Pete reaching down to support me. "It was?" All these weeks I'd been so sure Kelly had been murdered. Barb had been certain for years. How was I going to tell her she was wrong? How was I going to tell Maude?

"Of course it was." Cindy giggled. "I didn't mean to kill her. It was an accident. Just like that college girl. And Amy. Accidents, all of them. Like when that brick almost fell on you? Accident. They happen, you know."

Pete's hands gripped my shoulders and I felt the solidity of his legs against my back. "Yes," I said slowly, "they do."

"Exactly!" Cindy said triumphantly. "I didn't mean for Kelly to drown, I just meant to scare her. It's not my fault. I mean, she was supposed to be this great swimmer," she said, rolling her eyes. "If she was that good, you'd have thought she could hold her breath a little longer. Sure, I pushed her head down with the rowboat oar, but still."

Oh, Kelly. I'm so sorry. So so sorry.

"And the college girl?" Pete asked. "She had an accident, too?"

"Well, yeah. People shouldn't stand so close to deep water. Especially in winter. You never know when you're going to slip and fall on the ice. Safety first," she said solemnly, then laughed.

"Amy," I said.

"That woman." Cindy shoved the words out of her mouth. "She was trouble from the beginning. Trouble when we were kids and worse trouble now. She should have stayed away from Keith. She had no right to him. No right!" The *T* hit her teeth hard. "Oh, I knew all about the way he visited her at night. I saw; I watched it all."

"You spent a lot of time watching him," I said.

She nodded fiercely. "I had to stop her from seeing him. All I was going to do was scare her a little with those wasps. Just knock on the back door and get her outside with a story about a poor, sad little kitten in the bushes. So easy, in spite of those cans of bee killer. I got one away from her, you know. And, anyway, how was I supposed to know she was so allergic? An accident, see. It was an accident."

Nausea rose in my throat, bitter and sharp. I stood up so fast that blackness threatened to overtake me.

"I have a lovely accident planned for you," she said. "So lovely. Bookstores can be dangerous places, you know. All those books, all those shelves. I'd lay money that not all of them are fastened to the walls properly."

Her smile curved up slowly and became the ugliest expression I'd ever seen on a human face.

She laughed. "Scared, little Beth? When I took that dumb notebook of yours, I thought it would tell me everything, but your handwriting is so horrible, I could hardly read it. You can't be that smart if you can't write."

Scared? Yes, I was scared. Scared and nervous and anxious and wishing with all the wishes granted to me that the police were here right now.

"You think you're so smart, but who's the smart one now?" Her hands burst free of the leash. She scrambled to her feet faster than light and hurtled toward me.

Spot barked wildly and danced around Cindy, nipping at her ankles, darting away from her kicking feet.

"Leave me alone, dog!" She aimed at his midsection. "I have to find an accident. There's got to be one here somewhere."

Pete had shouldered his way in front of me, but Cindy shoved him to the ground with a strength few women have. "Hah. Gotcha." She stood in front of me, laughing. "And I got you good, smarty pants."

I stared into her eyes. Why I wasn't scared, I had no idea. Calm ran through my body like a deep river. There was no need to fear. She would not hurt me. Peace filled my lungs, my smile, my eyes.

Cindy's hands were inches from my throat.

Don't be afraid.

I should have been, but I wasn't.

Cindy's eyes flared wide and she stopped dead. Whirled around. Threw her head back and looked up at the trees. "Kelly?" she whispered. "Kelly?" Her whisper turned to a shout. "I killed you! You're dead!" She flung herself around and reached for me again. "It's you! You're tricking me! I'll kill you for that!"

She grabbed my throat, shaking me like a small dog. Pete had scrambled to his feet and his hands were fastened on her wrists, but he couldn't break her grip. "Let her go!" he shouted. "Let go!"

And all I could do was stare into her mad eyes and feel sorry for her. The poor woman. All she wanted was love, and she was never going to get the love she wanted so badly. The poor, poor woman.

Spots of light sparkled at the edges of my vision and a curtain of darkness started to descend. Cindy was killing me, and still I wasn't afraid.

Jenna, honey, I love you.

Oliver, sweetie, I love you.

I'm so sorry. . . .

My knees went soft and I sagged. Cindy crowed with triumph, Pete shouted, Spot barked. The world went black . . . it was then, almost too late, that the police came. Gus and Sean and sheriff's deputies and EMTs. From my kneeling position on the ground, I watched as law enforcement officers wrestled Cindy down and handcuffed her.

The EMTs set down their boxes of equipment. "Ma'am? We need to make sure you're okay."

"I'm fine," I croaked through a raw throat, but they didn't pay any attention to me.

Gus nodded at Sean, who colored an adorable shade of pink and read Cindy the Miranda warning. Accompanied by the sheriff's deputies, Sean marched her off, and Gus came over to me just as the EMTs declared me of sound mind and body, packed up their equipment, and went off.

"She's going to be fine," he said.

I blinked. Gus was talking to me. He was actually talking to me. And not sounding as if he wanted to shout me down into silence. "She . . . will?" I glanced down the trail, where we could all hear Cindy shouting at the EMTs to leave her alone, to not touch her because she was saving herself for her soul mate.

Gus smiled at me, and it was as if the dark clouds of forty days and forty nights had broken clear. "Stage one cancer only, and they got all of it. She'll have to do radiation treatments for a few weeks, but they're saying a complete recovery."

"Winnie," I whispered. Suddenly, all became clear. Of course, it could have been clear for weeks if either Gus or Winnie had chosen to confide in their friends, but that would be a topic for another time. "Oh, Gus, I'm so glad."

He looked at me. Glanced at Pete. Studied the light in the trees. Looked back at me. "I owe you an apology, Beth. I haven't been a very good police chief the past few weeks. I haven't followed up on what I should have, and I'm sorry."

I touched his arm. "Apology accepted."

He gave my hand a quick squeeze, then let it go. "And," he said, so quietly that it almost wasn't audible, "I haven't been a very good friend, either. For that, I'm even sorrier."

I inhaled sharply. This was an apology I hadn't expected. "Um . . ."

"Well, I need to get going," Gus said. "Got to follow up on what the youngster does. Beth, I'll see you at rehearsal on Wednesday, right?" He hitched up his utility belt, and was off.

Pete made a "hmm" sort of noise, which covered pretty much everything.

We stood there a moment, neither one of us saying anything, until we heard voices and footsteps coming toward us so fast that we barely had time to get off the path before a pack of runners swirled on by, chattering about splits and barefoot shoes and carbs.

When they'd passed, the mood had changed. Pete and I had shared a traumatic experience and I'd been far too close to death, but right now I wanted—needed—to go home and not think about it. We could talk about it later. Just not now.

I looked up at Pete. "Um . . ."

He smiled easily. "Disc golf on Tuesday?"

I smiled back, nodding, and he sauntered off, hands in his pockets, whistling. I watched him go, happy that he was my friend. Actually, there were a lot of things I was happy about: all the questions about Amy's and Kelly's deaths were now answered, Cindy wouldn't ever cause any more accidents, and I could finally, with complete confidence, tell both Maude and Kelly's mother what had really happened that night.

There was only one thing left to do—call Marina and tell her that I'd helped capture the killer without her help. She'd play at being annoyed, of course, but—

A sharp noise cracked through the trees.

I jumped and whirled, looking for the threat, breathing fast, trying to see, trying to see . . .

Don't be afraid.

"I'm not," I said out loud. And I wasn't.

The branch that had broken off a nearby tree rattled down through the upper limbs and tumbled down to earth. I walked over and kicked it off the path, deep into the undergrowth.

No, I wasn't afraid at all.

I put my hands in my pockets and walked off, whistling, with Spot at my side.

Epilogue

The middle school auditorium was filled to standing room only. Once word spread that the PTA story project was complete and that the children and their story partners were going to appear together on stage to read excerpts, everybody in town wanted in on the fun.

From the phone calls and e-mails, it quickly became evident that the elementary school gym was going to be at least two sizes too small, so the principal got together with his middle school counterpart and moved the whole kit and caboodle across town to the school Jenna would attend come September.

I bit my lower lip, thinking over the things that moms worry about. Would she like middle school? How could she possibly be old enough to be headed here? Was she going to feel lost in this huge building? Was she going to make new friends? Was she going to be okay?

After I'd successfully tied my stomach into knots, I took a few deep breaths and took stock of my surroundings.

I sat on the stage at the end of a long row of chairs. Some were regular chairs, some were wheelchairs, and walkers and canes were scattered everywhere. Each student sat next to their story partner, and they were all chatting and laughing, looking like they were having the time of their lives.

There was Oliver with Maude. My heart smiled at the sight. A happy but unforeseen product of this project was how Oliver had blossomed. Though he was still shy, and might always be, he'd enjoyed meeting Maude and learning her story. He was even asking questions about the stories in our own family.

This was good, of course it was good, but if he decided to research certain family members, things might become sticky.

Marina, out in the audience with Zach, caught my eye and waved her copy of the *Story Book* at me. "Got 'em!" she called, grinning hugely.

When the books had gone on sale last week, she'd made it her new life goal to get the autographs of all the kids and all the seniors. She'd stopped by to tell me so on the Sunday afternoon of Cindy's arrest and had found me on the sunny deck, reading through the galleys of the story project. The printer had told me I could make a few changes at this stage, but please, not very many of them.

"How goes it?" she asked, dropping into a chair.

I put down my red pen and stretched. "Almost there. The kids did a great job."

After a companionable silence during which we both sat with our faces turned up to the sun, Marina said, "You've changed."

I kept my eyes closed. "Have not."

"Sure you have. Think about it. Two years ago, would you have taken on a project like this? No way. You might have helped out a little, but you wouldn't have come up with the idea, presented it to the PTA, persuaded them it was a good thing to do, and then followed through."

"Would too."

"Nah." She slid down in the chair, down far enough to rest her head against the back. "You've gotten gumption. Or maybe you had it all along, and now it's finally surfacing."

I closed my eyes again, enjoying the warmth of the day.

"Either way," she said, "it's a good thing."

"Mmm."

She snapped her fingers. "Almost forgot why I stopped by. You, mah deah, are the winner of the weight loss contest! By one small pound, you have overtaken the rest of the contestants. I declare you the winner, with all its responsibilities and commitments." She beamed.

I squinted at her. "I didn't know there were any responsibilities or commitments."

"Are you saying you don't want to wear a crown and a sash and ride a float in parades all summer?"

"That's exactly what I'm saying."

She put her chin in her hand. "Disappointing, but not unexpected. As such, I revoke all of that and instead, award you the grand prize." She opened her purse, pulled out an envelope, and handed it to me with a grandiose flourish. "Yours for the keeping, little chickadee."

Using my thumb, I ripped open the envelope and looked inside. Frowned. "I thought the prize was going to be a trip to a day spa."

"Yeah, sorry about that. The deal fell through."

I extracted the gift certificate to Sabatini's. "So instead, my prize for losing ten pounds is a meal at a pizza place?"

Marina shrugged. "If you don't want it, I can give it to the second place winner."

"Who came in second? You?" I held the envelope out to her.

"Claudia."

I snatched the envelope back, tucked it into my waistband, and gave it a pat. "They have good salads, if you don't mind iceberg lettuce." And the twenty dollars I would make sure to collect from Claudia would be the sweetest I ever spent. If I didn't frame it, that is.

Now the big hand on the large clock on the back auditorium wall was only a couple of minutes away from the starting time. I looked at Erica, down in the front row, but she was deep in conversation with the parent to her left.

Along the row of chairs, I heard Maude's clear laughter. Her clear, perfectly healthy laughter.

After Cindy's arrest and before I went home, I'd hustled over to Sunny Rest. I'd rushed inside, anxious, hoping to find Maude conscious, hoping that she hadn't slipped further away. I'd race walked to her room and found it empty. Stricken, I'd stood in the doorway, and hung on to the doorframe. She was gone. I was too late, I'd taken too long, I'd done my best and it wasn't good enough. She was gone. . . .

Tracy, the nurse's aide, stopped, a pile of linens in her arms. "In the solarium."

I blinked at her. "What?"

"You're looking for Maude, right? She's in the solarium. Down the hall on the right." She put a hand to her waist. "Beeper. Gotta go."

With slow measured steps, I walked down the hall. In the solarium. Probably had her wheelchair placed so she could enjoy the sun. She couldn't have many days left and would want to soak it in as much as possible. She'd probably be asleep and she'd be—

She slapped a card down on the table. "Right bower. That's my trick and you, my dear friends, are euchred."

Auntie May cackled. "Way to go, partner."

I stood there, gaping at the scene. "You're not sick." The four women at the table turned to me as one. "You're not sick at all!"

"Oh, honey." Maude's face filled with concern. "Let me explain, I—"

"You were making it all up!"

Auntie May rolled her wheelchair around. "I'm the one who made her do it. If you're going to be mad at someone, be mad at me." She stabbed at her chest with her index finger.

I had a sudden flash of Marina and me, forty years hence. I'd be Maude and Marina would be Auntie May and no one in Rynwood would be safe. I pushed the vision away. "You manipulated me. Maude is healthy as a horse. You . . . you lied to me. Both of you."

"As little as we could," Maude said. "My doctor did shake her head about crocheting, I didn't lie about that. But what I didn't say is that she was recommending cross-stitch, instead."

"Of course we manipulated you," Auntie May snapped. "Someone had to light a fire underneath your hind end. Only way to do it was play on that guilt complex you carry around on your back. Got to get results, kiddo, and that was the best way to do it."

"I didn't like it," Maude said. "But it was a lovely chance to act again."

"To . . . what?"

"Maudie here was a leading lady in the Rynwood theater for years," Auntie May said. "Only stopped when she broke her hip about twenty years ago."

Which explained why I hadn't known; she'd dropped out of theater about the same time I moved to town.

And Maude's theater experience must have been what people had been trying to tell me about for weeks.

"Besides," Auntie May said. "If you'd known Maudie was hale and hearty, would you have tried so hard?"

"Of course . . ." I stopped. Of course I wouldn't have. Maude's supposedly ticking clock had been one of my primary motivators. It had been the reason I'd lost so much sleep and the reason I'd barged into Amy's house.

I'd tried hard to be angry, but Maude had taken my hand and put it to her cheek. "Please forgive me," she said softly. "If I could have done it any other way, I would have."

So I'd forgiven her, and both Auntie May and I comforted her when I told her what had really happened to Kelly that long, long-ago night.

I looked down the row to where Maude and Oliver were deep in conversation and smiled. How could anyone stay angry with her? Not me; I found it difficult to be angry with anyone, even Faye Lewis, who had come into the bookstore last week, also begging for forgiveness.

"Cindy and I grew up together," she'd said in my office, tears streaming down her face. "I knew how she was about Keith, I knew how she could be, but I didn't want to know. I didn't want to see. I didn't want to . . ." She'd put her face in her hands and sobbed.

I'd finished her sentence for her. Didn't want to know that her friend was a killer. And who could blame her for that? "Nothing to forgive." I'd gone around my desk and hugged her tight until the tears stopped.

Now I made eye contact with Erica and pointed at my watch. She nodded and walked up the stage steps, head high, carriage straight, knowing without looking that she wasn't going to trip on the steps with her high heels. But instead of walking to the podium she came over to my chair.

"Here." She held out a sheet of paper.

Automatically, I took it. "This is the schedule for the assembly. You need this." I pushed it back at her, but she held her hands away.

"I'd like you to lead this assembly," she said.

"Me? I'm doing the project introduction, that's all. You're the PTA president. You do the real stuff."

"Dearest Beth." Erica shook her head. "You have no idea, do you? I don't doubt that you've been wondering why I've been so harsh with you the last few weeks. Ah, I can see you have and I'm sorry for that. But I had to see what you're made of."

"Flesh and bone." I pinched my skin. "See?"

She smiled. "But what I didn't know was if that skin could take the heat."

Clueless Beth did not, in fact, have any idea what was going on. "Probably not," I said. "I'm not good with high temperatures."

"And there you're wrong. You did wonderfully. Not only did you respond well to Claudia and Randy, but you completed the project on time, filled this auditorium, and got the attention of local media." She glanced at the TV camera crew stationed at the side of the stage. "Plus, you found another killer and have given this town a sense of peace it hasn't known since that poor young girl died."

I eyed her. Maybe she'd taken exaggeration pills.

"My point," Erica went on, "is that you're the best candidate possible. I want you to run for president of the PTA next year."

"What?" I sat up tall. "But you're president. I'm not going to run against you." No, don't make me do this. I'm happy being secretary. I'm happy behind the scenes. I'm where I belong . . . aren't I?

I glanced at the packed auditorium. Thought of the speech I was about to give, and realized I wasn't at all nervous. No, I was looking forward to it. I wanted to tell everybody about this project. I *wanted* to speak. Good heavens, how had this happened?

Erica smiled. "You've grown so much in the last two years that I almost don't recognize you. You're ready for this, and I'm ready for a rest. Consider it, please." She leaned close and dropped one eyelid in a wink. "After all," she said softly, "do we really want Claudia Wolff to be PTA president?"

She returned to her seat, the gauntlet thrown into my lap.

Oh, dear.

I swallowed. Looked at the schedule. Opening remarks. Pledge of Allegiance. Etc., etc., etc. Okay, I could do this. No problem, or at least not enough of a problem to cause paralysis or instant death. But . . . did I want to?

Maude's laughter punctuated my self-absorption. Maude. I wouldn't have met her without the PTA, wouldn't have met Barb, wouldn't have learned about Kelly, would never have learned what had happened to Amy, wouldn't have met Officer Sean and maybe wouldn't have learned how good a friend Pete would be. He was such a nice man that he was even here today, taking time away from his business to watch the assembly and take the three of us out for ice cream afterward.

But . . . PTA president?

No. Let someone else do it. I'd stay secretary as long as I was wanted, but president? No. I didn't crave drama. I wanted peace and quiet and long walks with my children and dog in the evenings. I was happy that Cindy wouldn't hurt any innocents ever again, but I was even happier that things were back to normal.

I liked normal. Normal was an excellent place to be.

Decision made, I stood and walked to the podium. Adjusted the microphone. Straightened the paper. Smiled at the crowd. Saw Marina's grin, saw Jenna's happy face, saw Erica's encouraging nod.

Then I saw Claudia Wolff glowering at me.

And I changed my mind.

ALSO AVAILABLE
FROM

Laura Alden

Foul Play at the PTA

PTA meetings at Tarver Elementary School can get pretty
heated. But after parent Sam Helmstetter is strangled in his
car following a meeting, mom and PTA secretary
Beth Kennedy and her best friend Marina fear there may be
a cold-blooded killer in the group...

"Excellent." —Fresh Fiction

**Available wherever books are sold or at
penguin.com**

"Like" us at facebook.com/TheCrimeSceneBooks

OM0072